BLOOD MAGIC & BRANDY

Emily Michel

This is a work of fiction. Similarities to real people, places, or events are entirely coincidental.

BLOOD MAGIC AND BRANDY
First edition. April 12, 2022

Copyright © 2022 Emily Michel

All Rights Reserved.

No part of this book may be reproduced in any form or by any electronic or mechanical means, including information storage and retrieval systems, without written permission from the author, except for the use of brief quotations in a book review.

Cover design by **JJ's Design & Creations**

For whichever family member gifted me a copy of
Grimms' Fairy Tales when I was young.
In the best way possible, this is all your fault.

Author's Note

Please be aware this book contains elements that may upset some people. These include past death of parent, controlling stepparent, brief description of a murder scene including blood, threatening the life of a child, and mind control. The author welcomes comments on her website should you find something upsetting not mentioned above.

Chapter 1

Like everything in her life, including her name, Rane's fairy tale began with an accident. She balanced precariously on a thick, knobby branch and stretched for the rosy apple just out of reach. Her dog circled the tree, barking and whining in warning. Rane teetered for an instant, but a triumphant smile flourished on her lips as her fingers closed around the fruit. Catching herself on the trunk of the tree, she yanked on the apple, and it pulled away from its branch with a satisfying snap.

"Easy, Bash," she said to the distressed hound. "I'm fine."

Bash let out one last low whine and settled into a small hollow in the tree's roots. It wasn't her fault she was so protective. The fairy hound had been bred to be a loyal companion and a guardian to keep Rane safe from dangers both known and unknown, even when she herself was the danger.

She slid down the trunk until her ass hit the branch of the oldest tree in the ancient orchard, one of the few places away from prying eyes where she could be herself. Dangling a leg in the air below, she polished the fruit on her threadbare tunic. Rane bit into the firm, snow-white flesh. Nothing tasted so good as a stolen apple on a beautiful autumn day.

She should have been in the castle today helping to set up for the big feast tomorrow instead of taking refuge among the twisty trees and ramshackle sheds. The ambassador from Teruelle was due later, and her mother had asked—no, ordered—her to help the steward with the guest quarters. That being the last thing she'd wanted to do, Rane snuck out right after breakfast, leaving the details to her much more obedient and efficient siblings.

Besides, wasn't it more important she take advantage of the last two months before she turned twenty-one than help old Radclyffe make a few beds? The orchard was an excellent place to disappear for a few hours. Her life would change after her next birthday, and not for the better. New duties, less fun, and it would be time to pick a husband from her limited options. The thought ripped away a bit of her joy and soured the apple she held. Rane pulled out her knife and cut off a piece.

"Here you go." She dropped it.

Bash lifted her head, tail thumping against the ground, and snatched the small piece out of the air. The dog resembled a normal hound for the most part, but her eyes were as blue as the summer sky, and the pattern of her coat was too symmetrical, with three perfect circles of dark brown fur along her spine. Rane smiled and bit into the apple, its sweetness restored. If nothing else, she'd always have Bash.

A low rumble drew her attention to the road. A dust cloud hung over the wide thoroughfare, and two mounted guards led a trio of carriages surrounded by another ten guards. The coat of arms shone through the dust kicked up by the horses and wheels of the lead carriage. A red saltire crossed the crest from corner to corner behind the crouching green dragon on a field of gold, announcing the ambassador from Teruelle was ahead of schedule. Well, shit, it appeared her morning adventure would be cut short.

She'd left her mare in a meadow on the other side of the road. Rane would have to ride like the wind to beat them to Avora once the delegation passed. But they didn't pass; they slowed.

The mounted guards fanned out to the edge of the old orchard. The doors to the carriages opened, spewing their inhabitants onto the dusty road. From the lead carriage, a young man emerged. He wore travel-rumpled clothes that seemed a bit too big, as if he wanted to hide in them. There was a placid, almost vacant, expression on his face as he helped a woman exit with a flourish worthy of the most insipid dandy in the Lorean court. This must be the young ambassador, Lord Nevar of Otero, and the advisor sent along to help the novice diplomat not fuck things up. Idoya, Mother of All, help them. King Armel had sent a sycophant as ambassador.

Most of the party stayed close to the carriages, a few heading into the woods on the other side of the road. The lordling waited until the woman's attention was drawn elsewhere before shuffling into the orchard, heading toward Rane in an awkward zigzag, a guard following in his wake.

"Go hide, Bash."

Bash could sniff out a shady character from a furlong away and run faster than a horse. Should the ambassador prove a threat, the dog would be at his throat before Rane could call for help. The hound whined, whipping her tail back and forth in protest. Rane gave her the hand signal to go, and Bash obeyed, taking off like a shot. The undergrowth barely trembled with her passing.

Rane drew her leg up and huddled against the tree trunk. The leaves would shield her from discovery if the goddess looked favorably upon her. She stilled her mind, wishing she hadn't left the invisibility charm with her horse. Sunny wouldn't do much more than search for greener grass to munch on, but Rane hadn't wanted her to contend with the bears she'd heard snuffling around during her journey out. Though she hadn't heard, smelled, or otherwise sensed them, the occasional fey creature also wandered this area, hunting for easy prey.

She certainly wouldn't waste her single boon from her godmother on retrieving the charm when her own stealth should be sufficient. Rane dared to look toward the road again.

The ambassador gesticulated clumsily at the man trailing him, who then glanced over his shoulder, his attention on the woman traveling in the lead carriage. The ambassador said something with a feeble smile, and the guard mirrored the smile before striding off toward the rest of the party.

As he slipped away from the guard, the ambassador's strange, shuffling gait and blank expression vanished. The further he wandered from the road, the taller he seemed, gaining an inch or two, and he walked with a distinct spring to his step. He transformed before her eyes from a vacuous little lordling into a confident man, leaving her to question why he felt the need to hide his true nature.

His long strides brought him to her tree in no time. She noticed his square-jawed face right away. How could she not? He wasn't just handsome. He was goddess-blessed beautiful. His reddish-brown flawless skin, strong nose, full lips, and tight black curls were something out of a dream.

She leaned out from her well-hidden perch, desperate to figure out what made this man different from any she'd met. The leaves fluttered and crackled around her. He looked up, his eyes as sharp as bronze knives. She gasped at the intensity of his gaze and let go of the branch she held for balance.

"Fuck," she said as she lost the battle and slid off the tree.

Chapter 2

The more distance Nevar put between himself and his stepmother, the better he felt. A weight he always forgot he carried in her presence lessened, and he dropped his charade, finally moving like the trained warrior he was.

A rustling in the trees above him had him loosening his sword from its scabbard. It wasn't people he feared. Rumor had the woods near Lorea full of many strange beasts. Fairy, some claimed. Others suggested monsters, but most likely the usual wolves, bears, and lynx.

Nevar looked up, unsure whether he'd need to run or draw his sword to fight off whatever was trying to close in on him. What he didn't expect was a delicate, heart-shaped face and shining eyes the color of the moss on the north side of a tree. The woman teetered on the branch she sat upon and toppled over, swearing as she fell.

Frozen in place by his surprise, his mind wasn't quick enough to realize she was directly above him. She fell out of the tree and landed on him with a thump and a crackle of twigs. They collapsed to the forest floor, knocking the wind out of him and sending legs and arms akimbo.

The brush under the trees quivered and before he could regain his breath or his feet, a flash of brown and white bounded out and growled at him. Nevar raised his arms to fend off the attack, but the dog stood its ground a couple paces away, hackles raised and teeth bared. The woman's warm body rolled off his, and the hound took a menacing step toward him. He gripped his sword once again, the angle extremely awkward from his prone position, but he refused to go down without a fight.

"Don't." The woman stood and studied him. Coming to some sort of conclusion, she pursed those lovely lips and whistled, high and sharp. "Come, Bash."

Her firm voice was used to giving orders and having them obeyed. The dog instantly backed off and returned to her mistress, sitting placidly at her feet, tail thumping softly against the fallen leaves. The mystery woman patted the hound's head.

Nevar raised himself on his elbows to get a good look at the young woman. About average height, she had more curves than most, shown off by the tan breeches she wore instead of a skirt, and a plain leather jerkin over a white tunic nearly transparent from wear. Her chestnut hair escaped the braid she'd tried to corral her locks in, tendrils curling softly around her face. It wasn't every day such a beautiful woman almost killed him by misadventure.

He sent out a prayer of thanksgiving and ignored the breach in decorum. "Are you all right?"

She held out a hand. "I'm fine. You?"

He took it and pulled himself up. Much like his own, her hand had many calluses. He had earned his with hours of sword practice. How had she earned hers? Perhaps she was a gamekeeper or maybe a farmer's wife. Nevar fervently hoped for the former.

"The only thing injured seems to be my pride."

"I apologize for falling on you. I wasn't expecting company in the orchard today."

"Are you supposed to be here? I believe this is a royal holding. I doubt a stranger climbing his trees would please the king."

Her lips curved into a half smile, and something reckless gleamed in her eyes. "Your concern is noted, but the king and I have an… agreement."

"An agreement to climb his trees?" Was it possible this young woman was the king's mistress? The notion was disappointing.

"Something like that."

"Why were you in the tree?" If she was going to be cagey about this agreement, at least he could find out why she was climbing trees. It could be important if, for example, she was evading some of those wild beasts he'd heard rumors about. Although the dog was still calmly sitting at the woman's feet, he glanced around to ensure no more surprises lurked in the shadows.

She shrugged. "I enjoy climbing trees."

"You should be more careful. It's easier going up trees than down."

"Any cat could tell me that, but I find it gives me a new perspective on things."

"Oh? And did you like what you saw?"

Her half-grin blossomed into a full smile, and her gaze roved from his head to his toes. "I didn't *not* like what I saw." Her voice dropped low, and something deep within him thrummed with possibility.

Nevar cleared his throat, grasping for control around this puzzling woman. He searched desperately for a proper retort to her backhanded compliment, but he came up empty. All he wanted was to spend as much time as possible in her company. He grabbed a stray thought and hoped it would suffice.

"The scenery is nice today." Oh, God, how was it he had a line of noblewomen back in Otero waiting for his attention, and the best he could come up with when faced with a beautiful farm girl was, *The scenery is nice*?

A raucous laugh erupted from her, drawing her hound's attention. This only made her snort, and a tear dripped down her face.

"You're not very good at flirting, are you?" she said when the snorting subsided.

"It's not usually necessary."

"I imagine all the Teruellan ladies throw themselves at your feet."

"How did you—?"

She gestured in the direction of the unseen carriages. "Your carriages carry the coat of arms."

Ah, yes. But who was she to recognize the coat of arms so easily? The mystery surrounding this woman made him want to get her to spill her secrets. A tree-climbing, callous-having, beautiful woman who happened to recognize a foreign sovereign's coat of arms had to be worth knowing. She was far more interesting than all those ladies who lined up back in Otero.

"Are you in need of a ride? I'd be happy to offer you one anywhere between here and Avora."

She snorted again, but examined him with a new, appraising light in her eyes. "I appreciate your courtesy, but I can make my own way home."

"My lord?" A voice carried through the trees from the direction of the road, breaking whatever spell had settled over them.

"I should let you return to your carriage." She glanced toward the voice. The hound followed her gaze.

"But—"

"I've kept you too long. Safe journey." She stepped away, but stopped when the hound let out a low whine. "Fine, you can say goodbye."

The dog sprung at Nevar, and he raised his arm again to fend her off. But she placed her paws gently on his shoulders and licked his cheek. The woman whistled once more, and the hound dashed away into the brush at the edge of the orchard, her white-tipped tail marking her passage through the undergrowth.

"I'm Nevar," he called out as the woman followed the animal. "You can find me at the castle in Avora."

She glanced over her shoulder, another half-grin on her lovely face, those green eyes sparkling in amusement.

"I know."

Then she disappeared into the brush, as if she'd never been there.

Just in time, too. A flash of dark blue and silver caught his eyes as the guard he'd waved off a few moments ago trudged into view. Nevar hunched his shoulder, relaxed his muscles, and blanked his face, transforming himself from a muscular, intelligent warrior into a soft, simple lordling.

"Her ladyship is becoming vexed at your absence, my lord." He enunciated the words slowly with a hint of exasperation, as though talking to a six-year-old.

"Yes, of course." He glanced around the orchard as though he had no idea where he was or how he got there. "Lead the way."

Together, they slouched back toward the road.

"It's about time, Nevar." His stepmother's voice grated on him. Most would consider it to be a lovely voice, but he did not. Nearly every word out of her mouth attempted to humiliate him. She told him he was lazy, insinuated he was stupid, and yelled at both him and his little brother for each mistake. Long ago, Nevar had learned to wear his indifference as armor. The more she assumed he didn't care, the less she would probe for any weaknesses. "Where did you find him?"

"He'd wandered under the apple trees, Baroness." The guard's voice held the apology she wouldn't get from Nevar.

She shook her head, her lips pinched and a crease in her brow. Only fifteen years his senior, she'd been patronizing enough at their first meeting that his five-year-old self had sensed it. To this day, she insisted on treating him like an infant.

"I am not a child, Jocelyn," Nevar murmured sullenly, keeping his exasperated sigh in his chest.

He had honed his skills at subterfuge since his father, Baron Leon of Otero, had taken ill some four years ago. He had to play his part for a little while longer before he showed her, showed everyone who—and what—he truly was. Pushing away the urge to smile, he climbed back into the musty carriage.

"Then stop acting like it," she snapped back, her hazel eyes flashing with irritation as she sat across from him. "Your dawdling could make us late, and that would be a bad first impression."

Nevar wanted to tell her she'd requested the stop, but it would only prove her point. Instead, he allowed icy disdain to fill the space between them, ignoring the waves of scorn coming from his stepmother, as he always did. Except for her request for a stop by the orchard, the silence had been their companion all day.

They would be in Avora, the capital of Lorea, before the end of the day, a little early. If King Rowan didn't send a ceremonial escort soon, they would still be greeted with pomp and circumstance in the castle courtyard. At least the weather on this autumn day was clear and warm. Pomp and circumstance was a nuisance on the best days, but in foul weather, it was a nightmare.

Jocelyn stabbed her needle into the embroidery she carried with her while he gazed at the passing scenery through the window. At least she had something to do. Nevar only had his plans.

Yet those plans, which hadn't stopped churning through his mind since King Armel of Teruelle had finally assigned him to this mission two weeks ago, were replaced by the lovely face peeking out from the branches of the apple tree. Who was she? He kept pushing visions of her messy hair, sparkling eyes, and wry smirk away, trying to grab hold of those plans once more. It was important to keep his mission in mind. If he succeeded, he could prove his worth to his king and begin reclaiming his birthright. If he failed…

Nevar regarded his stepmother out of the corner of his eye. She was still a lovely woman, with long, dark hair. A white streak ran from her temple and wove its way through an elaborate hairdo. Jocelyn seemed ten years younger than she was. He would have assumed she used some dark magic if she didn't hate and fear it so thoroughly.

"What are you looking at?" Jocelyn barked, jabbing the needle through the cloth.

"Nothing," he mumbled.

"Keep your mind on the task at hand, Nevar. I'd hate to report back to King Armel that you failed at this simple assignment."

She said it with all the venom of a shadow viper. Jocelyn had never been a kind woman, never had time for her stepson. Never had time for her own, either. Poor Orom. Since his brother was old enough to remember, Nevar was the only member of the family who had ever spent any time with him. He missed the boy. Kind and easy-going, Orom was everything his mother was not.

Nevar brought his mind back to the present. The woman in the tree, no matter how lovely and intriguing, had nothing to do with why he was here. Thoughts of her would have to be relegated to the dark hours of the night, when loneliness and doubt overwhelmed him. Though it always was wise to keep an eye on his stepmother, alert for any treachery, she wasn't his immediate concern.

"I won't fail," he said.

The only thing he needed to do was to negotiate the hell out of these mineral rights, proving he could run the barony himself. This would force Jocelyn to step away, and he would wrest control back where it belonged—with him. He could keep Orom safe from her negative influence and rebuild what had gone to seed over the past several years.

"You owe me. I recommended you to King Armel, and you still haven't thanked me."

As usual, she made everything about her. The baroness had only recommended Nevar after he'd called in all his favors from the young lords of the Teruellan court. Once she realized it was inevitable, she had insisted on an audience with the King. Nevar had no room for error. Jocelyn would take any opportunity to control the negotiations.

"I'm sorry, Jocelyn. You are right. Thank you for your endorsement." Placating her now would lower her suspicions.

She sniffed and pulled out the small hand mirror she always kept nearby. Jocelyn gazed into it at least a dozen times a day. He'd never met a more vain person in his entire life, though she was beautiful enough for it to be understandable. She pursed her lips at whatever her reflection held and tucked an errant strand or two of hair back into her coiffure.

She finally responded with a coy smile on her lips. "You are welcome. Although I'm not certain you're up to the challenge, you deserved a chance to make your father proud."

That would never happen. His relationship with his father had been rocky from the start. It was difficult to win the love and approval of a parent when they held you responsible for the death of their beloved spouse. Since the baron's illness, Nevar wasn't sure if his father was aware of what went on in the barony or his family. He smiled nonetheless as his stepmother proceeded to ignore him again.

It was going to be a long ride to Avora.

Chapter 3

Sunny sped through the gate, Rane grinning ear to ear as they left minor chaos in their wake. The guards' eyes had widened as they approached, dashing to the side to avoid being run over. Of course, Rane would have reined in Sunny or the horse would have easily jumped over them, but once they saw Bash, there was no doubt who approached the gate at such a madcap gallop.

Rane glanced behind her, catching the glowers the uniformed guards sent her way. She was certain they had cursed her name, but she was too far away to catch anything. They'd best keep it to themselves, though, because Captain Jadran rushed out of the guardhouse to check on them. The frown on his face caused a momentary pang of guilt. He'd forgive her once she explained. Hopefully.

Rane pulled Sunny to a halt at the stables. She leaped off and tossed the reins to the stable hand.

"Keep her warm. I won't be long."

Jadran stomped in her direction. She didn't have time for this. Rane gave him a half-hearted salute and ran into the castle, Bash at her heels.

She tore through the halls, but as Rane rounded the last corner before the Council Chamber, her feet scrabbled for purchase. She grabbed onto a suit of armor to keep from sprawling in an undignified mess onto the stone floors, pulling it into a marble statue.

"Idoya's tits." Rane screeched to a halt.

She gaped as the statue fell to the floor, making a boom that could compete with the midday cannons. The Council Chamber door burst open, and guards poured into the corridor, searching for the enemy. The arm of the statue rotated lazily a few paces away, and the nose skittered to her feet.

The guards noticed her and stopped examining every nook and cranny of the hallway for the perpetrator. Her history with accidental destruction in the wake of her perpetual lateness was more than enough of an explanation. They trudged back into the chamber.

"Ladies don't swear," said a quiet voice behind her, parroting her least favorite governess from her childhood.

"Good thing I'm a fucking princess, Ebon."

Rane glared at her brother, who merely chuckled. His neat, close-cropped hair was the same shade as hers, but while she was of average height and curvy, he was tall and lean. She brushed some imaginary dust from her tunic to avoid giving him the upper hand.

"A fucking princess who was absent without leave for her duties this morning. Mother is livid and Father is—"

"Disappointed?" Guilt should prick her conscience, but years of disappointing her father dulled the sharpness of the word.

Ebon half-grinned, a wry twist to his lips. "I'm not covering for you."

"I don't expect you to."

This time, a cynical laugh escaped from her brother as they strode down the hall. It didn't matter she had been running before. She needed to show as much proper decorum as she could muster now there were witnesses.

"Sure, Rane. And I have a magic portal to Faerie."

"Fine, I don't need you to this time. I have important news."

"News that will make them forget you disappeared *and* missed the Council meeting?"

The guards bowed as the siblings passed.

"Not forget, just defer the shouting match."

They entered the Council Chamber, the large space dominated by an oversized oak table surrounded by twelve tall, gilded chairs. The windows were flung open, allowing the breeze to cool the stuffy chamber and bringing the sweet smells of early autumn. The ripening grain, fresh-cut hay, herbs, and flowers in the garden would all fade away soon enough.

The Council members meandered toward the door and bowed their heads in her general direction before leaving, trying to escape the coming storm. Her father and mother remained seated as she approached, frowns firmly affixed and their eyes thunderous. Rane paused by her father's taller, even more gilded chair and bowed. A curtsy while wearing breeches would have looked ridiculous. Her brother, a step behind and on her left, did the same.

Bash slunk off to the corner where her sister waited, surrounded by various and sundry animals. Betony's own personal court consisted of her mother's two small white dogs, the kitchen cats, and Ebon's two greyhounds. Even a few mice slept on her sister's lap. All perfectly content to wait at Betony's feet until dismissed or called by their masters.

"My apologies for missing Council, Your Majesty," Rane said. It wouldn't do to address him as merely Father when she was in trouble. "But I bear important news."

"What kind of important news is worth disobeying us and missing Council, Ranunculus?" Queen Beatrice asked with a touch of acid.

Rane winced. No one used her preposterous given name unless she was in serious trouble. She glanced at her father. His green eyes, so similar to her own, gave away nothing.

"The ambassador from Teruelle is early. He should be here soon."

"And how did you discover this?" King Rowan asked in his deep baritone.

Heat reddened her cheeks. She couldn't very well tell her father she'd fallen on the ambassador from another country and flirted, albeit poorly, with the man.

"Saw the carriages near the old apple orchard."

He flicked a glance at Ebon, checking the veracity of her words. Rane didn't blame him; she wasn't exactly known for adhering to the truth when an exaggeration or a fib would do.

"I was here all morning," Ebon said. The glare he shot her added, *unlike some.*

"I'm not lying." Rane tried to keep the whine out of her voice. She almost did it.

Her mother's dark eyes glittered with annoyance in the same

heart-shaped face shared by each of her progeny. The queen examined Rane from head to toe. Her children never knew if it was mother's instinct or the small amount of fairy blood running through her veins, but when it mattered, Beatrice always knew when they lied.

"She tells the truth."

King Rowan signaled a guard, who dashed away to inform whoever needed to be informed.

"Duly noted. Have a seat, Rane."

She stepped toward her sister and the two other plain chairs set against the far wall.

"No, here." Her father gestured to the chair on his left.

Rane swallowed the bitter retort on the tip of her tongue. Not only wasn't she ready for that seat, she also had no desire to ever take it. Nevertheless, as crown princess, it was hers, whether she wanted it or not, whether she deserved it or not. Rane pulled out the chair and sat gingerly on the edge.

"You are excused," the queen told the other two siblings.

Betony rose with her usual grace, and the animals followed the cranberry-haired princess out of the room. If the unusual hair color didn't scream fey, the way her menagerie obeyed would tell anyone her sister was special. Even Bash followed, though the hound looked back forlornly. Rane signaled her to go with Betony. Ebon hesitated, but at their mother's sharp glare, he left and pulled the heavy doors closed with a deep boom. King Rowan placed a hand on Rane's shoulder and gently cupped her chin, compelling her to meet his gaze.

"Rane." Disappointment dripped from the single word.

She broke eye contact and stared at the intricate carvings on the edge of the table.

"You must do better. As my heir, you will soon have a seat on the Council."

"You have only made things harder on yourself," her mother said.

"I know." Rane could not keep the frustration out of her voice.

"This kingdom will be yours someday," the king said. "Right now, my advisors and ministers aren't sure you are ready to assume the duties of crown princess, let alone queen."

They weren't wrong. It was one reason she disappeared so

often. No matter how much time her parents spent training her, Rane was certain she couldn't handle the duties that would soon be thrust upon her. Even her training with the Queens of Faerie was insufficient to the task. Unfortunately, she couldn't find the words to explain that to her father.

"I'm not even twenty-one yet. You'll live to a hundred. Why should I be ready to deal with all those assholes now?"

Her father sighed. Her mother shot knives at her with those darkling eyes.

"Be that as it may, it is time to step up to your duties as crown princess instead of running from them. I am entrusting you with formally greeting the ambassador in the hope you will show the Council the side of you I know exists."

"Deep, deep down," her mother added, deadpan.

"Fathoms," Rane agreed.

A wry smile crinkled the corners of her mother's eyes, and the worried expression on her father's face eased.

"We don't have long before they are here if you saw them at the old orchard," her father said. "I've never met Lord Nevar, though I vaguely recall meeting his father a time or two. Is there anything you learned?"

She could have told him most of the truth. She should have, but there was something about her encounter with the lordling Rane wanted to keep to herself. Her mother's eyes narrowed, but she didn't say anything. Rane shook her head.

King Rowan sighed. "Do what you can to determine what kind of man he is."

"Can I take Ebon?"

Her brother was well versed in the long history between the two kingdoms. He'd be invaluable. Maybe she could take her usual step back and let him handle the delegation. It could even play into her father's plans of trying to determine what kind of man he was. Ebon could handle the advisor and the functionaries, while Rane could get closer to the young and handsome Lord Nevar. The idea made her pulse race.

"No." Her father didn't even seem sorry for telling her no. "The chain of command must be clear. Having Ebon along muddies it."

Damn. He knew her too well.

"Take Bash, though," her mother added.

Of course she would take Bash. Her loyal companion, whom she trusted absolutely, had decided Nevar was worthy of trust. Rane needed to figure out why.

"I'll take Jadran and his company, too," she said.

Captain Jadran had trained her since she was old enough to hold a sword. Not only did he excel at his job at keeping her safe, but he also put up with her nonsense without losing his temper. He was the closest thing she had to a friend since she turned thirteen.

"Excellent choice." Her father's expression was impassive and his tone even.

"They're already set, aren't they?"

King Rowan smiled. "You trust no other captain as much as Jadran. *I* trust no other to keep you safe. One day he will make a fine choice as your Commander of the Guards."

"Father," she protested.

He held up a hand. "It's fine, Rane. Go, now. I'd hate for the ambassador to reach the gate while you argue with me on an obvious choice."

"Yes, Father."

Rane took a tentative step toward the doors, and when no one stopped her, walked so quickly she was nearly running out of the Council Chamber. Her parents stood close together, talking softly as they often did. No fond glances or surreptitious displays of affection. Theirs wasn't a love marriage. A monarch of Lorea couldn't afford one of those. However, they were friendly and made a strong team, both in raising their children and ruling the kingdom.

She opened and closed the great doors as quietly as she could. Betony waited patiently for her outside. Most of the menagerie had dispersed, but Bash remained with her sister.

"Father is aggravated when you're late," Betony said, her dainty arms perched on her slender hips and her bright green eyes glinted with irritation.

"I know."

"Just because you're the crown princess—"

"I *know*, Bet," Rane said, unable to keep the exasperation out of her words. "But I don't care as much as you."

"Well, obviously." Her sister relaxed and a little of the

annoyance faded. "I don't understand why you do it, though."

"When your twenty-first birthday is two months away, we can have this conversation again."

Rane walked away from Bet. She didn't have time for a long conversation in the hall. She had to make herself presentable for the ambassador. The image of what his face would look like when the official emissary from King Rowan turned out to be the woman who fell from an apple tree made her smile.

"What does *that* mean?" Her sister's slippered feet tapped after her, her skirts swishing around her ankles.

"It means I won't have time to flout court conventions. I'll be too busy practicing being queen and finding an appropriate consort."

"What's wrong with that? Weren't you tired of being treated like a child?"

They passed more statues on plinths, decorative vases and other small sculptures, and some portraits of their ancestors as Rane rushed through the halls on the way to her room. Bash kept right behind, a big doggie grin on her face.

"If it was only learning how to be queen, taking on some extra responsibilities, that would be fine, I guess. Have you given any thought to how limited my options are for finding a husband, little sister? My marriage must benefit Lorea. I've met five men who meet those qualifications. And if I make a good match, you and Ebon have much more freedom in choosing your future partners."

Bet's face fell and her cheeks turned rosy with chagrin. "I didn't think of that."

Rane stopped and Bet nearly ran into her. "I'm glad you don't have to. But I do, and I hate it, so sometimes I decide to put me first while I still can."

Betony threw her arms around Rane. "I'm sorry."

Rane tucked her sister's head under her chin and patted her back. "Being born first sucks balls, but if it means you and Ebon get better choices, I don't mind too much. I merely want to put it off as long as I can."

Bet giggled and let go. "Okay. I'm in. Let me know what I can do to help."

"Well, for now, getting out of my way so I'm not late twice in the same day would do."

Her sister stepped to the side, and Rane raced away. Bursting into her rooms, she pulled up short. Her brother lounged in a chair, legs over the plush arms, sipping something from a flask.

"Want some?" Ebon held it out.

"Not you, too." Rane snatched the flask out of his hand, hoping it wasn't cider or lemonade. The warm sting of her father's best brandy slid down her throat, the sweetness of the apples soothing in its wake. "Better not let Father catch you stealing his brandy."

Ebon could get away with a lot. Some of that was because he rarely caused trouble, spending most of his time happily in the castle library with his tutors. Some was because when he did cause trouble, he didn't get caught.

"Not me, what?"

"I got lectured by Father, Mother, and our little sister. I don't need one from you, too." She took another sip from the flask. Ebon grabbed it away.

"Oteran apple brandy, dear sister, the last in the castle. Go easy. I'm not here to lecture you. I'm here to help."

"Oh, really?"

"Yes, really. Especially since I don't have to play second fiddle to you and can lounge in the library reading all the books I want this evening."

"Fine, tell me about Otero."

He raised his brows and gave her an enigmatic grin. Of course, her brother would know nearly everything about the barony and the family who ruled there. It was what Ebon was good at, knowing things.

"As you're off to meet the ambassador, who is from Otero, you should enjoy a taste of their best-known product. The harvest was bad a couple years ago, so it might be the last for a year or two. If you showed up for lessons, you would know this stuff, too."

She stuck out her tongue. His grin blossomed into a full smile, and they laughed together. Rane wasn't a terrible student when she bothered to pay attention, but there were many more interesting things to do, such as riding, and hunting, and swimming, and combat practice, and otherwise evading her responsibilities.

"That's why you're around, brother mine. To give me the answers I need."

Rane walked over and ruffled his hair, the same color as hers. He smoothed it back, glaring at her with their mother's darkling eyes, black as midnight with pinpoints of light like stars, a rare gift from a fairy ancestor. They couldn't be more different in temperament, but it worked well for them. Rane was always glad for his advice and knowledge, and Ebon seemed to appreciate her ability to take the spotlight and lead him on adventures.

"Fine, but you owe me one. Actually, you owe me at least five. I will collect someday, sister dear." He took another swallow. "Lord Nevar is Baron Leon's heir and could inherit any day. The baron has been sick on and off for years. The baroness has been ruling in his stead as he became ill shortly before Nevar's majority. She has a lot of friends in the Teruellan court, and they didn't want to rock the boat until the baron croaked. If I recall correctly, he has a younger half-brother about twelve years old."

Rane rolled her eyes. "You always recall correctly."

Ebon spent his spare moments digging through the library, the archives, and Father's old papers. He assailed his tutors with endless questions and never forgot a single insignificant fact. Her brother would make a wonderful advisor to their father someday, and she would count herself lucky to have him by her side as she stepped into her official role in the coming months.

"I was trying to be modest." Ebon grinned before sipping his drink.

Lord Nevar had been in a strangely ambiguous position, granting him heaps of free time. She had to shirk as many of the responsibilities her parents assigned her as she could to have more than a few hours to herself each month.

"Since his mother rules, what does he do with all his spare time?"

"Stepmother. Apparently, he doesn't do much. Reports have him spending most of his time in brothels and gambling houses. Rumor has it he is lucky at cards. He's soft, using carriages instead of riding. I can find no records of any duels, battles, or tournaments he's participated in. He may not know how to fight, as best as I can tell."

A timid, lowly baron's son sent as ambassador. That had been her first impression, too. Rane trusted her second impression more. His calloused hands spoke of sword training, his sharp eyes told her of his intelligence, and his strangely rumpled clothes screamed cunning. If his stepmother ruled in his place, it would explain the subterfuge. She recalled the woman traveling with him. *The stepmother must be the advisor.*

"I believe there is more to him than meets the eye," Rane said.

"You have a sharp mind when you choose to use it." Ebon held out the flask once again, but Rane waved it away. "I'll leave you to it. Have fun, Rane, but not too much."

As soon as he left, she walked into her bedroom. A beautiful steel blue riding dress with a split skirt lay on her bed. Rane stripped off her breeches and stepped into the riding dress. Her sister had embroidered the bodice with silver fern fronds, which shone in the bright light of her room. Thank the Goddess it was simple laces rather than a corset. After the confrontations with both her siblings, she had no time to call for help to dress. Rane pulled the laces snug and slid her feet into the slippers someone had left at the foot of the bed.

She paused by her dressing table, where the final piece of her outfit rested. Rane glanced in the looking glass hanging on the wall. Oh, her hair was a rat's nest. Rane undid the braid, brushed out her hair, and re-pinned it into a simple twist. She picked up the silver circlet, her headwear for official business. Thin strands of fairy-wrought silver intertwined in an intricate pattern like fine silk thread. At the front was a small, pink enameled flower. It was a ranunculus, her namesake.

A low woof of approval issued from Bash as Rane adjusted the circlet. Together, they dashed out the door and ran full speed all the way to the stables. The guards milled around the courtyard, saddling their mounts. An air of anticipation swept through the courtyard for the easy assignment on a beautiful day. The stable hand still held onto her amber colored mare. Rane leaped onto Sunny's back and dashed off, eager for another encounter with the new ambassador.

"Mount up!" Jadran shouted at the guards as she rushed by.

She caught a mutter about rash princesses and lead-asses before leaving them all in the dust.

Chapter 4

"Tell the driver to make haste. These people will surely move out of the way of a royal carriage." Jocelyn looked up from her embroidery and scowled at him. Her tone was as sour as her frown.

The pastoral scenery he'd enjoyed most of the past four days had changed since they'd left the apple orchard and that most unusual woman. The rolling hills, fields of grain, and forests had morphed into well-made houses, busy markets, and industrious people crowding the road. Their pace had slowed as they dealt with more carts, horses, carriages, and pedestrians.

"It's busy, Jocelyn. I'm sure the driver is doing his best." He kept his own voice neutral and his posture slouched. No need to give her any clues.

The sourness changed to irritation. Nevar sighed. She would continue to harp on it until he spoke with the driver. The past four days had been the most time he'd ever spent alone with his stepmother. At least she still had no idea who he truly was. He needed to keep it that way.

"His best is not good enough, and if you were the man your father hoped for, you would ensure your retainers always performed at their peak."

Nevar wished for the frosty silence of earlier. He bit back the first idea that popped into his head. *If you were the wife and mother my father had hoped for, they'd all jump to do your bidding.* Instead, beneath her beautiful exterior lay a predator, ready to pounce on any weakness, hoard any amount of power, and remove any obstacle. Since Baron Leon had taken ill those many years ago, Jocelyn had assumed his duties, even after Nevar had attained his majority. The king and the court admired her, trusted her.

He stuck his head out the window to speak to the driver, but the words caught in his throat. Looming ahead were the city walls of Avora. Above the city, an impressive castle topped a still-green hill, a great hulking white bear guarding its territory.

"We're here," he said quietly.

Nevar was impatient to be getting on with these important negotiations. He'd cultivated the persona of a lazy, entitled, tiresome aristocrat coasting on his father's good name. One small favor, one task at a time, Nevar amassed the political capital he would need over the past four years. Every late-night visit to a brothel to keep a fellow young nobleman out of trouble, every game of dice he lost, every hand of cards he won and refused to keep his earnings, had paid off with this plum assignment. Behind the scenes, he had utilized the Oteran library to study history, diplomacy, and law. The only people more well-versed in Teruellan and Oteran laws were King Armel's closest advisors.

He'd called in every favor and won an audience with the king. Trading off his father's reputation and having well-placed courtiers vouch for him, Nevar convinced the king he was the right person for this job. When he successfully negotiated mineral rights with Lorea, he would be in an excellent position to suggest it was time his stepmother spent more of her hours nursing her poor, ailing husband and leave the running of Otero to the rightful heir.

Jocelyn shifted her attention away from her embroidery and glared out the window. She sniffed in derision, but her hazel eyes sparked with interest. As pleasant as the small barony of Otero was, as opulent as the Teruellan court was, Avora was far more majestic.

"Get the man to stop, then, you dolt."

He didn't have to. The driver pulled the horses to a stop, and Nevar bounded out of the carriage, forgetting for an instant to hide his strength and dexterity. He kept his mind keen and his body fit.

Outside the city gates stood a gathering of guards dressed in the green and brown of the Lorean royal house. Seated on a fifteen-hand tall mare in front of the rest was a woman dressed in steel blue, her silver coronet catching the late afternoon sunlight and gleaming like a beacon. King Rowan had honored him, and thus

King Armel, by sending one of his daughters to greet him.

"What's going on?"

He tore his eyes away from the approaching welcome party and looked into the carriage. It must have been a trick of the light, but his stepmother seemed weathered for a moment, her lips drawn back in a sneer and her fingers changed to claws as she gazed into her mirror. In a blink, she was back to normal, but he was left with a sinking sensation that not all was well.

"There's a delegation from King Rowan. Would you care to greet them with me?"

Nevar trusted the instinct that told him his stepmother was dangerous. He'd long suspected his father's illness wasn't natural, and only one person benefitted from Baron Leon's illness. Instinct also told him if he made any accusation against Jocelyn without sound proof, his father's life would be in danger.

"You have snow for brains, Nevar. The slightest effort of thought, and it all melts. Of course, I would."

He held out his hand for Jocelyn, ignoring the old insult and careful not to show his burgeoning excitement at the official start of the mission which would turn the tables on his stepmother. He hunched his shoulders in his usual slouchy manner and willed his face to stone. A low bay caught his ear, and he jerked his head toward the approaching welcoming party.

A familiar hound paced alongside the amber mare. His gaze met the heart-shaped face he'd seen in the tree. A mischievous smile pulled up the corners of her lovely pink lips, and her eyes twinkled with suppressed laughter. Nevar froze in place with raised eyebrows and dropped jaw.

"Nevar." His stepmother growled out his name, bringing him back to his senses.

"Sorry, Jocelyn," he murmured, hoping she hadn't noticed the change in him.

"One would think you hadn't seen a princess before," she snapped.

The guard riding directly behind the princess, a captain by the epaulettes on his uniform, called out, "Her Royal Highness, Crown Princess Ranunculus."

Nevar bowed and Jocelyn curtsied.

"Lord Nevar of Otero, ambassador from his majesty King

Armel of Teruelle, and the Baroness of Otero," the driver announced in a hoarse voice.

The crown princess herself. King Rowan had pulled out all the stops. Keeping his slouch, he met her gaze. Those eyes still held amusement, but her features were schooled into a suitably somber expression. She dipped her head regally from atop her horse, acknowledging the greeting.

"Lord Nevar, Baroness. On behalf of King Rowan and Queen Beatrice, I welcome you to Lorea. I hope your journey was uneventful."

"Yes, Your Highness, quite dull." The sharp edge had disappeared from Jocelyn's voice, replaced by a simpering sweetness. It was a tone she frequently used when they were at court.

"Perhaps it's a good omen for the upcoming negotiations. My father has granted me the honor of escorting you to the castle."

"Thank you, Your Highness," Nevar said. "It is our great pleasure to be here. I look forward to fruitful negotiations."

"As do I." The princess bit her lip. It was a simple gesture, one he'd seen the ladies of the Teruellan court use time after time to draw attention to their perfectly painted mouths. This seemed a less practiced gesture, and she seemed unsure of what to do next. "Would you care to join me on horseback through the city, Lord Nevar? I believe it's your first visit to Avora."

"I would be most honored."

A bright smile lit up her face. "Excellent."

Nevar helped the dour baroness back into the carriage while a guard dismounted and sat next to the driver. He made himself comfortable in the unfamiliar saddle. The color rose in his cheeks when his eyes met the princess's, and she winked at him before wheeling toward home. The guards let them pass before falling into formation behind, and the remaining Oteran delegation followed.

Nevar couldn't keep his eyes off her as she set a brisk pace. He had never met a princess with a slobbery hound, a certain disregard for propriety, and a propensity to climb trees. Of course, the only princess he'd ever met before today had been King Armel's infant granddaughter. Princess Ranunculus—what a mouthful of a name—had a rebellious streak, but how far did it go?

Nevar allowed himself a few moments to admire her exquisite seat, fascinated as her hair once again escaped her coiffure and danced in the breeze of their passing like silken streamers on a windy festival day. Her hair delighted in being unconfined just as much as the princess did.

He dragged his mind away from the lovely woman riding next to him. He was here to negotiate with the King of Lorea, not his daughter. It didn't matter how tempting it was to watch her lush curves move under her dress, and to remember what her figure looked like clad in skin-tight breeches and a jerkin. He had more important goals for this trip than seducing an intriguing princess.

If successful, this mission would solidify his place in court, allowing him to manage his father's responsibilities until his health improved or… He couldn't allow his mind to follow the notion to its logical conclusion. There was a lot riding on these negotiations, and the mineral rights in the Calcolo Mountains between their two kingdoms was only one matter.

"Thank you for the invitation, Your Highness." He brought his steed alongside the princess. The mare she rode nuzzled the other horse. She was a friendly sort. Was her rider?

"I thought you might enjoy a ride after being cooped up in a carriage with your stepmother. She did not seem pleased at all. And I owed you for falling on you earlier."

He glanced at her out of the corner of his eye. A small grin curled her pale pink lips. He nodded his thanks again. A guard galloped past them and headed straight to the castle to announce their presence. Her captain dropped a length back, allowing them to precede the rest of the party. The hound kept a steady pace between them, deftly avoiding the horses. Their hooves rang out on the cobblestones, and the pedestrians in the streets cleared the way, bowing and curtsying.

They passed through the city gates, and the sights that greeted him took away whatever he was going to reply. A small forest sprung up in what would be a plaza in any other city. Tall birch trees, their leaves beginning to change from green to gold and rust, taller pines, and an overabundance of wildflowers filled an area larger than the courtyard of his own castle in Otero. People wandered through the tree-filled square, respectful but not frightened at their passing.

"Pixies got your tongue, my lord?" she asked when the silence stretched far too long.

Damn. "I'm sorry. I'm just not sure what to say to someone who fell on me."

She laughed. It wasn't the delicate laugh the ladies in King Armel's court practiced. This was a thing of glorious honesty, full-throated and decidedly unroyal. The princess's laugh was as appealing as she was.

"Good point. I will dispense with the normal pleasantries. 'How was your journey?' sounds trite after that."

Nevar chuckled. "It does."

"Excellent, we're on the same page. What would you like to know?"

A hundred questions popped into his head. It was his first journey away from Teruelle. He forgot to play the seasoned diplomat and blurted out the first thing that came to mind.

"What is this place?"

"A shrine, of sorts."

Ah, yes. Loreans worshipped Idoya, a mother goddess, and believed the best way to do so was in open air surrounded by nature. He'd never seen a dedicated glade before.

"It's beautiful. How do you keep it green in the city?"

"Magic, of course."

He swallowed nervously. While the idea of magic was intriguing, the practice of it was frowned upon in Teruelle. He'd met exactly one fairy in his life, and he was now in a land that had signed a treaty with the Faerie realm a hundred years ago.

"Magic?"

Her eyes fell on him and a brilliant smile spread over her lips.

"There's nothing to fear from magic. It's all around us. Many fairies choose to live in Avora." She pointed at a bakery ahead. In the window, a wooden spoon stirred dough in a bowl without anyone around to move it. Several paces away, the baker kneaded another batch. His mouth dropped open once more, and the princess chuckled. "A hundred years of peace, prosperity, and magic lets me forget the awe others experience. Wait until you see the lights in the castle."

Nevar closed his mouth and cleared his throat. He needed to

do less gaping if he didn't want to seem a backwater rube posing as an ambassador.

"But the fairies—I haven't seen a single set of pointed ears."

"Fairies with pointed ears are usually a bit wilder and dislike cities. Have you noticed any of the people with less-than-natural hair colors?" Her body quivered with suppressed amusement.

He checked. About one person in ten had hair pigments more at home on an artist's palette than on their own heads. Bright blues, greens, purples, and pinks added splashes of color to the throngs of people going about their business.

She cocked an eyebrow. "If I recall, Teruelle doesn't use magic. Is this your first time?"

Nevar narrowed his eyes. What exactly was she suggesting? Her lips twitched. Dammit, he was being teased by the crown princess. The tension eased from his back.

"You are correct, Princess Ranunculus." At her wince, Nevar guessed she didn't appreciate her name. "We prefer machines and workers over magic. It has allowed us to keep up with Lorea in most industries."

"Most, but not all."

"Not all. Teruelle is a productive kingdom, and King Armel believes there's nothing magic can do that his engineers won't figure out a mechanical solution for."

"I wish you luck. With all the many of wonders magic I've seen, I don't know what I would do without it, especially my fairy godmother."

"To each their own, Your Highness." He avoided using her name. Not only was it rude, especially in earshot of the guards, but if she detested it, the last thing he wanted was for her to associate the feeling with him.

"You may change your mind about magic when you see the city lit at night. Perhaps someone will convince you to take a night tour."

Her gaze wandered over his body. He caught her staring, and she winked at him. Heat rushed through him. *Do not flirt with the princess.* Too much rode on his assignment, and enticing princesses had no part of his future.

As they approached the castle, the inns and houses grew bigger and more elaborate. Even more parks appeared, compact groves of trees and flowers, with children playing in grassy plots. They paused to greet the caravan. The city was prosperous, and its population seemed content and safe. Impressive.

They turned another corner, and the castle loomed large above him, its creamy limestone walls reflecting the golden light of the late afternoon. It was a fortress, yet small details lightened its massive presence. High, arched windows looked down upon them as they passed under the portcullis into the courtyard. Standing at the far end, surrounded by guards, were a tall man and a small woman, their gold crowns catching and reflecting the sunlight, glowing as though lit from within.

They slowed to a walk until grooms ran up to take their reins. The crown princess dismounted, and he followed suit. She brushed out her skirt. There was no way she was getting rid of all the wrinkles, but he understood the instinct. In fact, he straightened his doublet behind the horse before approaching the king and queen. He bowed with a flourish.

"King Rowan and Queen Beatrice, I present Lord Nevar of Otero, Ambassador from King Armel of Teruelle." Once again, the princess spoke with authority. "My lord, King Rowan and Queen Beatrice of Lorea."

"You are welcome, Lord Nevar, as is your lady mother," King Rowan said in his sonorous voice, rich and deep as the earth.

"Thank you, Your Majesty." It always stung when others identified Jocelyn as his mother. Though he'd never known the woman who birthed him, he would have preferred no mother to the woman his father married. "I hope our negotiations will be beneficial to both our kingdoms."

"As do I."

"You must be weary after your journey," the queen said. "Our servants will show you to your quarters. Supper will be served in your room tonight, but tomorrow is the welcome feast."

A shuffling behind him drew the attention of the king and queen.

"Ah, Baroness, it has been too long," the king said, bowing slightly.

His stepmother rose from her deep curtsy. "That it has, Your Majesty. Thank you for your kind welcome."

King Rowan smiled warmly. Queen Beatrice's sharp gaze

darted between the two, but when a servant came out, the royals walked back into the castle without another word.

"I leave you in good hands. I will see you tomorrow night." The princess held out her hand.

He bowed low and placed a soft kiss on the back of it. She smelled of horse and dog and something else, something earthy and green. The princess's fingers tightened on his for an instant before she reluctantly released him.

"Good night, Your Highness." He gave her his most seductive smile.

Her eyes widened, and an answering smile bent her round, pink lips upward. She turned and disappeared into the castle but cast one last look at him.

"Milord, this way," said the servant, gesturing to the left.

Nevar followed the servant through the brightly lit halls. The fairy lights floating below the ceiling cast a yellowish glow upon them as they walked up a winding staircase and down a hallway lined with paintings and statues in between doors. Finally, the servant stopped at the last door and opened it.

"Where will the baroness be staying?" he asked the servant.

His stepmother's sharp voice whirled up the stairs.

"Why are we all the way at the top of the castle? Shouldn't our quarters be nearer to—"

"Never mind."

He slammed the door on the servant's quizzical face before Jocelyn could see him. Nevar hated being rude, but the last thing he wanted was another conversation with his stepmother after they'd been stuck in a carriage together for days. He needed a quiet night away from her complaints.

Nevar glanced around the small sitting room. A roaring fire cast flickering shadows across two plush, blue velvet chairs, and a delicate writing desk stood in a corner along with another magic lamp. It was cozy, not opulent. Perhaps that was the way in Lorea. If so, Jocelyn would be unhappy. She was used to much more lavish accommodations when they visited King Armel.

A carafe of water and a brown bottle stood on the desk with a cut crystal goblet catching the lamplight. Nevar poured himself a glass of amber liquid and sipped it. Spiced rum flowed over his tongue and sent a pleasant warmth through his chest. It wasn't

Oteran apple brandy, but he could get used to it. He took another sip.

A knock drew his attention, and he set the goblet down. Nevar opened the door to find a pair of servants carrying his trunk. They lugged it through the second door into the bedchamber and placed it on a stand at the foot of the large bed, its dark wood gleaming in the firelight. A young woman with light brown hair followed them in and set a tray on the writing desk. Her dark brown eyes raked over him, her rosy cheeks coloring even further.

"Thank you," he said.

"You're welcome, milord. Ring the bell and call for Alize if you require anything else this evening. Anything at all."

It was an invitation he couldn't miss, but he needed to be wary of spies.

"I am tired from the journey. That will be all."

She seemed disappointed but curtsied before leaving, shutting the door quietly behind her. It hadn't been a lie, not exactly. The journey had been taxing, and some relief of the sexual kind would not be amiss, but not tonight. Tonight, he was grateful for the quiet after spending so many days with his stepmother. With any luck, she wouldn't seek him out this night to pepper him with more advice and questions he didn't want to answer.

Nevar sat at the writing desk, pulling the silver dome off the tray. Roasted chicken and potatoes with honeyed carrots greeted him, the sweet herbal smell filling the small room. The food at the inns along the way had been adequate, but this was divine. He went to bed with a full belly, and the image of the intriguing and lovely Princess Ranunculus whirled through his dreams.

Chapter 5

"Remind me why we're doing this, Rane," Ebon said the next morning in the kitchen garden.

He lunged at her, his blunted blade nearly hitting her shoulder. She brought up her own practice sword to block the strike with a satisfying clang.

"Because Jadran is too busy to practice."

She parried the thrust and stepped back, probing for an opening. There was none. Ebon was too good, and ever since he'd gone through his growth spurt three years ago, he had the advantage of his reach. She'd always had to rely on cunning and luck to win, but she won few matches these days.

"It doesn't have anything to do with Commander Miren and Mother's recent conversation about appropriate self-defense tactics for a princess, does it?"

He swept his blade at her knees. Rane saw it coming and jumped, allowing the blade to cut the air under her. She flashed a quick, impish grin and stepped closer, too close for him to hit with his sword.

"No," she protested weakly.

It was exactly because Mother and the commander had decided the time spent with Jadran would be better applied to more appropriate pursuits for a princess. Pursuits such as etiquette, law, music, and picking a husband. Boring.

A mischievous spark lit his eyes. "You have to admit they have a point. If you ever have to defend yourself, Jadran has failed in his duty."

He shoved her away and backed up a few paces. They circled

each other. Rane feinted a thrust, but Ebon didn't rise to her bait. He merely twisted away, keeping his eyes on her face, watching and waiting for her tells. Her brother was as good as Jadran and a decade younger. He would be a formidable foe before long.

"He would only fail if I'm dead. None of us want that, least of all you. Then you'd have to wear the crown. Whose ass would warm your favorite settee in the library if you're king?"

She got to him. He lunged at her once more, and she deflected his blade. Using the momentum, she put more distance between them.

"What do you think of the ambassador?" Ebon turned the conversation away from things they never talked about. If Rane was queen, their father was dead. And if Ebon was king, Rane was dead. A sad fact of being a royal.

Once again, they circled, blades pointed at each other.

"I'm not sure, yet. I only had one conversation with him."

"It didn't seem so from where I sat," Betony said in a bird-like twitter, watching in amused tolerance from her perch in the old apple tree in the corner. She'd never joined in their practice, preferring the wooden quarterstaff to hard steel.

"Oh, and where were you sitting, little sister?" Rane asked. Bet had a habit of finding things out, and nobody knew exactly how.

"Wouldn't you like to know?"

Yes, she would, but she had no more attention to waste on her sister's whereabouts yesterday. Her brother pressed her skill enough neither of them could speak.

"He's a diplomat," Ebon said when they broke apart again. "You don't know what he's capable of."

"Bash approves of him."

Ebon's eyes widened in surprise. Fairy hounds were rarely fond of many people. Bash liked Rane, her siblings, her parents, Jadran, and tolerated everyone else. A few people had learned to stay far away from the dog when she consistently growled at them. It almost always turned out they were up to no good.

Rane took advantage of his momentary shock and closed the distance between them once more. The ringing of metal on metal as their swords clashed together filled the garden. Unable to concentrate on anything other than her brother's blade, Rane thrusted and parried, jumped and ducked, circled and jabbed at her brother. Rane and Ebon's swordplay roamed the entire kitchen garden, sending them past raised beds of herbs drowning in buzzing bees, hoping for the last nectar before the cold set in. Turfed benches, their green grass bright in the morning light, surrounded the round wrought-iron table in the center of the garden. Rosemary draped over the edges of planters, and several were cut into elaborate topiaries. Her mother loved rosemary, and it was a key ingredient in the soap produced by the staff.

Rane tired, and the glint in her brother's eyes told her he knew it. He pressed her harder, their blunted blades clanging even more loudly in the quiet morning.

Lord Nevar appeared in the door to the kitchen, and Rane froze. His loose tunic caught the morning breeze, pressing the fabric against his muscular form, giving lie to the need for the extra fabric. She stepped toward him, heart pounding, suddenly desperate to be next to him, only to trip over a stone peeking out of the ground and ending up on her ass. The tip of her brother's sword rested under her chin.

"I yield." She took the hand Ebon graciously offered.

The ambassador clapped. "I didn't know princesses could do that."

"What, fight?" she snapped.

"No, fall on their ass."

She glared at him, but his bronze eyes softened from hard metal to soft silk in the morning sun. His gaze dropped slowly down her body, sending shivers up her spine. The right corner of his full mouth twitched ever so slightly. He was teasing her.

Rane suppressed the smile threatening to form. She struggled with what kind of princess to be, torn between what her parents expected, what her kingdom needed, and what she wanted. Whatever Lord Nevar saw in her, he approved. She didn't need his approval, but it felt splendid being appreciated for who she was, all of her, and not only for what she was.

However, she couldn't let him get away with the insult.

"A princess doesn't fall on her ass. She takes a tumble." Rane adopted the supercilious tone many of the ladies at court used much too often on the castle staff.

A low rumble erupted from the young man, starting low in his chest and working its way out. He threw his head back, and the laugh filled the garden.

He was handsome, but when he laughed, he was gorgeous. His muscles released their tension, and his brown skin glowed, changing him from a warrior ready for whatever may happen into an enticing man. She shook away the image of him letting go, of his muscular neck thrown back in laughter, and tried hard not to imagine how he'd look if she kissed his neck.

"You can make it up to me," Rane said playfully.

A spark of something dangerous danced through his eyes. "How?"

"Ebon, hand him your sword."

"I am not sparring with a princess," Lord Nevar protested.

"That is not a good idea, Rane," her brother said.

"Chickens, both of you," she said.

"I am a diplomat, my lady. It is generally frowned upon to fight the heir to a throne."

"I'm with him," Ebon said. "What if Mother finds out?"

"Give him your sword or I'll have Bash sit on you."

The hound's ears perked up at the sound of her name.

"You wouldn't!"

"Do you want to find out?"

"Fine, my tutor awaits anyway. He gets cranky if I'm late. Good luck, Lord Nevar." Ebon handed the blunted blade to the ambassador, who held it as gingerly as one might handle a wild animal. Her brother dusted off his hands and glared at Rane.

"Make sure you don't get ink on your hands today. It irks Mother," Rane warned him.

"Who, me?" Ebon mouthed, ducking into the kitchen before she could offer any more sisterly advice.

"He complains, but there's nowhere else he'd rather spend the day than in the library," Rane said. "Come on, sword ready."

"I don't want to hurt you." Lord Nevar's gaze darted from his sword to Rane.

"You won't." The set of his mouth told her she would need to sweeten the deal. Hadn't Ebon mentioned he gambled? "Fine, how about a wager?"

Interest lit up his face. "What do I get if I win?"

"A personally guided tour of the castle grounds by the crown princess herself."

Heat flashed in his eyes and his gaze roamed over her body once again. If he didn't stop looking at her like that, there was no way she would best him. Maybe she didn't want to.

"And if I lose?"

"What do you have to give?"

A wicked grin flashed across his face and heat flooded her body and settled in her core. She lowered the tip of the sword to the ground so it wouldn't give away her trembling.

"My last bottle of Oteran apple brandy."

"Deal."

"What about your sister?"

Bet stood as far from them as she could get, paying no attention whatsoever to the verbal sparring between the two. She crumbled a slice of bread she'd pilfered from the kitchen and scattered the offering to the birds and mice gathered around her.

"She won't tell. Some things are meant to stay between sisters."

Before Lord Nevar could ready his sword, Rane brought hers up and attacked. She had wearied herself sparring with her brother, and the element of surprise was her only chance of winning. He fended off her blows quickly and easily, the grin going nowhere.

Rane's moves grew more wild, more frenzied as she tried to exploit any opening he offered. Trouble was, he offered none. The ambassador was an excellent swordsman. Perhaps if her limbs weren't leaden from the workout with her brother, she might stand a chance. But it quickly became obvious her opponent was merely humoring her.

She jumped back and tossed her sword at his feet.

"You win," she said.

This only widened his grin. He picked up the sword and placed both weapons on a turfed bench.

"Only because you were already fatigued."

"You are too kind. You would be quite the foe even for Commander Miren. I am impressed."

She walked over to the copper hand pump in the middle of the garden, washing her hands with the rosemary-scented soap. His gaze lingered on her back, and Rane fought the urge to return it. Instead, she stared at the trellises of roses walling off the garden and breathed in their sweet perfume. The bright splashes of pink, red, yellow, and white would have faded weeks ago in any other garden, but her godmother had enchanted it to bloom year-round.

A commotion at the kitchen door drew her attention. Cook was attempting to corral a couple of toddlers. Rane smiled.

"We're done, and Betony will love the company. Can you bring out something to eat for our guest, though?"

"Of course, milady."

The toddlers ran to her sister, drawn to her as much as the animals were. They raced around chasing cats, butterflies, and each other with Bet in the middle of it all. Happy giggles filled the air.

"I don't want to be any trouble," Lord Nevar protested.

"Don't be ridiculous. Cook would be offended if I didn't offer you something, and Mother would have my head."

"Ah, well, I wouldn't want that. Thank you."

He went to wash his hands as she had a moment ago. She finally had an opportunity to consider the young lordling. The timid, shiftless noble was gone, replaced by a warrior, alert and self-assured. He was a fascinating study in contradictions. Her experience with young noblemen had been underwhelming. Most had few interests outside currying favor with her father. This one seemed to have secrets and some sort of strategy. She didn't know what his end goal was. The way he looked at her, it was possible it could be her.

Which was unfortunate. There were five men considered appropriate suitors for the crown princess of Lorea, and the eldest son of the Baron of Otero was not among them. Besides, with his father ill and his younger brother nearly ten years from his majority, there was no one else to run his barony should he ever get out from under his stepmother's influence.

Perhaps that was his goal. It made sense. Use a successful negotiation with another kingdom to assert his birthright. It was a tactic worthy of the Faerie Court. Was he using her to ensure his success?

"What has you thinking so hard?" His voice cut through her reflections, and Rane jumped in her seat.

"Nothing," she said.

He raised his eyebrows, but she was saved the follow-up question when a maid carried out a tray with a pot of tea, fresh bread, eggs, and a few apples. Catching the whiff of food, Bash bounded over from where she chased the children and, true to her name, threw herself into Rane's legs. Rane shoved the hound away and poured the tea.

"Thank you." Lord Nevar sipped and made a face.

"Not to your liking?"

He flushed. "I'm afraid I prefer coffee."

"Oh, you should have said something. We keep some on hand for visitors."

"No, don't trouble the staff. It will be fine with a little honey."

Rane smiled and playfully shoved the pot across the table, where it promptly landed in his lap, spewing honey all over his breeches, the table, and the flagstones below. He gasped and his body stiffened. Bash ran over and did her best to clean up the mess, starting with the young lord.

The color left her face. She'd really stepped in it this time. Their guest's face was red, and she'd just sicced her dog on his fucking lap.

Instead of an angry remark, more laughter tumbled out of him as Bash licked his face. Determining the lordling was clean enough, she began work on the flagstones.

"Are you all right, Lord Nevar?" Rane asked in a small voice.

He waved a hand at her as he dabbed his napkin at his eyes. "Yes, I'm fine. Better than fine. I haven't laughed like that in a long time."

Bet appeared, a dampened napkin in hand, and handed it to the ambassador before spinning away, once again chasing the small children. With a smile, he wiped the honey from his fingers and did his best to remove what Bash had missed. All he accomplished was a sticky, wet mess on his breeches.

"These don't fit right, anyway." He placed the napkin to the side and leaned back in his chair.

"I'll send someone to take them to the laundry after breakfast. They'll look almost new in no time."

"If losing a pair of breeches is the price I pay for such good company, it will be well worth it."

A warm tendril of delight wound through her and nestled close to her heart. Rane suspected others merely tolerated her company for what she was instead of enjoying her company for who she was.

Rane needed to be careful, though. This lordling had proven to be a good actor, putting on different faces depending on the situation. She suspected he was his true self now.

"Thank you for the compliment," she said with a smile.

"Oh, I wasn't talking about you. This bread is amazing."

She couldn't help it; she laughed. The bread from the royal kitchen was the best she'd ever had. If he teased her, he saw her as a person first, not a princess. Rane liked the thought a lot, maybe too much.

A squeal of delight drew her attention to the corner where Bet swung the children around, Bash barking and the birds swooping. It was chaos, and it was beautiful.

"Your sister…" Lord Nevar's question died on his lips. His amazingly luscious lips. He cleared his throat. "How does she get her hair that color?"

Betony's bright cranberry hair soaked in the sun, making it a bit more pink than usual. It wasn't a secret, but it wasn't something they really discussed to all and sundry.

"She was born with it. Betony is fey," Rane said.

"A changeling?" He sucked in a breath.

Rane hated the legend. On occasion, maybe every hundred years or so, a fairy child might be left in place of a human one, usually due to a tragedy. But the way the stories promulgated, he could be excused for assuming it was a common occurrence.

"No. That's more legend than truth." His relief was almost palpable. "Those with distant fairy ancestors sometimes are born with fairy characteristics. Betony is the first in our family since the Treaty of the Argent. The Queens of Faerie were ecstatic. They had hoped for something of the sort when they put in the stipulation that a Lorean of the royal family marry a member of the Faerie Court within a hundred years."

"What will happen to her?"

Rane appreciated the trepidation in his voice. Until King Armel had signed his own armistice with the Fairies a few years before her birth, any born fey in Teruelle were exiled or killed. That wasn't the case in Lorea.

"Sometime in the next couple of years, Betony will foster full time with the Queens."

"You'll allow your flesh and blood into the Faerie Court?" The outrage colored his cheeks and his eyes gleamed like polished bronze.

"If she doesn't go, she may become a danger to herself and others. They can teach her how to use her magic."

"But no one ever returns from the Faerie Court. You'll never see her again."

Rane laughed darkly. The Queens would be thrilled to hear the rumors they'd spent centuries spreading had done their job.

"I have traveled there freely for the past eight years."

He closed his mouth and looked away in shame. She touched him lightly on the hand. Once again, a frisson of yearning traveled up her arm and along her spine. Rane focused her attention back to the matter at hand.

"My sister may choose to stay when her training is complete, but she will be free to leave. We have stayed with the Faerie Court for two months each year since turning thirteen. All Lorean royal children have done so since the treaty, and for the past several decades, most noble houses have sent at least their oldest children for a few months."

"Is it safe? I've heard—it doesn't matter." He smiled wryly. "It seems most of my information regarding the fairies is inaccurate or woefully out of date."

"So it seems." She appreciated he was able to admit he was wrong. It was a skill lacking in many men. "We are safe enough as guests of the Queens and are treated with respect. Those who do not come with an invitation or introduction are at more risk."

"Risk for what?"

She smiled at him. "You know, I never asked. I doubt the consequences would be pleasant, though."

"Oh. What's with the animals?"

"Bet has always had a way with the beasties, but this entourage is new. I'm afraid we may need to send her to the Queens sooner than we hoped."

The ambassador studied her with eyes as sharp as any blade she'd ever wielded. "That makes you sad."

"Yes". She bit her lip. Her parents didn't want to send their youngest off to the Faerie Court yet, but they might not have much choice. As annoyingly perfect as Betony could be, Rane loved her sister with a frightening ferocity. She would make a good queen if her people would accept a fey on the throne. They weren't there yet. Centuries of prejudice couldn't be overcome quickly.

"I need to be getting on with my day. You probably do, too." She had a long list of chores to finish before getting ready for the feast tonight. "Grab some dishes and help me clear the table."

He arched an eyebrow at her but gamely assisted when she picked up an armful of dishes and balanced the remaining apples on top. They deposited the dishes into a sink filled with soapy water.

He bowed. "This was the strangest breakfast I've had in a while, Your Highness."

"In case you get hungry later, my lord." Rane handed him an apple. He clutched it, but kept his gaze firmly fixed on her own. Her voice came out much huskier than she intended. "I look forward to seeing you tonight. Will you save me a dance?"

"Of course, my lady. And don't forget, you owe me a tour."

He turned and walked down the corridor, tossing the apple up and catching it, over and over. She admired his muscular form and tried not to imagine how his silken skin would feel beneath her lips.

"Oh, I won't forget," she murmured and headed to the stables.

Chapter 6

There was more to life than a beautiful woman, even a sword-wielding one. Even when the sword-wielding woman wore curve-hugging breeches, leaving nothing to the imagination. Even when he'd much rather see her out of those breeches and in his bed.

Nevar leaned against his chamber's door and groaned. He couldn't afford any distractions. Too much was riding on his mission to Lorea and seducing the heir to the throne was a good way to get his ass expelled from the kingdom. These fantasies sneaking into the cracks of his imagination weren't helping. He needed to concentrate on his goals.

The king had charged him to secure a compromise over a gem mine in the Calcolo Mountains. The mine entrance was on the Teruellan side of the border, but it seemed the vein went over into Lorean territory. Until they could come to terms, the mine, the miners, and the town supporting both lay idle. If he could deliver a signed and sealed agreement with Lorea, not only would he put his people back to work, but he'd also prove he was a valuable member of the court, equal to if not surpassing his stepmother. Once the king trusted him to carry on the Otero tradition of negotiation and political finesse, his stepmother would have no further reason to hold him back from his rightful place as his father's heir.

Of course, Nevar could not prove she'd relegated him to insignificance a few months before his majority on purpose. The best doctors couldn't figure out what was wrong with his father, and Teruellan law was unclear who should assume the duties of a member of the peerage who could not fulfill their obligations. Since he hadn't reached the age of legal majority, Jocelyn gained control of the barony. She'd managed to hold tight to her power ever since.

Nevar walked into his bedroom and pulled the documents from his trunk. Formal negotiations would not begin until tomorrow, but he had time to review the maps, a draft agreement, and similar agreements his father had negotiated in his prime. It would take his mind off the lovely princess. Nevar spread the papers across the writing desk in the sitting room and poured a cup of tea from the pot left there. He missed the coffee served at home.

A sharp rap at the door startled him. Before he could stand to open it, Jocelyn strode in as if she owned the place, snapping her little mirror shut. He covered his work as best he could with blank pages.

"My lady." Nevar bowed.

He always treated her with courtesy, and for now, it was important to keep up appearances. It irked her, but he would give her no reason to poison him, too, if she was in fact poisoning his father. Suspicion was one thing, proof another. He would eat nothing his stepmother offered.

"Where were you at breakfast?" she demanded.

"I went for a walk to clear my head."

Her hazel eyes flashed with suppressed anger. She was used to controlling nearly his every waking moment. Late at night, when she believed he slept, Nevar would sneak out. Sometimes he would meet with a few trusted men-at-arms outside the walls of their fortress to train. Sometimes he would meet other young lords also desperately trying to escape overbearing parents. Together, they would find all sorts of trouble.

Jocelyn made it clear she resented her secondary role in these negotiations. She much preferred being the center of attention, but there was little she could do unless he fucked up. Another reason to leave the princess alone. The baroness would be more than happy to step in should he find himself up to his neck in a scandal.

"As if there were anything in your head that needed clearing. What are you working on? Perhaps I can lend a hand."

She stepped toward the writing desk, but he kept his body between her and his work. A thin scowl flashed over her face, and her fingers twitched like they wanted to push him out of the way and grab the papers.

None of your business. Though tempted to say it, he held his tongue. Nevar didn't need to escalate matters yet. There would be plenty of backlash after the feast tonight. He pretended her words had no effect. He was neither stupid nor lazy but hearing it over and over again always made him doubt himself. If he gave her an inch, she would try to take credit for his ideas. Worse, if it seemed he took his cues from her, it wouldn't help his cause at court.

"Writing letters to Orom and Father," he lied smoothly. Years of practice made it much easier than it should be.

Jocelyn waved a thin, well-manicured hand in dismissal.

"You'll be lucky if your father is well enough to read a letter from you, and your thickheaded brother can't sit still for more than a few moments."

Nevar gritted his teeth and bit back a retort. It was cruel to imply his father might die while they were away. He already carried enough guilt for the death of his mother, but not being at his father's side should this be the time he passes on was a calculated risk. Though Orom preferred riding, hunting, fishing, questioning a farmer, visiting with the stable hands, and snatching treats from the cook to almost anything, he wasn't slow-witted. Nevar would argue the opposite, but Orom did hate his studies. Well, he hated his tutors, who were the harshest, most critical ones Jocelyn could find.

"It's still a good idea. Is there anything else I can do for you?" He struggled to keep his tone even. Any emotion would only serve to inform her she'd gotten under his skin.

She eyed him with a deadly glare, and a cold pit of fear formed deep in his belly. In the next instant, her face softened from murderous to disdainful.

"You should prepare for negotiations tomorrow, not waste time on letters. I also expect you to escort me to the feast tonight. Do not forget to wear your best."

With a last longing glance at the papers, she turned and swept out of the room, leaving the door open. He sighed, both at her lack of courtesy and her treating him like a child. To be fair, he'd played the lazy layabout to perfection for the past several years. Nevar prided himself on his deception, but he didn't appreciate others treating him according to the façade he wore.

Patience. A few more hours and he'd show them all.

Nevar shut the door and dashed off two quick letters, fulfilling his words to his stepmother. No need to give her any reason for suspicion. He lost himself in his plans.

The light streaming through the bedroom window took on golden tones as the day progressed. A light tap on the door brought his attention to the present. He rubbed at his eyes and stretched out his back. The tapping sounded again. He stood and answered it.

The same pretty young woman from last night dipped a proper curtsy, peeking at him under her long lashes. He hadn't seen such an obvious come hither look since his last visit to the Teruellan court months ago. Her rich brown dress and emerald green bodice, well made though plain, hugged her lean form.

"Yes?" he prompted.

Under any other circumstances, he'd invite the woman in to stay for a while. Or better yet, to come back after the feast and stay the night. But not only did Jocelyn's recent behavior have him on edge, he couldn't help comparing this lovely maid to the crown princess and finding her—not wanting, not exactly. It was Princess Ranunculus whose laugh teased him, whose voice distracted him, and whose body he craved.

"I've been sent to see if you needed anything before the feast this evening." Her voice was warm and smooth, like the best brandy, and the double entendre was obvious.

"Sent by whom?"

The question caught her off guard. She didn't have a ready answer and stared at him openmouthed until she stammered out, "The, the steward."

The color rose even further in her cheeks, red and blotchy now, instead of the rosy pink of a moment before. He'd eat his shoe if the steward had sent her. From the hunger in her eyes, he'd bet a gold coin she'd made herself available to the visiting ambassador on her own initiative. Nevar tapped his fingers against his thigh as he considered.

"I could use your assistance with a small matter," he said at last.

A smile bloomed on her face as she stepped into the room. She moved to pull the door shut.

"Leave it open. This will only take a moment." The smile faded, but she nodded. "Wait here."

He went into the bedroom and pulled out the clothes he planned to wear tonight. A black silk tunic, black leather breeches, and a sapphire velvet doublet embroidered with gold thread in an intricate pattern of rings and diamonds. The tunic was a wrinkled mess. He brought it out to the young woman.

"Could you please have this pressed, Alize?"

She clasped the tunic, shoulders slumping. "Of course. I will have it back in two shakes of a lamb's tail."

Bobbing another curtsy, she turned and left. He stuck his head out the door to make sure she wasn't hanging around outside his room. It was also possible his stepmother had recruited a spy. The maid was gone.

He packed away the papers he'd been studying all day and pulled out the bottle of his favorite apple brandy, the one he'd wagered in his sparring with the princess. The harvest three years ago had been meager, due in part to a too warm and dry spring. After aging two years in oak barrels, they'd finally been able to bottle and consume it. This vintage was rare, and few had been sold outside of Otero. It was a reminder of how past events could shape the future.

He poured a tot into the teacup he'd used earlier and sipped. The sweet, sharp sting of the alcohol coated his tongue and warmth flowed through his body. The tension in his shoulders melted, and the kink in his neck released its grip.

Nevar warmed the ewer of washing water next to the fire before he downed the rest of the cup and tucked the bottle back into his trunk. He would require his wits tonight, and more liquor would only increase the likelihood he'd give into the temptation presented by the crown princess. He needed to be on his best behavior, his most charming, his most canny, perhaps his most guarded. It was hard to do so while inebriated.

He poured water into the bowl and added a couple drops of cypress oil for a light fragrance. He stripped off his plain doublet, tossed it on the bed, and loosened the strings of his tunic. Using the cloth hanging on the table, he wiped his face and neck and thoroughly scrubbed the ink from his hands.

Another knock at the door announced Alize. She gave him a

slow, delighted glance before dropping into a curtsy and handing over his tunic.

"Thank you, Alize."

"My pleasure, milord. Do you require anything else tonight?"

Her eyes boldly met his, and a lusty smile turned up the corners of her plump pink lips.

"No, but I appreciate your attentiveness."

Alize lifted a finger and trace the deep V in his tunic. He'd forgotten to tie it. Nevar stepped away. She must be a highly placed servant to be this brazen around a noble. Or perhaps her advances had never been stymied.

Her lips pouted, but she made no further movement toward him. "If you should change your mind, pull the bell cord next to the bed. I'll come running."

She curtsied again and left. Nevar cleared his throat and shut the door. He didn't want to know if she lingered this time.

The setting sun sent red-gold tendrils of light through the wavy glass of the bedroom window. He dressed quickly, fastening on a black belt and pulling on his tall black boots. Nevar added one more accessory, an affectation he'd picked up from the Teruellan court. He clasped a small gold hoop into his earlobe. Glancing into the mirror above the washstand, he was pleased with the results. He looked refined and sure of himself for the first time in years.

Tonight was the night. Nevar, the wastrel, the lazy good-for-nothing, was dead. In his place stood Lord Nevar, ambassador and heir to Otero. Let the cards fall where they may.

Chapter 7

"Where is Alize?" Rane tried to tighten the laces on her corset herself.

"She's been assigned to the Teruellan delegation, Rane," Betony chided.

Idoya's tits, now she remembered. Alize's cheery good nature and light hand with corset stays usually made dressing for these formal events, if not pleasant, at least bearable. If it weren't for these damned corsets, she'd wear dresses more often. There was a reason she preferred breeches and jerkins. For a moment, Rane couldn't help but imagine the look on Lord Nevar's face when he saw her in this.

"Can you help me, Bet? I'm shit at this." Rane stared at Bet, but her sister didn't turn around. "A little help here."

"Yes?" Betony's voice was sweet and even and as irritating as ever.

Her jewel-bright eyes turned toward Rane, and the little brat smiled. Rane ground her teeth. She would have to contain her temper and ask politely to get what she wanted from her little sister.

"Could you please tighten my corset? Please?"

There. It was a grudging request, but she hadn't used a single swear word and had said please twice.

"I'd be delighted, sister dear."

Bet swished over in her butter-yellow chiffon dress, an intricate design embroidered with emerald green thread. Unlike Rane, her sister had sought help from one of their mother's ladies-in-waiting. Bet's nimble fingers quickly tightened the laces just enough for

Rane's dress to fit, securing them with her signature easy-release knot.

"You are much better suited for this crown princess crap."

Rane slipped on her dress, a wry grin on her lips. She whirled around, her skirts twirling in a satisfying flurry of silk, the same emerald green as the embroidery on Bet's dress. Butterfly brushes on her back tickled as her sister buttoned her into the gown. Embroidered with golden ranunculus, it was easily the most elegant she'd ever worn. As her majority approached and she tackled more official duties, her clothing became more complicated, more elaborate, and more uncomfortable.

"Maybe, but *you're* the crown princess, not me."

"I could abdicate. Ebon would, too."

If anyone wanted the crown less than her, it was Ebon, but she couldn't actually abdicate until she was queen. By then, Ebon and Bet would be off living their own lives. They might annoy the shit out of her, but that didn't mean she wanted to burden either of her siblings with the crown.

"You could, but you won't." Betony fingers stilled, and her eyes grew unfocused. "Holding the crown is not my destiny. It's yours."

Stupid fey visions.

"What else do you see, Bet?"

The silence grew. Rane opened her mouth to ask again, but before a word passed her lips, her sister blinked and shook her head, eyes refocusing to the present.

"Only you wearing the crown with someone worthy standing behind you."

"Any idea who this worthy person is?"

Bet arched her eyebrows and faked innocence. "Have anyone in particular in mind? Lord Nevar, maybe?"

"No," Rane said quickly. Too quickly. Her sister smiled suggestively.

"I like him. He seems a good man, but he's not being completely honest."

"Should we expect complete honesty from a diplomat?"

"Perhaps not. Whatever—whoever—your destiny, you don't need to suffer for it." Her sister's trilling laugh filled the bedroom. "Rest easy, Rane. I would wager the more you wear your corset loose, the others will as well. You are becoming an influence at court, you know."

"Great, now I'm an influencer," she muttered.

Rane walked over to the dressing table and picked up the silver circlet. She arranged it around her thick hair, coiled and pinned to the top of her head, wispy tendrils framing her face.

Betony's circlet was as detailed as hers. The silver fern fronds were so realistic one could be excused for believing they'd been plucked and dipped into molten metal that morning. Rane turned around and pinned it into her sister's hair. Bet wore her hair loose, and with the circlet in it and her diaphanous gown, she'd never looked more fey.

"Ready?" Rane forced a smile. Her cheeks would hurt by the end of the night, but what choice did she have? Run away and live with the pixies in the forest? *If only.*

"Always." Betony's smile seemed easy and natural.

"Are you sure you don't want to be crown princess?" Rane couldn't resist bringing up the joke one last time.

"Not for all the jewels in the kingdom."

"Crap. Guess I must convince Ebon."

Rane opened the door.

"Convince me of what?" Ebon stood on the other side of the door, mid-knock.

"To be crown prince," Bet said, sweetly. She darted into the hall, away from Rane's scowl. *Clever brat.*

"And give up all my library time? No, thanks."

"Fine, I'll do it. But you can't make me enjoy it."

The three siblings strolled through the castle, a sister on each of Ebon's arms. He wore a thick brocade doublet of emerald and gold over a brown silk tunic. His leather breeches matched the color of his tunic, complete with polished boots and a belt.

The only one missing from their usual procession was Bash. Relegated to the kennels until the night's festivities were over, the hound had stared at her with those blue eyes, begging to come along. However, dog slobber and formal events did not go together.

As they took the back stairs, trumpets sounded, telling the guests to assemble in the dining hall. The royal family was announced next to last, so there was no hurry in their steps. The crier's voice floated up, calling out the names and titles of the guests as they entered the hall.

They approached the entrance near the dais where Mother and Father waited. The king wore an outfit almost exactly opposite his son, green tunic and leggings, a brown brocade doublet. The queen's gown was green velvet, elegant in its simplicity, with pearls beaded on the bodice. Golden crowns sat atop their heads, reflecting the lamplight in the hall.

Mother stretched out her hands, a warm smile gracing a face similar to Rane's own. Rane held her mother's hands, and they exchanged pecks on the cheek.

"You look lovely, Rane."

Her father took over from the queen, holding her hand tight in his. "An understatement. You are a vision."

Were those tears in her father's eyes? Her parents may not have a fairy tale marriage, but they loved their offspring fiercely and were proud of their accomplishments. Looking pretty wasn't usually enough to garner tears. The king and queen were up to something.

Oh, Idoya help her, no. It was a feast, and she was almost twenty-one. She'd bet her best blade there were at least a few suitable bachelors on the guest list. Although she wouldn't officially search for a consort until her birthday, her parents—no, the king and queen; this was kingdom business, no personal feelings allowed—would see no harm in inviting a few likely contenders.

Rane bit her tongue, the sharp pain reminding her to not pick a fight before a formal state affair. However, she'd be mentioning this incident at the earliest possible moment. Boundaries. They needed boundaries.

She gulped some air. Perhaps it wouldn't be as bad as she thought. After all, these sorts of things would become even more common until they came to an agreement on an acceptable consort. If only attraction and passion could be considered as much as political gain and treaties. Such were the prospects for the heir to the throne.

Boot heels clacking on the floor drew her attention. Captain Jadran led their honored guests down the hall. The Baroness of Otero wore a black velvet dress with tiny sapphires sewn around the neckline, sparkling like the sun off ocean waves in the lamplight. Her straight black hair hung loose, the white streak brushing past her cheek.

But it was the man beside her who drove everything else from Rane's mind. Lord Nevar cut a fine figure in his blue velvet doublet, the black silk of his tunic an intriguing contrast to his brown skin. For once, his stride and posture reflected the confident man she met in the orchard and who had sparred with her this morning. His gaze swept over her, and for a moment, a spark of something wild and sensual flared. Heat flooded her body and settled in her belly.

A jerky motion drew her attention to the baroness. Jocelyn stared at her stepson, her eyes glittering darkly in the low lighting, and a sneer curled her lips. Her fingers were claws ready to slice at him. Cold dread replaced the heat from an instant before, and Rane froze. Surely the baroness wouldn't do anything rash. It had to be a trick of the light. Before Rane could say anything or move between the two, Radclyffe, the steward, opened the door.

"Are you ready, Your Majesty?"

The baroness relaxed, plastering on a smile and tucking her hands into her skirt. The moment passed, and Rane could almost convince herself she'd imagined it, except the woman's eyes still sparked with something dangerous.

"Yes, thank you, Radclyffe."

The steward stepped back into the hall, and Captain Jadran held the door. Radclyffe's voice rang out, announcing each of them. He called the baroness first and seated her far from the king and queen's places. She shot jealous glares at her stepson who, as the most honored guest, took Rane's usual chair. Ebon walked to the far end, next to the baroness, and Bet sat next to him. Rane flinched when her formal name rang out, and her mother flicked her elbow. She sat next to Lord Nevar.

Her mother didn't just walk in. She glided as though carried by the breeze, but her presence was a rock-solid weight lending gravitas to the gathering. All remaining chatter hushed in awe of her. Or perhaps fear. Beatrice looked every ounce the queen she was raised to be by the Faerie Court.

Her father broke the spell his wife cast over the crowd. All bowed and curtsied to their sovereign, and chatter returned.

"Lords and Ladies, Honored Guests." King Rowan's baritone

filled the large space, reverberating off the walls and silencing those gathered. "We are here tonight to welcome the Ambassador and his Lady Mother. We pray to the goddess Idoya and the God of Teruelle to bless our coming negotiations."

The king bowed his head for a moment to allow for the silent prayer of those who wished to join him.

"Thank you for being here. There will be dancing after dinner. Let's eat!"

A muted cheer rose from the crowd, along with some table thumping, but it died down when the servants brought out the first course: bread, a cold cucumber soup, and assorted savory treats, such as deviled eggs and almonds roasted with chili powder. Rane ate sparingly. After breakfast, she'd spotted Cook preparing tonight's dessert and wanted the largest piece of berry cake she could eat.

The court musicians played quiet, up-tempo music to encourage conversation. She would have been happy to eat in peace, but after a brief exchange with the King, Lord Nevar turned to her.

"Ranunculus is a unique name, Your Highness."

"Ridiculous, is what you mean." She snorted, and he replied with a small, non-committal smile. She was tired of explaining her name, but if she ever wanted him to call her anything else, it was better to get it over with. "Do you have fairy midwives in Teruelle?"

He shook his head and frowned. "The only fairies I know of are those who are part of the diplomatic contingent at King Armel's court. Even if there were some, my stepmother would never allow magical beings to settle in Otero. There is great distrust, even fear, of magic and magical people in Teruelle."

Outside of the capital of Avora, her own people had held similar beliefs. Queen Beatrice had spent most of the last three decades changing hearts and minds. She had been mostly successful.

"The royal family has had them since the Argent Treaty a hundred years ago. They are not only well trained but versed in both herbalism and magic. When a fairy midwife presides over a birth, mothers and babes have a much better chance at survival."

"Does everyone benefit from these midwives?" His face held

only curiosity, and his relaxed body language saved judgment like a true diplomat. Something important for her father to recognize before negotiations commenced.

"There's always a price to pay for fairy intervention, a debt. In our case, the midwife becomes the godmother, tying our kingdom to Faerie. We offer them free trade and easy movement between our kingdom and theirs and give aid in times of crisis. It is a mutually beneficial arrangement."

"That is all well and good, but still doesn't explain your name."

The dishes were cleared from the first course, and plates of venison and vegetables replaced them. The savory scent of roasted meat made her stomach rumble. Lord Nevar cocked an eyebrow at her.

"I'm saving room for dessert," Rane said. "You should, too."

A wide smile crossed his face, and his eyes danced in the lamplight. She could get lost in those constantly changing eyes. Rane cut a dainty piece of venison and chewed, buying her more time to answer the question.

"Your name, Highness," he reminded her after watching her swallow. His voice seemed huskier than it had a moment ago.

It was the first accident of her life, but far from the last. "According to family lore, my birth was a difficult one. My mother's midwife, her mentor in Faerie, gave her a powerful painkiller. When she was asked what to name me, Mother suggested Ranunculus. She claims it was the most ridiculous name she could think of. Before Mother could explain the joke, Hyssop had performed the Naming. No going back once that happened. My godmother has an odd sense of humor."

He pressed his full lips together, and those eyes now glimmered with laughter.

"Go ahead and laugh. It's the most bizarre name for a future queen I've ever heard. Or read. Or even imagined."

He chuckled but didn't laugh outright. "It suits you."

"It does not."

"It does."

"Do I look like a fu—" Rane caught her mother's quirked eyebrow. Right. No profanity at formal events. "A cursed flower?"

The smile stayed stubbornly on his lips, and a sudden urge to kiss it away overcame her. Rane turned back to her plate, refusing to look at him.

Lord Nevar leaned closer, his warm breath tickling her ear. "You look like the most beautiful woman here."

The compulsion to turn her face into his and kiss him grew. Instead, she shook her head.

"No, my mother—"

"Your Highness, are you trying to argue with the Teruellan ambassador when he has paid you a compliment?" He shook his head in mock outrage.

His hand was a fingerbreadth from hers, and a shock of yearning traveled from where he didn't quite touch her to chase away the foreboding his stepmother's earlier behavior had planted. Before she could deny it or give in to the fancy to kiss him, a crack of thunder filled the room, and the doors to the great hall blew open.

A tall woman stalked in. She moved with the confidence of a wolf, her long, vibrant yellow hair streaming behind her. Her eyes, the violet color of amethyst, glittered in the bright light of the hall. Her dress matched her eyes and clung to her thin frame like a second skin.

The steward scurried to his place beside the head table.

"The Lady Hyssop of Faerie." His voice warbled in his haste and, perhaps, in fear.

A tight grin pulled up the fairy's pale lips. It should have softened her face, but it only made her seem more a predator, a wolf trying not to bare her teeth in threat. King Rowan stood, and the entire hall rose with him.

"Welcome, Lady. Please, join us."

As a servant rushed a chair to the head table, Hyssop inspected Rane, her keen eyes missing nothing. She peeked at Lord Nevar, taking him in with one glance.

"You look well, child," Hyssop said, returning her sharp gaze to the princess.

Rane dipped a curtsy. "Thank you, Godmother. As do you. Not a day over three hundred."

"Impertinent." The smile on the fairy's face softened finally, and the wolf left the hall.

After sharing some whispered words and knowing smiles with the queen, Hyssop made herself comfortable next to Rane.

"You're in time for dessert. Cook made berry cake," Rane said.

"Ah. I sensed it was important to be here tonight. The presence of berry cake proves me right."

The servants cleared away the main course. With Rane's attention on her godmother, Lord Nevar was now engrossed in a discussion with her father. She missed the intensity of his gaze.

"Is that why you came?"

Hyssop had a standing invitation to any function, formal or informal, and she made an effort to show up at least once or twice each year. One never knew if a fairy would show or what they might do when they did, but chances were it would be interesting.

"I dreamed today would be important for you, and you might have need of the boon I owe you. What kind of godmother would I be if I wasn't by my goddaughter's side for all her important occasions, whether she knew it or not?"

"A normal one."

Hyssop laughed, a rich, tinkling sound that reminded her more of Betony's laugh than anything.

Cook wheeled in a cart carrying a large cake coated in white icing, pink flowers, and berries of many hues of purple and red. A spun sugar crown graced the top. When Cook cut into it, the cake was a rich purple from all the berries baked into it, and it was Rane's favorite food in the entire world.

She took a bite, and Hyssop chose that moment to ask her next question in a quiet voice.

"Who's the lordling next to you?" It seemed a casual question, too casual.

"Lord Nevar of Otero, the Ambassador from Teruelle. Why?"

Rane glanced to her other side, but he hadn't heard her, still involved in a lively conversation with her father. That boded well for the next day. Of course, the entire point of a welcome feast was to break the ice and allow them to get to know the new ambassador.

Her godmother took another bite of cake, purposefully delaying her answer, keeping her features neutral as though she hadn't planned this theatrical pause.

"Because, when I walked in, all eyes were on me. Except for his. He couldn't take his eyes off you."

Chapter 8

From the moment he'd seen the crown princess in the hall, Nevar could think of nothing else. He'd tried replacing their moments together with dull mining surveys, old treaties, and plans for tomorrow, but the way the fairy lights hit her tawny, silky skin in the hall reminded him of the mountain lynx of his homeland. She was a goddess made flesh, surrounded by a green as bright as the summer forest, and he could almost smell the pine resin in the air and hear the twittering of the songbirds.

A desire so strong it was a compulsion swept through him. The brief contact they'd made that morning only made him crave more. Now she was here in front of him, her dress baring her arms, shoulders, and her bountiful décolletage, he needed to know her, to touch her. When he was seated beside her, his heart soared. The rational part of his mind kept insisting he had other, more important things to do. The irrational, lust-marinated part of his mind beat it into a pulp. He would kiss her before the mission was over. It was the only certain thing in his world.

When the fairy had swept in, unease set his teeth on edge. He focused wary attention on Ranunculus's reaction; if she gave any indication of fear, he'd take matters into his own hands. He brushed his fingers over his belt, searching for his missing dagger, forgetting no weapons were allowed in the king's presence. It didn't matter—he'd use a fucking spoon if it kept her safe.

Nevar only relaxed once the princess embraced the fairy. The godmother, he now recalled. He'd met one fairy before today, an ambassador at the Teruellan court, when he'd been a boy of twelve. His father had kept him well away from the Faerie delegation for their brief stay, but Nevar had snuck out of his room and wandered to the ramparts. His favorite spot for watching the sunset had been taken by a short, stocky man with hair the color of green grapes and yellow eyes like a cat's.

Too young to know better, too old to show fear, he'd joined the odd man and watched the sunset in silence. The ambassador had risen, ruffled his hair as he passed, and left. Nevar hadn't felt this kind of alarm.

Against his better judgment, reluctant to leave the princess to what he suspected were the none-too-tender mercies of her godmother, Nevar turned to the king and engaged in polite conversation regarding the Calcolo Mountains. Nothing too close to the subject they would discuss tomorrow, but general questions about villages, roads, and scenery. He knew the mountains on his side of the border well but had never ventured further.

He lost the thread of the conversation, though, when his name crossed the crown princess's lips. A liquid heat flowed through him, and he wanted nothing more than to hear her speak his name every day for the rest of his life. What had come over him? He was a lovesick fool, and he'd met this woman yesterday.

Nevar was grateful when a servant placed a slice of cake in front of him. It meant the dinner was almost over, and he could go back to his room and regroup. An obligatory dance with each woman at the head table and his duty for the evening would be complete. Then he could try to figure out what was wrong with him before he had to sit at the negotiating table with the King of Lorea. He couldn't allow his attraction to the princess to destroy everything he'd worked for.

When the king and queen finished their desserts, the steward stood at the front and made an announcement.

"Their Majesties King Rowan and Queen Beatrice invite you to stay for dancing and games."

Several musicians set up their instruments near the head table as the servants buzzed by, clearing dishes and refilling cups.

The king leaned toward Nevar. "I'm not one for dancing. We will stay for two official dances and retire to the gaming rooms with our older guests. Please stay and dance as long as you like."

"Thank you, Your Majesty, but we have a long day ahead of us tomorrow, so I will turn in early."

"Suit yourself, but there are many lovely young ladies here tonight who would be excellent matches for you."

Nevar smiled stiffly and bobbed his head. There were, but he only had eyes on one. He doubted it would please King Rowan to know which of the young ladies in the room had caught his eye, much less what his body wanted to do with her if he ever got her alone.

The musicians struck up a tune. The king led the queen by the hand to the dance floor. A cheer filled the air.

"Give them a count of thirty and escort me out," Jocelyn said in a low, venomous voice.

"I know, my lady." His father and tutors had given him plenty of protocol lessons. Even Jocelyn had spared a few moments now and then ensuring his appropriate behavior. Yet she persisted in treating him like the boy she'd first met all those years ago.

"You are too smart for your own good, Nevar."

Icy disdain dripped from her mouth. He recognized it for what it truly was: desperation. He didn't shoot back a final retort. Instead, he courteously offered his hand. The same ice that dripped from her lips flowed from her fingers. He shivered at the maelstrom of hostile emotions she barely controlled. Nevar had never been so glad to be surrounded by a hall full of witnesses.

They joined the king and queen for a turn around the dance floor. Other couples joined them. He caught a glimpse of the princess dancing with a boy several years younger than her, her movements sure to his gangly awkwardness.

On the next song, Nevar danced with the queen while the king danced with the baroness. Queen Beatrice blushed prettily as he took her hand, lending youth to her features and looking more like Princess Ranunculus's older sister than her mother.

The king and queen left after the second dance. A gaggle of young women stood nearby. The last thing he wanted to do was dance the night away, at least not with anyone who wasn't a particular princess. His eyes darted to the woman who held his attention. She edged her way out of the great hall next to her godmother.

"Your Highness!" he called out above the crowd. She spun his way, and her dress caught the light and glowed like a gemstone. A lovely blush rose from the swell of her breasts up her neck before settling in rosy circles on her cheeks. "I believe you owe me a dance."

The fairy gave her a small shove toward him, an enigmatic smile on her face. He stepped closer and bowed. She curtsied in return but looked as if she wanted to say some choice words.

"Go, child. I will amuse myself while you're away," Lady Hyssop said.

Princess Ranunculus placed a dainty but strong hand in his, and Nevar led her to the dance floor.

"I thought you wanted to dance with me," he said, keeping his voice light and teasing.

"I did. I do."

"But?"

"But things always get interesting when Hyssop is here. I didn't want to miss any of the fun."

A shiver ran up his spine, and he spun the princess away from him to hide it. When she was once again in his arms, he whispered, "She's a little scary."

Her throaty chuckle caused the soft flesh peeking above her neckline to quiver in an incredibly appealing way.

"Yes, she is, but she's my godmother. She will offer no harm here. You should ask her for a dance."

Another shiver shook him. He couldn't hide it this time, but he caught a wicked grin flash across the princess's face.

"No, thank you."

"It's either her or the noble daughters searching for a husband. You'll be safer with her."

He sighed. She was right. It would be better to dance with a scary-as-fuck fairy than a dozen marriage-minded aristocratic damsels.

"Besides, now that you've drawn attention to me, I'll have to dance with all those young noblemen who are torn between lining up for me or asking one of the women waiting for you. One of them may even be my consort someday."

"Which is the most likely contender?" He shoved down the jealousy that turned his blood green. She wasn't his, couldn't be his. He had a birthright to win back, a brother to raise, and his own barony to protect. To assume he had the rank necessary to make a good match with a princess, let alone a crown princess, was hubris even Jocelyn wouldn't be capable of. Otherwise, it would have been on the negotiating table long ago.

The princess made a funny face, halfway between revulsion and resignation. She pointed her chin at the young man she'd been dancing with.

"That is young Lord Iban. He is fostering with my father's cousin for the next couple of years so he can court me."

"Iban, Duke Marko's second son?" The duke was one of King Armel's top advisors. He saw the family resemblance, though Iban favored his mother's side more than his father's. "Isn't he a little young?"

"Yes, yes he is. But he won't be in a year, and he is of sufficient rank to be on the list." She gestured at a man dressed in outrageous finery, tall and lean and handsome. "That is Count Tahvo, Father's exchequer. He has no lands but is brilliant with money. He would serve the kingdom well."

Nevar couldn't imagine the princess stuck with a dandy who would always compete with her for attention. *It's not my problem.* He wished it was. For now, he enjoyed her soft body under his hands and banished the thought to the deepest recesses of his mind.

"The admiral's son, Radomir, is a fine naval officer, and he has my father's trust, but he's out to sea often. I've only met him twice before tonight, but Mother and Father went all out to ensure most of my suitors were here for an unofficial courting event."

She said the last without emotion. It seemed the princess was as enthusiastic about her marriage prospects as he was.

"Who else is here?" He failed at keeping his tone even, and the words came out gruff.

"Why? Are you going to protect my honor? Not only am I perfectly capable of protecting it myself, you're about five years too late."

He blinked at the wicked grin on her lips. When her words sunk in, he itched to get her out of this hall and somewhere more private. Instead, he leaned in and murmured in her ear.

"Oh, I think I'm right on time."

Goosebumps rose on her skin, and he held her close enough to feel the shiver travel over her body. The wicked grin vanished from her lips and moved to his. Her eyes softened and her lips parted. God, he wanted to kiss her.

The song was almost over, and Count Tahvo waited impatiently at the edge of the dance floor.

"I believe you still owe me a tour of the grounds, Your Highness."

Her gaze darted toward the approaching suitor with trepidation. "Yes, I do. Do you mean to collect?"

"Let's make a bargain."

"Said the diplomat."

It was his turn to chuckle. "I will dance with your godmother while you dance with the approaching count. Excuse yourself for some air. I will do the same, and you can pay your debt."

He spun her away again before she could answer, both to give her a moment to consider his words and to hide how the idea of having her to himself made his heart race.

She returned to him, a wide grin on her lips. "Deal."

The music ended, and he brushed his lips across the knuckles of her hand. She trembled at the simple touch. He wrapped the thrill of it in a bow and stowed it away for later. Nevar approached the Lady Hyssop.

"My lady, would you care to dance?"

She eyed him, and a predatory smile stretched her pale lips.

"Thank you, Lord Nevar."

She placed her hand in his, and icy dismay settled in his heart. Frozen in place, the fairy tugged gently on his hand before he could command his feet to follow her to the dance floor. He held her in the proper embrace for this dance, but his legs were wooden. Keeping tempo with the music was a feat, let alone the graceful moves he'd spent years perfecting.

"I apologize, Lady Hyssop. I am usually a better dancer."

"I have seen." Her smile showed the points of sharp teeth. "It is I who should apologize. I am afraid I'm the reason for your clumsiness."

Nevar gulped. He didn't want his fear of her to give offense. "You?"

"I am an oracle among my people, seeing glimpses of the future. Some humans react to that." A silvery laugh escaped, and for a moment, the apprehension vanished. "That unease is your destiny approaching."

The disquiet returned, and he swallowed. "What, what is it?"

Her eyes lost focus, turning inward. "I do not know for certain, but it is a tangled mess of danger and hope, love and loss. Whatever comes, it comes soon, and you may not survive. If you do, you will experience joy."

When the song ended, the fairy glided away. After a quick stop to kiss her goddaughters farewell, she exited the hall, her gossamer hair trailing in a faint breeze. He didn't see Hyssop turn left or right; she merely vanished in the space of a heartbeat.

Princess Betony waited expectantly. He owed her a dance, but Nevar made his excuses, begging for a moment or two of fresh air.

She eyed him with her iridescent green eyes. "What did Hyssop tell you?"

"She said my destiny approached."

She snorted, a much more delicate sound than he had expected given her sister's broad laughter. "She says that to all the young lords. Don't worry about it. Fairies enjoy scaring people."

"But is it true?"

"Our destinies always approach, Lord Nevar. It is difficult to outrun them. But that doesn't mean you should fear it."

The princess seemed wise beyond her years.

"What about you? Do you enjoy scaring people?"

"I am fey, not fairy. Mostly human. I prefer to offer kindness. Go get your fresh air. Tell my sister hello."

Warmth colored his cheeks as she pushed him toward the door. He gave her a wry grin and a deep bow. He walked out of the hall and found the nearest exit from the castle. Crown Princess Ranunculus waited for him in the soft, golden glow of a fairy lamp, looking even more like a goddess.

"Your sister says hello," he said, offering his arm.

She smiled and took it. "Betony is too smart for her own good."

They followed the path, the warm light of lamps illuminating their way. The air was cool, but his skin was too hot, wanting more than her arm in his.

They chatted about the dinner, about the music, nothing consequential, both at ease with the other. When the castle was a collection of lit windows floating in the night, the princess tugged on his arm, pulling him off the path and into a copse of trees. Mighty oaks mingled with silver-barked birch and the red-berried mountain ash. She seemed to know the way from memory, not needing the dim light of the crescent moon. He, on the other hand, only avoided a few low-hanging branches by a hair's breadth. They emerged in a small clearing ringed by trees. A crumbling fountain stood in the middle, and the patter of falling water filled the air.

"This is my favorite place."

Ranunculus threw an arm out and gestured wildly, dropping all pretense of propriety. Nevar spared a quick glance around. The shadows from the trees should have made the glade seem menacing, but they merely added to the magic of the place. Maybe it was the company more than the place. His gaze kept returning to the woman before him. The moonlight glinted off her moss green eyes, giving them a distinct fey appearance. Tendrils of her hair, nearly black in the low light, curled softly around her face.

Nevar had seen plenty of beautiful women and had slept with many of them, but none were as luminous, as fascinating, or as seductive as the one standing next to him in the moonlight. He wanted to kiss her, and the way her lips parted, she might want to kiss him, too.

He tugged on the arm he still held, pulling her into his body. She placed a hand on his chest. Surely, she must feel his heart racing beneath her fingertips. A flash of dismay crossed her face. Had he read her wrong?

"I'd very much like to kiss you." Nevar's voice was a raspy mess. He'd never wanted anything as much as he wanted this.

Something hot and dark blazed in her eyes. She stepped closer and bit her bottom lip. "I'd very much like you to kiss me."

Nevar lowered his head, ready to do her bidding. His heart soared, and other things twitched at the anticipation of kissing her, but she placed a cool finger on his lips.

"But it would be a bad idea."

He expected the smile to disappear from her face. He expected her to step away from him. He didn't expect what she said next.

"I like bad ideas."

She stood on tiptoes, only a breath between them. Her cheeks were smooth beneath his fingertips, and she smelled of berries and buttercream frosting.

Somebody crashed through the trees, making a tremendous amount of noise. Rane jumped away, and Nevar placed himself between the oncoming disturbance and the princess.

Jocelyn broke through the tree line a heartbeat later. The moonlight did her no favors, enhancing every fine line and dulling her hair. Once again, her hands curled into the talons of a raptor. She stalked toward them, tucking away a glinting object. Her damned mirror.

"There you are. I've been looking all over the castle for you."

"Didn't you retire with the king and queen?" Nevar asked.

He had barely spared Jocelyn a thought, so taken with the princess he'd been, but there was something cold about his stepmother tonight, something dangerous. He may have pushed her too hard, revealing himself at the feast. It had to happen sometime, and he couldn't bear being the vacuous lordling for his first official event in Lorea. There seemed to be enough of them in court.

"Your head is thick, but it isn't right, leaving your kin to wander a foreign castle alone."

He didn't even notice these minor insults anymore. Nevar glanced at Rane. The wistful spark in her eyes had disappeared, and she'd pulled on the mantle of crown princess once more, lovely but distant. He immediately missed the warm woman he'd come to know over the past day and a half. When she wasn't busy being the heir to the throne, Rane was ten times as beautiful.

"Please, do not dally on my behalf." Even her voice was a mask, using the formality of court to cover—what, exactly? "Escort the baroness back to the castle. I can navigate the grounds blindfolded."

"Thank you, Your Highness." His stepmother's obsequious voice was like nails on a slate.

"Good night, Princess," Nevar said.

He might as well have spoken to a statue. Her attention was now on the fountain, and they had been effectively dismissed. Lights shone through the trees, enough for him to lead Jocelyn back to the castle. As he stepped into the copse, he heard a murmur in the breeze.

"Good night, my lord."

Chapter 9

Rane didn't sleep at all. She tried, but every time she closed her eyes she saw *him*, Lord Nevar of Otero.

There were a thousand reasons it would have been a bad idea to kiss him. She had made it a point since discovering sex to stick to strangers who wouldn't recognize the Crown Princess of Lorea in bed or out of it. Her first had been a stableboy attached to the household of a duke. Amused by the young woman who visited the duke's horses late at night, he'd kissed her. In retrospect, their kisses had been sloppy, but for a little while, she was a person instead of a princess.

None of the likely contenders for her hand had piqued her curiosity, let alone her desire. They'd all been perfectly polite, perfectly handsome, and perfectly dull.

Then the Teruellan ambassador strode into her orchard, into her castle, and into her head. What was it about him that drew her in? Like all the other lordlings she'd met, he was handsome and polite, but he wasn't perfect. His smile was a little crooked, and his eyes were a little wary. He'd dropped the layabout persona he'd worn as a mantle at the feast last night, and when he touched her, molten want wove itself into her mind and body.

Alize tiptoed in. She'd always hated waking Rane.

"I'm awake." The words came out as a groan.

"Good morning!" Alize traipsed across the bedroom and drew open the curtains with aplomb.

Rane threw an arm over her eyes. She was awake, but who needed the sun streaming in when they hadn't slept?

"Your tray is out in the sitting room," Alize said cheerily. She'd always been a morning person. Fuck her. "Cook made cherry bread."

Sniffing the air, Rane detected the faint scent of her favorite morning treat. She should get out of bed and enjoy. With fall in the air, it wouldn't be long before all the cherries were gone. She tossed the covers aside and padded into her sitting room.

Alize chased after her with a dressing gown. Rane waved her away. Her maid was only doing her job, but Rane didn't care who saw her in her chemise. Nobody would be shocked after she'd spent most of the last decade running around in breeches and a tunic whenever possible.

"You're not even supposed to be here," she mumbled around a mouthful of cherry bread.

With a sigh, Alize draped the dressing gown over the other chair in the sitting room. She cleared her throat delicately.

"The baroness didn't take kindly to me."

No one offered more jovial company than Alize. They'd run through the halls and gardens together as children, and there were few people then Rane would have preferred to spend time with.

"Everybody likes you. What happened?"

Alize's cheeks reddened, and her chin jutted out in defiance. "I flirted with the guards. She said they weren't there to flirt with some low-born *servant*."

Alize mimicked Jocelyn perfectly, and Rane chuckled. The baroness had picked the wrong woman to insult. Alize was the daughter of the Commander of the Guard. Though she didn't share her mother's aptitude for weaponry and tactics, she excelled at managing others and the many tasks required to run a castle. When Radclyffe retired, Alize was his most likely replacement as steward.

"And what did you say?"

"I told her to stuff it and left."

Jocelyn didn't seem to be a kind woman, let alone an egalitarian one. Alize's words probably went over poorly.

"Now why would you go and do something like that?"

"I asked myself what *you* would do."

Alize returned to Rane's bedchamber, her brown eyes sparking in victory. Good for her. She would need every ounce of nerve to keep the castle running and protect Rane's time and attention when she was queen.

The creak of hinges and smell of cedar assured her that although Alize disapproved of her choice not to wear the blasted dressing gown, she was still going to ensure Rane was presentable today. The first day of negotiations required the crown princess's presence.

Her duties grew more burdensome the closer she came to her investiture at the winter solstice, shortly after her twenty-first birthday. Some days she took them seriously, but the reality of having a voice and a seat at the table was terrifying, so she escaped at every opportunity. Time drifted away too quickly, and the freedom she had now would soon disappear.

Rane ate quickly and ducked back into her bedchamber. Alize was brushing off a pair of plain gray slippers. On the bed, she'd laid out a linen shift, a green petticoat with simple curlicues embroidered in silver thread, and a gray silk kirtle with lace trim. This was business; proper, sedate clothing was in order.

At least it was a kirtle and not a corset. She'd slip into her usual attire as soon as the business of the day was complete.

Dressing as quickly as she'd eaten, Rane was soon shoved into a chair, and Alize worked her own special magic on Rane's tangled mess. Tossing and turning all night and trying not to think of a certain ambassador had left her with something resembling a bird's nest. The brushing was unpleasant, but soon silken waves framed her face. Alize braided it back and pinned the end under. No need for her coronet today, as she didn't have an official role to play.

"Lovely as always, Your Highness."

Rane smiled at the woman who had once been her friend. At thirteen, Alize accepted a place at the castle as a lady's maid, and Rane had missed her greatly. Though she often attended the princess, too much had changed for both women, and their friendship had evolved into a warm, semi-formal rapport.

"Thank you, Alize. Can you put out clothes for me to change into at the end of the day?"

"Do you want the sneaking out of the castle outfit or the fiddle about in the stables one?" Alize grinned. She still knew Rane well.

"I'm not sure yet."

"I'll put out both, and you can decide later."

Rane's skirts swished nicely through the halls of the castle. Her mother had long abandoned trying to force Rane into elaborate dresses for everyday activities. Why would she, when it only meant ruining fine clothes?

For once, she wasn't running late. There would be no fanfare about this, but at least her sleepless night had one benefit. She rounded the corner at a normal pace, and every statue lining the hall stayed upright. With her hand on the door to the Council Chamber, a commotion around the corner drew her attention.

"Shit!" a low voice called out right before the tinkling of broken glass drowned whatever words came next.

Rane rushed around the corner to see who would get the blame this time, a small part of her overjoyed it wouldn't be her. Nevar knelt next to a marble plinth, picking up pieces of a glass sculpture that had perched there since before Rane was born. He looked up at her footfalls, chagrin adding more color to his cheeks.

"Good morning, my lord," she said with a sly grin.

He dropped the pieces and rose, bowing stiffly. His rumpled clothes and mussed hair suggested his night was as restless as hers.

"Good morning, Your Highness. I apologize for my clumsiness. My valet failed to wake me in a timely manner. It's not a great excuse, but it's what I have."

"Don't worry. You're not late yet."

She stepped closer and flicked off a piece of glass embedded in the fine embroidery on his doublet. Without hesitations, she smoothed the shoulder of the garment, making the ambassador a smidge more presentable. The heat rose in her own cheeks when she realized what she was doing.

Nevar froze and seemed not to breathe. Rane stilled her hand and stepped back, going against every instinct telling her to get closer. She might be in trouble.

"I should find a maid and apologize to His Majesty."

"I'll take care of it. Breathe. You'll only have this one chance to open negotiations. You need to look the part." She threw propriety into the hands of the Goddess. May the Mother of All grant her mercy. Rane tugged on his doublet, straightening out a few wrinkles and aligning the laces. He smelled of cedar and earth. "Turn around."

He gave her a crooked half-smile, but did as she ordered, his entire body twitching in amusement. Nevar ran his hands through his hair, and it fell into place. She tugged a bit on the back of his doublet, unable to ignore how good his ass looked in his breeches.

"Good enough, my lady?" His voice warbled with humor.

"It'll do. My father is much more impressed by good ideas than proper dress. Act like you belong and know what you're talking about, and it won't matter how wrinkled your clothes are."

Rane stepped away, and he turned, a quizzical expression raising his brows and thinning his lips.

"Why? Why help me?"

She gave him her most enigmatic smile. "You're anything but dull. Go, or you *will* be late."

Rane nudged him toward the Council Chamber. Nevar took a few steps before glancing back. She liked that he checked to see if she still watched. Perhaps she liked it too much. He straightened his shoulders and pulled open the door, the epitome of confidence.

Rane found a maid and arranged for the mess to be removed. The bells rang as she finished giving her orders. Oh well. No one expected her on time, anyway. She entered the chamber as her father motioned for the council and ambassador to sit.

King Rowan glared at his daughter. Rane approached and curtsied.

"I'm sorry I'm late, Your Majesty. There was… an accident in the hall."

The king sighed. "What ancestor do I need to apologize to this time?"

She smiled brightly. "None. It was the ugly glass sculpture from the Duke of Ibai's grandfather."

He groaned. "Go sit with your mother. I'll draft a letter later. You will sign it personally."

Rane curtsied and joined her mother. Her gaze met Nevar's as she sat in the uncomfortable chair set to the side. His eyes were bright, and an intriguing half smile lingered on his lips. It made her want to kiss him even more than before. She buried a groan.

His stepmother stared at her, then at Nevar. Rane had never seen a more calculating expression on anyone's face, not even her godmother's. And no one was more calculating than a person raised in the Faerie Court.

"If you were on time, you wouldn't have to rush through the

halls, Rane," her mother hissed at her, keeping a neutral face through her anger. It was a trick Rane had yet to master.

"I already apologized, Mother. And it was one of the uglier pieces out there."

Her mother's eye twitched. She'd moved it where it was harder to see. She hated that piece.

"The point is," she ground out, "you should be on time."

Rane was not going to tell her mother she had been on time, or she was only late because she'd stopped to rescue a lordling in distress. It wouldn't help Nevar, and she would only get a different lecture.

The morning dragged on. It would have been less dreary had the baroness not tried to interrupt Nevar nearly every time he opened his mouth. She seemed to have an insatiable need to make everything about her. Half the time, her suggestions were nonsense, and the other half she merely rephrased what the rightful ambassador said. Nevar had to spend valuable moments shutting down her more outrageous suggestions politely. Rane understood better the iciness between the two of them.

His masterful handling of the situation, though, had all others at the table appraising him with new eyes. His opening offer was slightly less than reasonable, giving the Loreans plenty of room to negotiate but neither underselling nor overselling what Teruelle and Otero had to bargain. She even caught her father with the tiniest grin, though it disappeared before she could blink.

The only thing that made the morning bearable was catching Nevar staring at her more than once, always with his crooked smile. Their eyes would meet, and sparks of desire would prickle her skin before he turned his attention back to the negotiations. Something warm grew in her belly, a desire mixed with curiosity and delight.

They broke for lunch. Her mother and father retired to his study for some privacy, leaving Rane to play host. Though she preferred riding, hunting, and caring for her animals, this was a role she found straightforward and comfortable. Ensuring everyone had enough to eat, making small talk, and otherwise playing the princess was all part of her family's commitment to serve the people of their kingdom. Rane gladly served her turn in the hospital, providing needed medicines and occasional first aid.

She loved playing with the children at the orphanage, missing them when she traveled to Faerie or other places in Lorea.

She poured tea for the baroness and Lord Nevar in a corner of the Council Chamber. The other members of their delegation, an engineer, a cartographer, and a scribe, joined their Lorean counterparts at the large, round table.

The Baroness of Otero sipped the tea and winced.

"The tea isn't to your liking, my lady?" Rane asked.

"I'm sorry, Your Highness. We have coffee in Otero. I find tea unsatisfying." The woman's pinched face made it seem nothing satisfied her.

"I like it. What's in it?" Nevar asked.

Rane raised an eyebrow. Yesterday, he wasn't fond of tea. He kept his face neutral. Was he purposefully goading his stepmother? If so, why?

"I have no idea. Cook never shares her recipe," she replied carefully.

Jocelyn sniffed. "That would never happen in my household."

"Mother believes autonomy is important, probably because she was raised in the Faerie Court."

The baroness paled. It was hard to tell, as she was as fair in complexion as any person Rane had ever met, but the rosiness left her cheeks.

"Oh, the poor dear." Jocelyn wore a false attitude of concern.

After all the time Rane had spent in the Faerie Court, she could spot insincerity a mile away. She answered honestly, anyway. "She missed her father terribly, but the Queens ensured she had everything she needed. They even made her a queen in her own right."

"But the magic. Being around magic must have been terrifying for a child." Something in the baroness's voice struck the wrong chord. The words seemed to come out of her mouth in a knee-jerk reaction.

Rane waved away her words. "When you are raised with something, it is no longer terrifying. Magic is a tool and reflects the intentions of the wielder. Is an axe evil?"

"No," said Nevar. "But someone could use it to build or to destroy."

"Exactly. The lights in this castle, the prosperity of our

kingdom, the ease of travel between Lorea and Faerie, all because of magic."

"But magical weapons killed the queen's father," Jocelyn persisted.

"And magic saved my mother and grandmother from the barbarians of Fuartir. Because of my grandfather's sacrifice, the Queens gave his family an honored place in court, which led to my mother's marriage to the king. It is natural to fear things we do not understand, but magic is just another part of life here in Lorea."

The baroness shuddered, and Nevar examined Rane appraisingly. She wanted his opinion, but her parents returned, and business resumed.

Rane tried to pay attention. She really did. But, from her position away from the table, the warm day, and staring at Nevar whenever he wasn't looking, she found her mind wandering to inappropriate places, like her bedroom, or the cool grass near the fountain, imagining how he'd appear without the linen doublet.

Her mother nudged her shoulder gently and brought her back to the boring old Council Chamber. "You seem flushed, Rane."

That was the goddess's honest truth. Maybe a prayer to Idoya would banish these lustful thoughts, at least until she was alone and could take care of them in a more efficient way.

"I'm fine."

The queen tsked. "Think it through, love. Not everything is about you."

Another test she failed. She prevented herself from rolling her eyes but couldn't stop the exasperated sigh from escaping her lips. Of course, she couldn't tell her mother exactly why she was flushed, but now that she mentioned it, the room was a little warm. A refreshing drink would be in order. And if she felt it, their guests did as well. Her mother believed there was no task beneath a member of her family. If a servant could do the job, so could a royal.

"I'll fill the cups," she said. Not only would it be more efficient but also honor their guests if she performed this small chore.

"You always get there eventually." Her mother smiled wryly.

Rane slipped over to a small table holding cooled wine. The magic table cooled anything set upon it, yet another benefit of their close relationship with the fairies. She picked up the silver pitcher and filled the goblets.

The Council and the Teruellan delegation were intent on their negotiations, and nobody noticed her. Some murmured thanks, others ignored her completely. Rane worked her way around the table until she stood by Nevar. A frisson of yearning started in her belly and worked its way to her hands.

The pitcher trembled as she poured his drink, chiming lightly against the cup. He looked at her, the only person at the table to do so, and smiled widely. His perfectly crooked smile made her want to kiss his full lips and lose herself in his warm brown eyes.

The pitcher dropped out of her hands, spilling its contents over the papers in front of the Baroness of Otero. Rane watched in horror as the liquid dribbled over the edge and onto the cream silk gown, leaving purple stains which would be nearly impossible to get out, even with fairy magic.

The baroness, however, hadn't looked up. Rane had an apology ready to go, but the other woman beat her to the punch.

"You clumsy nitwit!" she sputtered in indignation. "This dress is worth more than you'll ever see in your lifetime, girl!"

Conversation ceased. The smile faded from Nevar's lips, and his skin grew ashy. His stepmother, acting in her capacity as advisor, had insulted the crown princess. To be sure, she'd believed Rane was a servant, and in many places that would excuse such behavior, but not in the capital of Lorea, not in front of King Rowan and Queen Beatrice. Another lesson instilled long ago had been simple courtesy for all.

Rane glanced at her father. The tension in his shoulders and the set of his jaw were the only indicators of how angry he was, but he waited to see how she would handle this. Her lips twitched into a smile, and she fought the urge to wink at Nevar. She could handle this and do it without offering or taking insult. Business could resume quickly and without the major cause of the day's delays.

"Oh, I doubt it," Rane said calmly, positive no one had spoken to the woman that way in some time. This was more fun than she deserved.

The Baroness of Otero's face reddened with outrage, and she finally looked up. Rane bit her tongue to keep from laughing as all color drained from the older woman's face. Her mouth opened and closed like a fresh-caught fish. As she would with the fish, Rane put the woman out of her misery.

"My apologies for my clumsiness, Baroness," she continued, pretending she hadn't noticed the lack of respect. "Ask anyone here, it's a marvel I haven't ruined more dresses or broken more bones. We will, of course, clean your dress or replace it if we cannot. Let's get the laundress."

"I, I…"

"Come along. The longer the stain sets, the less likely she'll be able to remove it."

Rane offered her arm to the baroness, who had to take it. One didn't refuse a reasonable request from a princess one had insulted. Her father beamed with pride, not sensing her nefarious purpose. She honestly hadn't meant to spill the wine, let alone on the prickly baroness, but now she had, Rane wouldn't let the opportunity to remove Jocelyn from the negotiations pass her by.

"Of course, my lady."

Pages swarmed the area as soon as they left, cleaning her mess. The intensity of Nevar's gaze on her back as they exited was all the reward she needed.

Chapter 10

"Lord Nevar?"

King Rowan's deep baritone drew him back to the business on the table and away from the suggestive sway of his daughter's hips. Sweet fires of hell, what was he doing? Once the king realized he had Nevar's attention, he smiled all too knowingly and tapped the table.

"As I was saying, the terrain leading to the mine's entrance is tricky. Oteran donkeys can handle it," Nevar said, picking up the thread where he'd dropped it when his stepmother had embarrassed herself. He would take greater satisfaction if she wasn't his official advisor. Everything she did reflected not only on him, but also on King Armel.

"I'm sure they can, but we have access to good donkeys here," the Lorean chief mining engineer insisted.

Nevar had accepted these negotiations would take longer than a day, but they hadn't agreed on a single thing, and here he was arguing about donkeys. Donkeys!

The sun hovered over the horizon by the time they agreed to use Oteran donkeys with Lorean grain for their feed. Progress at last. His father always said negotiations started with fights over the small things to see what the other side was willing to give up and what was truly nonnegotiable. With that out of the way, business should move apace. Even better, his stepmother had not yet returned by the time the king ended the session for the day.

The strange fairy lamps brightened as he walked to his room. Before leaving the Council Chamber, he'd requested to have his dinner brought to him. The Loreans fed them well, and he was looking forward to another magnificent meal.

"Psst."

The noise stopped him in his tracks. It seemed to come from a darkened hallway off the main staircase. Nevar could make out nothing in the darkness. Maybe he was hearing things. He stepped away.

A firm hand closed on his upper arm and yanked him into the darkness. Nevar didn't have a chance to ready himself for a fight, but the scent of rosemary washed over him, quelling his response.

"Don't make me knock you to the floor, Lord Nevar. I'm not just a pretty princess."

At the sound of Rane's gentle alto, his body relaxed. How had he missed her? It wasn't that dark.

She wore clean but plain breeches, a simple cotton tunic in blue, and a leather jerkin buttery soft with age and use. From her fingers dangled a small, carved stone on a cord. A fairy rune glowed with an odd purplish light.

"How?" Nevar asked.

"Invisibility charm. I, uh, borrowed it from my sister."

The princess's luscious pink lips curved with a mischievousness that had him willing to go anywhere and do anything to keep the smile on her face.

"What can I do for you, Your Highness?"

"Stop calling me Your Highness, for one."

"What should I call you?"

"Rane will do nicely."

Oh, no, that went against every moment of training from his father and his tutors, but he could avoid royal titles.

Nevar tilted his head to the side, neither agreeing nor disagreeing. "And for two?"

Her grin widened and her eyes lit up. "Join me for dinner."

"As you wish, Your—"

"Ah, ah." She squeezed his arm in warning.

It should have been annoying, but all it did was make him wonder how her hand would feel on his bare skin. He clamped his mouth shut before he could say something he'd regret later. Perhaps keeping words to a minimum would allow him to leave his foot out of his mouth.

"Good. Follow me."

The princess let go of his arm, and much to his dismay, he found he truly missed her touch. She led the way to the end of the hall. Was there some sort of dining chamber here? She pressed a stone in the wall, and a door swung open. She grabbed his hand and tugged him along.

What in God's name was going on? Princesses didn't act this way, kidnapping ambassadors like some hero out of a story, or wearing peasant clothing to dinner, or spilling wine on a visiting noble. Did they? Admittedly, his experience with royalty was minimal, but this was not how King Armel ran his court.

Little blue fairy lights flickered to life on the ceiling of the low passageway as they walked.

"Where are we going?" he asked.

"Shh. The walls aren't as thick as you think," she whispered.

Nevar stopped dead and almost toppled over when the princess pulled on his arm.

"I'm not going anywhere until I know our destination."

"I said shh."

He yanked his hand out of hers, the warm air of the passageway no substitute for her heat. He crossed his arms to avoid reaching out to her and set his face into his best impression of his father when he'd become fed up with Nevar's antics as a teenager.

"I can wait here all night," he said, his voice rising in volume.

She grinned, a wicked one this time. The blue glow of the lights floating above lent an otherworldly air to her fine features. A shiver of foreboding ran through him.

"Are you sure?"

Her voice was barely audible. She muttered a word he'd never heard before, and darkness choked out the light in the corridor. Only the sound of her exhalations gave him any indication he wasn't alone in the void. This was hell as he'd imagined it as a child. Not fire, not torture, but pitch black and forsaken.

Her fingers glided into his, their solidness telling him he wasn't alone in the dark.

"Trust me." Another murmured word, and the lights flickered to life once more.

Of course, she had to demand the one thing he wasn't sure he could give. Rane led him down the passageway until it ended at a door. The princess pressed another stone in the wall, and they walked into a quiet alley. The castle loomed high above them, and the noises of the city filled the air. Calls of merchants, the clomp of horses' hooves, and the rattle of wagons and carriages replaced the silence of the passageway.

"I thought you might want to experience something other than fancy court life while you're here." She raised her voice to be heard above the throng.

"Is this a good idea? What about your guards?"

"Didn't I say I like bad ideas? I ditch the guards all the time. I'll have to apologize to Jadran later, but it'll be worth it. Don't you get bored with all the niceties of court?"

"Well…" He lost his train of thought when she dropped his hand and dashed to the end of the alley.

"And Cook's food is superb but wait until you try the meat pies at The Fiddle."

Rane held out her hand, eyes shining with glee, mouth turned up in a smile to melt the coldest heart. She bobbed on her tiptoes, ready for an adventure. An adventure with him. Nevar threw caution in the gutter and followed the mad princess, taking her outstretched hand.

You only live once, right?

They zigged and zagged through the still-busy streets. Most cities closed up shop after dark, but with fairy lights all over, the businesses of Avora were open until the bells tolled midnight. It was just past dark now, and there were hours of commerce left.

Jewelers and tailors and cobblers lined the street. He peered into a window to watch small people with brightly colored hair embroider fine details into a gown.

"I told you we had fairies," she said in a smug voice. "Those are brownies, sometimes called elves. They are industrious and are well compensated for their high-quality detail work for many artisans."

Rane led them past a street filled with brothels and pubs, commoners and nobles mingling together in the same establishments. A drunk man wearing plain clothing ran into a middle-aged lord dressed in velvet. Nevar waited for the explosion of entitlement, but the noble steadied the drunken fool and laughed.

Nevar couldn't keep his head from swiveling back and forth to take in all the activity. It was busier here under the starlight than it ever was in Otero. So many more people, so many more buildings, so many more things to see.

"You look like a tourist," the princess said with a hint of laughter.

"I *am* a tourist. This is my first trip out of Teruelle."

"Make the most of it. We're here."

She stopped in front of a vibrant blue building with a sign above the door lit by more of the fairy lights. Music spilled out of the open door, bright notes played on a fiddle, and a muted drumbeat made him want to tap his toes. *The Fiddle and Pipes* lived up to its name. The princess dragged him in and shoved him behind a small table in the far corner.

Before he could protest, or ask a question, or even catch his damn breath, she twirled off to the barkeep. Nevar watched in consternation as they chatted like two old friends. The Crown Princess of Lorea broke all the rules Jocelyn enforced in Otero. She swore—she wore breeches, for God's sake—and she seemed as much at home in this pub as she did at the welcome feast the night before. He couldn't figure her out, which made her all the more attractive.

She returned with two brimming mugs of ale and thunked them onto the table. Some of the liquid sloshed out.

"They'll bring the meat pies shortly."

"Are they worth all this?"

"Yes. Now drink up."

The princess gulped down her ale, a feat worthy of the thirstiest guard. Nevar sipped at his. The drink of choice in Otero was its apple brandy, and the Teruellan court drank wine. Ale was a rarity and good ale even more prized. This was excellent, and Nevar planned on savoring it.

A quartet of musicians played at the far end of the pub. Two fiddlers, a drummer, and a flute player kept up the merry tune he'd heard upon entering, and several couples danced a reel. Despite his best intentions, his toes tapped along.

"Now, isn't this better than spending another evening in the castle?" Her ale was half gone, her cheeks were flushed, and she studied him with those extraordinary eyes of hers. Curiosity gleamed brightly, and a smoldering longing drew him in against his better judgment.

"Why do you look at me like that?"

"Like what?"

"Like I'm an oddity in a menagerie or one of those meat pies you're raving about."

She barked out a distinctly inelegant laugh. It wasn't unpleasant but was brash and loud and free. It had him smiling along. Perhaps Lorean noblewomen had a different sense of what was proper for a lady. Certainly, this one did.

"You are an oddity, Lord Ambassador, a young man who should rule in his father's stead, but who has taken a subordinate role to his stepmother. A man who has a reputation for all sorts of naughty things yet behaves the perfect gentleman. A man who acts like he's been ambassador-ing for decades but is on his first official mission."

He chuckled. "Is ambassador-ing even a word?"

She waved his impertinence away and grinned her wicked grin, lowering her voice until the husky alto washed over him, drowning out the music and noise of the crowd, leaving only the two of them.

"If you haven't looked in a mirror recently, you are even more tempting than the best meat pie in the city. If you don't believe me, ask any woman here. And a few of the men, while you're at it."

The heat rose in his face, but he couldn't tear his eyes away. Desire flared between them, winding its way across the table, threading through them, and drawing them closer.

"I'm not the only oddity at this table, Princess."

He held her hand in his, thrilling at the touch of her calloused fingers on his. The smile vanished from her pink lips, but she didn't draw her hand away.

"It's not easy, being King Rowan's heir," she said quietly. "It's harder because I'm a girl who isn't exactly comfortable with a lot of girl things."

"If you're a girl and you do something, doesn't that make it a girl thing?"

A flash of teeth and the sadness disappeared from her tone. "I knew I liked you."

"Of course you do. Despite what my stepmother says, I'm very likable."

"What is it between you two?"

Nevar shook his head. "Jocelyn came into my life when I was young and my father was lonely. She can be charming when needed, and her skills at manipulation are so keen you don't even see it happening until she has you right where she wants you. Once she had my father, she took full advantage of his complicated emotions."

"How so?"

Despite his long years of holding back anything that could be used against him, Nevar found the words falling from his lips.

"My mother gave me two things before she died: my life and my name." He'd been born on the first snowfall that year, and it had been his mother's last wish to name him Nevar, *snow* in the old tongue. "I doubt my father ever forgave me, or her. Jocelyn seems to believe I've usurped something from my father, from my brother. Hell, maybe even from her."

"I'm sorry." She ran a thumb over his knuckles, and delicate tendrils of pleasure at her touch wove their way through his body. For the first time in a long time, he felt safe. How could he trust her this quickly? "If I recall Teruellan law correctly, as first-born son you inherit."

"The situation in Otero is… thorny. My father isn't dead yet, and the king granted Jocelyn stewardship as I wasn't yet of age."

He wanted to tell her more, tell her that was the reason he was here. If he could prove himself competent and valuable, he could make a case for claiming his birthright now instead of at his father's death. He didn't need to explain. A calculating crease graced her forehead, and her eyes lit with comprehension.

"Funny how I'd do almost anything to rid myself of my responsibilities, and you'd do anything to gain yours." A rueful grin crossed her lovely, kissable lips.

"A matched set of fuck-ups."

Another brash laugh erupted out of her lips, and Nevar joined in. The barmaid who delivered the famous meat pies looked as though she might call the authorities on the mad couple in the corner. He had to hand it to the princess; these pies smelled incredible.

One bite told him incredible was a drastic understatement.

"Oh my god," he mumbled around a mouthful of flaky pastry,

savory gravy, tender meat, and perfectly cooked vegetables.

She didn't reply, her own mouth full of pie, but amusement glinted in her eyes. He devoured the pie as if his life depended on it. He would've wanted more, but it left his stomach satiated. Other parts of him were decidedly not.

He watched in avid delight as she licked the crumbs from her fingers and the corners of her mouth. Had the damn thing been laced with some sort of aphrodisiac? He wanted her more here in this crowded, noisy pub, with the smell of ale, meat pies, and too many bodies wafting around them, than he had in the cool grove the night before.

The princess's eyes went wide, and her body froze for an instant before she scooted back, putting Nevar between her and the door.

"Oh, fuck!" She slouched and made herself as small as possible.

He tried to turn his head, but a tug at his hand stopped him.

"Don't look," she squeaked. "We need to go."

"Who is it?"

"Some guards from my captain's company. The ones who are supposed to accompany me on these excursions."

Fuck, indeed. If they discovered her with him, shit would fly. Her gaze followed the guards like a stalking cat. Nevar fought the urge to turn around and look. It would only raise questions he didn't wish to answer, such as, how did the Teruellan Ambassador get out of the castle without any guards noting it? Why the hell was he in a pub with the crown princess?

Her hand tensed in his as she watched and waited. A muscle in her cheek twitched, and she rose smoothly and calmly, pulling him along. Rane headed past the bar and straight out the back. They stepped into a dark, quiet alley.

"Why didn't you use your invisibility charm?" he asked.

"Idoya's tits!"

"You forgot you had it, didn't you?"

"Shut up."

He chuckled, and she shoved his shoulder gently. At no time did she let go of his hand. Nevar wasn't complaining. He enjoyed the feel of her. He allowed her to pull him into the less-crowded streets of Avora.

They wandered the city once more, and he couldn't stop gawping at the lights and people. A small shriek at a fruit stall in the night market drew Rane's attention. A large man grasped a child by the wrist, his face hot with anger, spittle flying as he yelled at the girl. Rane darted straight toward them.

"Princess," Nevar hissed, but she ignored him.

She stalked up to the man and tapped him on the shoulder.

"What?" the man snarled.

"Please let go of the child," Rane said.

"The thief, you mean. Why should I?"

She directed her attention to the child. "Did you try to take something?"

The child nodded, snot and tears streaming down their face.

"Are you hungry?"

"What does it matter? I want justice." The merchant's face went almost purple in rage.

Nevar tugged at Rane's arm. The ruckus was garnering a crowd, and they couldn't afford the scrutiny. She shook off his attempt and pulled out a gold piece from a pocket.

"This kind of justice?" Rane held her other hand on the dagger at her waist, back tense. "You take this gold piece and let the child go, or I will make you bleed. Your choice."

"You can't—"

Before anyone could blink, the tip of her dagger rested on the burly man's throat. Perhaps he could have pushed her away before she cut him, but the man was too much the bully. Content to accept a gold piece, he released the child. Rane snatched the apple from him and gave it to the waif.

The man made a rude gesture but turned back to his stall. Excitement gone, the crowd turned away, too. Nevertheless, Nevar put himself between the princess and the merchant.

"The next time you are hungry, go to the castle and tell the guards. They are under strict orders to provide food for any who ask, no matter how scary they seem," Rane said kindly.

The child blinked at her and dashed away, disappearing into the crowd.

"We'd better get back." Rane hooked her arm through his and led him back the way they'd come.

"You are unbelievable! You put yourself in danger for a thief."

Her green eyes snapped with anger. "No, I put myself in danger for a child. One of my people. Would you do the same?"

Would he? If he wouldn't, did he have the right to govern Otero?

"I didn't see it that way," he said with chagrin.

Some of the anger evaporated. "I can see it no other way. Everything I do, I must do for my people, for my kingdom."

"It sounds lonely."

"Why do you think I snuck out to eat pies at The Fiddle with a foreign ambassador?"

He laughed wryly. He could learn something from this princess about duty and honor. All too soon, they were back in the alley at the bottom of the hill, staring at the castle once more. She placed her hand on a stone. At her touch, it glowed green, and the passageway opened. Rane slipped inside, with Nevar close behind.

The fairy lights lit their way once again, the passage dark ahead and behind them. Her steps slowed as they grew closer to their destination. She paused at the end of the passage, her hand hovering over the door.

"I still want to kiss you," she murmured.

Nevar pulled her into his arms, tracing the line of her jaw with the backs of two fingers. So soft. Her moss-green eyes reflected the fairy lights in the ceiling, little stars in her eyes, and her pink lips parted, inviting him to kiss her. He was tired of fighting it. From the moment they had met, he'd wanted nothing more than to kiss her.

"What's stopping you?"

She pulled his head down, and her lips brushed his gently. Oh, God, it was better than the finest brandy. Rane drew closer, forming her sweet curves against his solid body. He let go of what little control he had left and pressed his lips into hers. A small groan escaped him, and he lost himself in the feel and taste of her. Her tongue darted out, tracing his lower lip. He tightened his hold on her waist, her hips supple beneath the fabric. He wanted to touch her skin, but there was too much fabric between them.

The thought of stripping her bare in the secret passageway caused his pulse to race. No, he couldn't do that. He tore his lips away from her delectable mouth and placed a tender kiss on her forehead, lingering there, savoring her taste a moment longer.

"Ranunculus," he breathed.

She whacked him on the shoulder with an open hand. It almost hurt.

"You can't kiss me and call me that. Everyone calls me Rane."

"But I don't want to be like everyone else, Ranunculus."

She hit him again, hard enough to hurt this time.

"Call me that one more time and I—"

Against his better judgment, he kissed her again, tasting her irritation and outrage and reveling in it. He could handle anything this woman threw at him. It both scared him and excited him. A thread of sadness wove through the moment. He couldn't have her. Not now, probably not ever. Besides being a conflict of interest, what would she think of him if he gave up his claim to Otero, to his people? He would have to in order to be with her. Rane was a crown princess. Lorea was her priority, and Otero was his.

He stepped away from her, and his heart cracked a little.

"This won't work, Rane."

She pressed her now-swollen lips together. He resisted the urge to stroke her cheek, clasping his hands behind his back. Rane nodded and bit her lower lip.

"I know. The heir to the throne cannot put her personal desires above the needs of the kingdom. You have negotiations to conduct, and I'm a damned princess who's not supposed to be kissing the ambassador."

Nevar couldn't argue. What they did here in the shadows was not possible outside these stolen moments. Shit.

He bowed low, ending the evening with a formality that split his soul. "I had a lovely evening, Your Highness. I look forward to seeing you at the negotiating table."

Rane seemed ready to cry, her eyes wide and shining with unshed tears, lips trembling. She took a deep breath, her breasts rising, tempting him to touch the skin exposed by the neckline of her tunic.

She opened the door. "Thank you for your company tonight, Lord Nevar."

Her quick steps led her into the lit hallway in the castle and away from him. It took everything he had not to chase after her. He gave it a few moments, allowing his pulse to slow and reason to reassert dominion over his emotions. Nevar walked through the doorway, his feet and his heart heavy.

He passed the steward on the way to his rooms, his booted steps echoing around him as he walked through the deserted corridors. In the dim light, strange shadows flickered off the plinths, vases, and busts tucked into alcoves. The empty eyes of the busts triggered a strange tension in his shoulders as a shiver made its way along his spine.

Nevar opened the door to his rooms. Someone had stoked the fire in the hearth, and cheery red-orange flames pushed away the eeriness from the hall. It had been a hell of a night, and the soothing normalcy of the fire helped him release some of the tension he still held.

He stepped into the bedroom and froze. On the floor lay one of his own men-at-arms, his leather jerkin and blue tunic stained with blood oozing from a gaping wound in his neck. The glassy eyes told him all he needed to know. The man was dead.

Standing above the dead guard, staring straight ahead and holding completely still, was the pretty maid who had flirted with him the past two nights. Her hand clutched his favorite dagger, a plain but well-made blade that had once been his grandfather's. Blood spatter coated the floor, the walls, and the quilted coverlet on the bed, but not the maid.

Her head turned slowly toward him, and her eyes were almost as glassy as the dead man's.

"What did you do!" Nevar demanded.

"Me? I did nothing." There was something strange about her emotionless voice, something familiar, but he couldn't place it.

"There's a dead man on the floor, and you're holding the knife."

"Oh, snow for brains, I am not holding the knife."

His blood turned to ice and his heart raced. Only one person used that insult.

"Jocelyn?"

His stepmother was afraid of magic, never went near the stuff. Except she obviously had, for what emerged from the poor maid's throat was not her own timbre and cadence. Jocelyn spoke through her.

"Who else?"

"But, why?"

"Why? I am a woman in Teruelle. My options were limited to

daughter, wife, priestess, or widow. I found another way."

"My father gave you a home, status, power. You're killing him, aren't you? Slow enough they'll never guess. And now you'll disinherit me and manipulate Otero."

"Don't throw stones. You haven't been entirely honest either. From your entrance at the feast last night, I knew you'd deceived us all. I'd hoped it was a fluke, an attempt to impress the princess you couldn't take your eyes off of. You played the cad for years and had everyone, including me, believing you incapable of ruling Otero. Now you seek to supplant me after all I've suffered from you and your father and your brother."

She'd been the youngest daughter of a land-rich and cash-poor count. Baron Leon of Otero had given her status as the wife of a wealthy and industrious landowner. Apparently. Jocelyn had wanted more than anyone could ever give her. If that was suffering, he'd eat his shoes.

"How will blaming this woman help you?"

"I'm not blaming her. The poor dear, she came here to flirt innocently with the handsome young ambassador. Pity he wouldn't take no for an answer. And more's the pity, one of his own men-at-arms ended up dead when he tried to intervene."

"But—"

She lunged at him, shoving him into the blood pooled on the floor. "I will give you a choice, Nevar. You can run, or you can turn yourself in to the Lorean guards."

"Why would I choose either of those?" He tried to rise, but his hand slipped in the blood.

A bizarre rictus grin formed on the lovely face of the maid. "Remember who has the power. If you choose not to take one of those alternatives, I will be forced to protect my interests. Your father won't live past dawn, and your brother will face the same fate before he attains his majority."

She dropped the knife on the dead guard, her eyes rolled up, and her face went slack as she fainted, collapsing in a heap at the guard's feet. A cold, leaden weight nested itself in his belly. What choice did he have? If he fought the trap Jocelyn had set, his stepmother would kill his family. He had to accept she had framed him for murder with a side of sexual assault.

"Fuck."

Chapter 11

It was all Rane could do to keep her heart pasted together during the race to her bedroom. She gulped down air, and tears streaked her cheeks. Tonight had been the best night of her life, finally finding a man who set her body aflame, sharpened her mind, and lifted her heart. Tonight had been the worst night of her life, because she couldn't have him.

She threw open the doors to her room. Bash rested on the rug in front of the fire, but her ears perked up when Rane stormed in. The hound whined in concern. Rane dropped into a chair, and Bash tried to crawl in her lap, licking away her tears.

"Thanks, Bash." Rane scratched behind her dog's ears. "I'm fine."

The hound answered with another whine, and her blue eyes peered into Rane's.

"Okay, I will be fine. I'm not used to not getting what I want."

Another swipe of the warm tongue on her cheek had Rane pushing away her best friend. Bash dropped to the rug, and Rane joined her. The two curled up together in front of the warm fire.

If only Nevar had more rank. If only there was a diplomatic reason to consider a union. If only she wasn't the crown princess.

Rane sighed. Bash panted in response, her tongue lolling out in a doggy grin. Even fairy hounds were hounds first and fairy second.

How did she get herself in this situation? Rane had always known her marriage must benefit her kingdom and her people, whether or not it benefitted herself. It wasn't romantic, but it was real. Hopefully, the man she married wouldn't be too much of a fool. If Idoya truly smiled upon her, perhaps she'd be able to build a comfortable partnership like her parents had.

She'd been prepared to accept her fate until she fell out of an apple tree and landed on her first interesting lordling. None of the noblemen who frequented court had ever ignited her curiosity, only discussing matters she knew inside and out: horses, hounds, and politics. Though she loved horses and hounds, she preferred to spend time with them, not talk about them. And politics made her uncomfortable. These subjects and men were too familiar to be intellectually or physically interesting.

For the past five years, she'd found some amusement and release among the visiting guards, footmen, and entertainers. Anyone who wouldn't recognize her face and wanted a no-strings-attached dalliance. Nobody expected a crown princess to find liaisons at a pub, and when they asked questions, she responded with half-truths and borrowed names. Thanks to her fairy godmother's special tea, she didn't have to worry about long-term consequences of her many affairs. They had only satisfied a small portion of her need, anyway. There was something different about Nevar.

Rane heaved herself off the floor and trudged to the bedroom, yanking at the leather thongs holding her jerkin closed, wishing Nevar's hands were there to undress her. She quickly disrobed and pulled on the silk chemise a servant had left on her bed. Dropping onto the little stool in front of her dressing table, Rane stared at her blotchy reflection in the mirror. She dashed away the angry tears leaking out.

Anger at her parents for taking away so much. Anger at her kingdom for the sacrifices it required. But mostly anger at herself for wanting something so impossible.

She pulled a stiff-bristled brush through her locks, thinking, something Ebon said she needed more practice with. From the time she was old enough to understand such things, her parents had made it abundantly clear she would marry for the good of the realm, with little account for her sentiments.

There would be no advantage to marrying Nevar. He was due to inherit a small barony in another kingdom, and her parents wouldn't trade her hand for mining rights. Perhaps they would for a rich merchant with trading relationships where her father had none, or the son of such a merchant. Perhaps the barbarians to the north would send an emissary someday soon, and an arrangement could be made to cease the uneasy antagonism between their realms. Perhaps a long-lost fairy prince would appear, cementing the Lorean and Faerie courts even tighter.

Just because she couldn't marry Nevar didn't mean she couldn't have him. As soon as his agreement was signed and sealed, Nevar would leave and probably never return. An affair might be feasible. Stolen moments in the passageways. Meetings in the gardens. Expeditions to *The Fiddle*. She deserved true passion at least once in her life before settling into her role as heir to the throne and a loveless marriage.

The brush dropped from her fingers, clattering against the wooden dressing table. Rane inhaled deeply and smoothed her chemise over her curves. The blotchiness had faded, leaving a rosy glow on her cheeks. She touched her reflection and went to search for her fur-lined slippers, made to keep her toes warm on the cold stone floor.

Bash whined as Rane passed her but seemed to know she didn't require canine company for this sojourn. On her way out the door, Rane grabbed a tightly woven shawl, her namesake flowers embroidered on a russet background, and the invisibility charm.

Rane knew where all the guards stood, the timing of their rounds, and the location of every nook and cranny large enough for her to hide. The corridors were deserted, and she had no use of the charm. Rane used the servants' stairs to the guest quarters but hesitated before opening the door to the hall. What if he said no? He'd be a stronger person than she. It might be for the best. She couldn't imagine any reason not to have an affair with the dashing young lord, but perhaps he could provide one.

Tiptoeing down the hall, Rane kept alert for any suggestion the Teruellan contingent stirred. Only silence and dancing shadows greeted her. The gaps under the doors were dark, except for one at the far end.

She stood outside, waiting a beat, building the anticipation. Rane giddily imagined the look on his face when he saw her standing in his rooms, almost naked.

"You can run, or you can turn yourself in to the Lorean guards."

A woman's muffled voice carried into the hall. Who was visiting him this time of night? What was she talking about? Why would Nevar turn himself in to the guards?

"Why would I choose either of those?" Nevar's voice held barely contained rage, the heat of it seeping out of the crack under the door.

"Remember who has the power. If you choose not to take one of those alternatives, I will be forced to protect my interests. Your father won't live past dawn, and your brother will face the same fate before he attains his majority."

Alarm shot through Rane like lightning. She opened the door in time to see Alize fall to the ground, next to an unmoving body and Nevar, both surrounded by a pool of blood.

"Fuck." She almost didn't hear him. He scrambled up and stared at the bloody mess at his feet.

Anger and fear battled for dominance. What had happened? Was Alize well? Was Nevar?

"Oh, this isn't good," she said, her voice weak.

Nevar whirled, eyes wild, face ashen.

"I—I—I—"

He seemed incapable of completing a sentence, and his gaze captured hers. Nevar held his hands up in a placating gesture. Blood coated them and streaked him from head to toe on one side. The emotion in his eyes wasn't guilt. It was fear. He glanced at the door.

Rane licked her lips and stepped toward the bodies on the floor. "I'm alone."

"Why? Why would you tell me that? You found me with a dead body and an unconscious woman. How do you know you won't be next?" His voice fluttered in panic, with maybe a hint of indignation.

"You didn't do it."

She knelt next to the two bodies. Alize's chest rose and fell, but the man in Oteran livery was perfectly still, flesh unnaturally pale against the red blood. It took a long moment for what she saw to sink in, but the gaping wound on his neck meant only one thing. She sent a silent prayer to Idoya for a quick journey to the afterlife and turned her attention to her maid.

"You can't know that." Nevar lowered his hands.

Rane shook Alize by her shoulder, but the woman's head lolled like a rag doll, and other than the pulse in her wrist and the movement of her chest, there was no response. Only the Mother of All knew what spell had been used on Alize and how much longer before she regained consciousness. "Yes, I can. My dog is an excellent judge of character. Bash approves of you, which is good enough for me."

"You're basing your belief in my innocence on the opinion of a dog?"

Rane stood, careful not to get the edge of her chemise in the blood. "Well, that and I caught the tail end of your conversation with Alize. She didn't seem herself."

Nevar let out a long sigh, mumbling about daft princesses and court politics. He moved toward the door, and Rane put out an arm to stop him.

"What are you doing?"

"Calling the guard. I'll turn myself in."

"Why? You didn't do it."

"She gave me a choice: turn myself in or run."

"But I was there. I can testify you didn't do it. That Alize wasn't in her right mind."

"Please don't tell anyone. If I don't do as she says, she'll kill my family."

"Who?"

"My stepmother."

Hot anger burned up her spine. "All the more reason."

"Can you protect them from this castle?"

Pain wove through his words, carving out a hollow place in her chest. The baroness had threatened a child and an invalid. Nevar's family. What would she do if somebody threatened hers? *Anything.*

"I don't know. I could try."

"I'm not risking their lives on maybe. I'll turn myself in and take the consequences. At least they'll be safe."

"Will they? With you incarcerated or…" Rane couldn't bring herself to say *dead*, but the word hung in the air between them. "You can't protect them if you're not there. She could change her mind at any time."

"What do you suggest, Princess?" He spat out the words with a bitterness Rane had never seen before.

"Under the circumstances, you can call me Rane."

He shook his head and the fight drained out of him. "What would you have me do? If I run, I look just as guilty."

Possibilities ran through her mind. She grasped one. "Hyssop. My godmother owes me a boon. She can fix it."

Nevar paled. "Please, don't. I can't risk it. I can't. If Jocelyn catches wind of any interference, I will never see my father or my brother again. Please, Rane. Your oath to never speak of this."

Rane bit her lip. She needed help to prove Nevar's innocence. As a princess, she was trained to govern, not to investigate. If she didn't give her word, he would turn himself in. The idea of him spending the rest of his days in a cell or his head on the executioner's block for something he didn't do was unbearable.

"What you need is time."

"Time?"

"Time to prove your innocence. Time to find evidence. Time for me to help you protect your family."

"And how do you propose to buy me time?"

A glimmer of a thought turned into an absurd idea.

"How do you feel about pixies?"

Confusion scrambled across his face, and his eyes darted around the room as though searching for any of the little folk.

"Pixies?"

"Never mind. Clean up, and pack a change of clothes and whatever else is helpful."

"No."

"No?"

"Not until I have your word. Orom is the only person in the world I care about, and I won't have my father's death join my mother's on my conscience. Your oath, Princess Ranunculus."

Rane gave in to the inevitable. "You have my word. On my honor as the Crown Princess of Lorea, I will keep what happened here a secret until we can bring Jocelyn to justice."

He nodded tersely, and some tension bled from his shoulders. She turned her back, giving him what privacy she could. Clothes rustled and water splashed, and Nevar cleared his throat a few minutes later.

"You can turn around."

He walked carefully through his bedroom, avoiding the pooled blood. Pulling a satchel from his trunk, he grabbed a tunic and breeches and shoved them into the bag. Nevar crossed over to his dressing table where a few plums, a loaf of bread, and a chunk of cheese sat on a silver tray and put everything that fit into his bag. He reached for the sword hanging in the wardrobe.

"Leave it," Rane said. "If you take your weapon, they will assume you mean to fight and will answer with equal force."

"But I'll need to protect myself."

"I'll give you one of mine. They won't check to see if I'm missing a blade or two, so they won't assume you're armed."

"Then I'm ready."

Rane held a finger to her lips and eased open the door. Only shadows greeted her. Nevar covered the lamp in the sitting room and joined her at the door. She twined her fingers in his. He pulled back, but she held tight and whispered a word. The world shimmered slightly as the invisibility charm worked its magic, and she pulled him after her. Quickly and silently, she led the way out of the guest quarters, through the castle, and to her room.

Bash's ears pricked up when they snuck in the door. She rose and calmly greeted Nevar with a snuffling kiss on the hand as if sensing the need for quiet. Rane uncovered a lamp and pulled a long, flat box from under her bed. Though her mother frowned on her fighting skills as she neared her majority, she hadn't stopped Rane from collecting a few blades of her own. Her favorites were hung on the wall, always at the ready, as Jadran had taught her. Many other weapons filled the box. Some were exotic swords, curved and etched with strange designs. Some were sturdy, but plain, blades. Some weren't blades at all: clubs, flails, even a war hammer. Gifts from nobles near and far.

She stood and met his eyes, twin points of molten bronze in the dim light.

"Help yourself. No one will miss anything."

"Why are you doing this?" His voice was rough and his shoulders tense, a heightened sense of awareness about him.

"I don't like the men I kiss to end up on the headsman's block," she replied flippantly, desperately avoiding her own reasons for helping him. The connection they had was strange in its strength after only a few days.

Nevar blinked, and a wry half-grin flickered across his lips, gone before she could return it.

"I'm a good kisser, Highness, but not that good."

Rane swallowed and gave him part of the truth. "I would do anything to protect my family. You were willing to turn yourself in, knowing you'd likely face the executioner. I respect that, but I also believe in justice. You deserve justice, as does your family."

Nevar's gaze met hers, his eyes searching for something.

"I appreciate you want to help, but I'm not sure it will do much good." He dug through the trunk, hefting the weapons. "I have long suspected my stepmother of poisoning my father. He fell ill not long before my majority, enabling her to maintain control of Otero and secure a place in court as a trusted advisor and ambassador."

"Do you have proof?" It was a serious accusation.

Rane moved into the bedroom and picked up her discarded clothes, leaving the door cracked so they could converse. She wasn't leading this man from the castle in her chemise. No telling what they'd run into while fleeing. Ease of movement and the ability to blend into a crowd may become important. She pulled the chemise over her head and folded it neatly on her bed.

"If I did, she wouldn't be here, and I wouldn't be in this position."

Good point. The thought of living with somebody who could have done such a heinous thing stuck like an arrow in her gut, ripping and tearing her up. Her parents respected each other and loved their children fiercely. She might not always appreciate her siblings, but she loved them and would ruin anyone who offered them harm.

It proved Nevar was not all he seemed. He was stronger and braver than she had imagined.

Dressing quickly in her tunic and breeches, she grabbed the worn leather jerkin and pulled the door open. Nevar made a forbidding figure in the flickering light, swinging around the strangest sword in her collection. On first glance, it was a typical long sword. Ribbons of iridescent metal swirled through the cold gray of the steel. The hilt was formed from the same shimmery metal, wrapped in sapphire blue leather.

He dropped the point to the floor when she entered.

"Like it?" Rane pulled the stockings out of her boots. They

smelled a little ripe, but time was of the essence. She could worry about clean stockings tomorrow.

Puzzlement drew a crease in Nevar's brow and pursed his lips. His highly kissable lips. Rescue first, kiss later.

"It's perfectly balanced, light and heavy at once. It's almost like it was made for me."

"It's fairy-wrought. Very unusual, as fairies rarely work with iron or steel."

Nevar almost dropped the sword. "I can't take this," he said, moving to put it back in the trunk.

"I insist. Besides being an excellent blade, it will warn you when danger is near. Every little bit will help you."

He regarded her, his eyes shimmering with too many emotions. Nevar slid the blade back into its scabbard and belted it on, treating it as a dangerous animal, his motions smooth and slow. He picked out a plain but serviceable dagger and tucked it on the other side.

Rane slipped on her jerkin and laced it. Snatching an apple off her desk, she tossed it to him. Nevar plucked it out of the air with extraordinary grace. Under other circumstances, she might have swooned.

"Take the rest of it while I write a note." She gestured at the remaining apples, a hunk of cheese, and a flagon of wine.

Nevar packed away the food, and she scribbled a hasty word to Lark on a scrap of paper she pulled out of the desk drawer. While it dried, Rane tucked her own sword and dagger into her belt. She folded the note and placed it in the pocket of her jerkin. Walking past him, she stopped at her dressing table and rummaged around in the silver tray on top. A small, plain stone encased in gold joined the folded note.

She grabbed an old bridle hanging on the wall. It was almost worn through, and she'd brought it back to her room to fix it days ago, maybe weeks. With any luck, it would do for tonight. Nevar joined her as she dug a saddle blanket out of a chest, all the accouterments she would need to help the young lord escape in her arms.

"Ready?" She stood to the right of her wardrobe with the blanket thrown over her shoulder.

He looked around the room once more, as though memorizing

it. "Yes."

Rane ran her fingers over the bricks. Where was it? Ah, there. She found the tiny R carved into one. The wall swung open, revealing a tight, winding staircase.

"Grab the lamp," Rane said.

Nevar lifted the small lamp from her dressing table and walked through the door without question. She appreciated that.

Bash whined, and her tail thumped against the wardrobe.

"Sorry, girl. You need to stay here. I'll be right back."

The dog whined again, but curled up at the foot of the bed, keeping her snout pointed at the opening in the wall.

"She's a good dog," Nevar said.

"The best. Go."

She followed him and pushed the wall closed behind her, waiting until the mechanism clicked. The rich smells of the kitchen wafted through the tight stairwell. They kept descending until a dank odor replaced the spices and bread of the kitchen. At the bottom, Nevar stepped out of her way, handing her the lamp.

Rane led the way through the escape tunnels deep below the castle. An ancient ancestor had constructed them in a time of war and surprise attacks. The tunnels hadn't been used in an emergency for at least decades, maybe even a century. She'd used them a time or two to make a liaison at an inn, or a barn, or—okay, maybe more than a time or two.

They arrived at the end of the tunnels, and Rane pushed open the door. A field of barley shifted in the wind, the moonlight turning the golden grain to ghostly tendrils, sighing a spectral song. She was unable to suppress the shiver of unease that traveled from the base of her spine to her fingers and toes.

"Are you cold?" Nevar's warm breath tickled the hair on her neck, causing a different kind of shiver; this one she was able to suppress.

"No. Just… a strange feeling."

"Now what?"

Shoving the stone door closed, she turned to Nevar with a wide, wicked smile on her lips.

"Now, we steal a horse."

Chapter 12

"We're going to what?"

Nevar didn't need to add an actual crime to the one Jocelyn had framed him for. What was this woman thinking? But the trust he'd placed in her had paid off so far. He wouldn't be spending the night or the rest of his life in a dungeon. Trust was hard for him, but his gut told him Rane was worth it. He followed her to the enclosed area next to the barley field. Rane stepped on the bottom rung of the fence.

"Give me some fruit." She ignored his question.

He had nothing left to lose. Nevar pulled the smallest apple he could find from his satchel. Rane snatched it out of his hand before he could ask any more questions. She whistled, low and slow, a series of notes that almost sounded like a familiar tune and blended into the night wind. No human would hear the whistle if they were more than a hundred paces away. He saw no buildings, no movement within that radius.

Rane pulled out her dagger and cut up the apple. She repeated the whistle, and a faint whinny carried over the breeze. A large, dark horse trotted to the princess, his hooves thudding in the grassy field. She stroked his neck as he delicately ate the piece of the apple from her hand.

"Hello, Grunnin. Long time, no see." The horse gave her a low whinny and nudged her hand with his head, searching for more apple.

"Can we hurry this along?"

The horse snorted and rolled his eyes around at the sound of Nevar's voice.

"Shh." She calmed the agitated horse. "This is my friend, Nevar. He won't hurt you."

She shoved the rest of the apple into his hand. "Here, give it to him. He won't hurt you if I'm here."

"Oh, that's reassuring." Nevar obeyed without conscious thought. She might not like being a princess, but she was damn good at it.

He fed the apple slices to the horse one by one. When the velvety horsey lips closed over the last slice, Grunnin gave him the same treatment as he had Rane. The horse nudged his hand, and Nevar stroked his long, sleek neck. Standing this close, he saw the horse as the true prize it was. A dark bay with white socks and a black mane and tail, well-muscled, and over sixteen hands high, the horse was a worthy mount for a royal.

"Grunnin is a real son of a bitch with strangers." Rane climbed over the fence and dropped next to the brawny horse.

"But you're not a stranger, are you?"

She walked along the fence and the horse followed her, not unlike an extraordinarily large dog.

"We're old friends. I helped train him."

"And who, exactly, does Grunnin belong to?" Nevar was pretty sure he would disapprove of the answer to his question.

They approached the gate in the fence.

"Commander Miren."

Of course it had to be the commander of the royal guard. "Are you sure you're not trying to throw me to the wolves?"

Rane's rich, low laugh would have flamed his desire under different circumstances.

"Grunnin's out to stud. The commander has another horse at the castle, and she will be busy searching for you. It won't cross anyone's mind that he'd allow himself to be stolen. He may even return before he's missed."

Beggars couldn't be choosers. Nevar was now in deep shit, no matter what choice he made. At least this one bought him some time.

She undid the gate and led the horse out of the paddock, murmuring to the splendid beast the entire time. Nevar closed and latched the gate. Rane slipped the bridle on, and Grunnin hopped a little. Not a rear, exactly, but enough to let them know he wasn't pleased with the turn of events. The princess stroked his neck and shushed him.

"Do you see the Argent Forest?" Rane pointed toward a smudge on the horizon. The bark of the birch trees caught the moonlight and gleamed like silver, living up to its name.

"Yes."

"Ride there as fast as Grunnin can go. Follow the edge west until you get to the main road, maybe a couple miles. Do not stray from the road."

"Afraid I'll get lost?"

"I'm afraid you'll get killed. The Argent Forest is fairy territory. The creatures there can kill you fast, kill you slow, or keep you alive long enough to wish you were dead."

Nevar shuddered. He had such high hopes when they left Otero a week ago, but now he fled for his life into a forest that would rather kill him than offer safe harbor.

"I'm going to repeat my question: are you sure you're not throwing me to the wolves?"

"Keep to the path. My friends will find you. Here." She fished around in the pocket on her jerkin, pulling the leather tight over her chest. He sighed. His night could have turned out so much better. Rane handed him a folded piece of paper and the stone on a golden chain. "Give the note to my friends when they find you. I expect the stone back the next we meet."

"How—"

"It's their job. They'll find you."

Nevar glanced back at the forest. He had little time to debate this, but he didn't want to leave her, either.

"Come with me. I've heard too many stories about the Argent."

"And they're mostly true."

"I'd feel better if you were around. I've seen you fight." He didn't want to let her go.

"You don't have to play the layabout with me, Nevar. I'd bet my kingdom you're as clever as I am with a blade."

He savored the sound of his name on her lips, though it sent a lance through his gut. He doubted he would ever hear that rare sound again after tonight. She said they would meet again, but would they? Could they?

"Besides, if someone raises the alarm before I'm back, they'll assume you kidnapped me, and you'd have to contend with the entire Lorean army. The pixies will keep you safe. They owe me."

She'd incurred a debt *from* a fairy? It usually went the other way around, to the detriment of the human caught in such a bargain. Once again, this princess surprised him. He may hide what he was capable of, but Rane's layers put his own to shame.

"Thank you. I don't know what I would have done had you not shown up."

"Made the wrong choice."

"Most likely."

Nevar trailed a finger down her cheek. Her lips parted, and he was reminded of the kisses they'd shared a couple hours ago. It seemed a lifetime. She leaned into his touch.

"You should go."

Yes, he should. He very much didn't want to. A few more minutes.

"I never got the chance to ask, but why did you come to my chambers in your chemise?"

In the pale light, a flush traveled up her neck and settled in her cheeks.

"You know why," she purred.

"Yes, I do."

A whirl of emotions flitted across her face. He lowered his lips to hers. Rane dropped his hand and grabbed onto his tunic, pulling Nevar even closer. She tasted sweet, like the berry cake they'd eaten yesterday. Her body pressed into his, her soft curves stoking a fire he was afraid he'd never put out. He wanted to lose himself in her.

Nevar pulled back reluctantly, Rane's fists still entangled in his tunic.

"I have your word you will speak of this to no one?" he asked once more to still the niggling doubt spreading its tendril in his head.

"Yes. I promise. Not until we have proof."

"You've given me a chance. It's more than anyone else would have. Farewell, Ranunculus."

A smile pulled up her lips. "Don't call me that. This is only goodbye, not farewell. I'll find you in a few days. Maybe it will be safe for you to return."

"Maybe."

He returned her smile with a sad one of his own. His hands rose to frame her face. Nevar placed a soft kiss on her forehead.

She let go of his tunic grudgingly and slung the saddle blanket across Grunnin's back. Nevar used the fence to give him a leg up on the formidable horse. As soon as his butt touched the horse's back, Grunnin ran off toward the trees like a pack of hounds after a fox.

"May the goddess protect you, Nevar," Rane called out.

Nevar held on tight, unable to look back at this remarkable woman who had saved his life. He owed her, too.

He expected to fall on his ass, thrown off the horse by a low-hanging branch. But Grunnin had sprinted directly to a narrow path skirting the forest. A soft fragrance filled the air. On the left side of the path, the small blue flowers of the flax absorbed the silver light of the moon, becoming as black as his stepmother's heart.

A part of him wasn't surprised. He'd never liked Jocelyn and had never trusted her. As the years passed, they came to an understanding. If he didn't bother her, she would leave him alone, too. Their tacit agreement was null and void, and he was left with few options. Even if he proved his innocence, without evidence of Jocelyn's guilt, the poor maid would be blamed. Somehow, he would make sure Jocelyn didn't destroy another life.

An hour passed. Grunnin had slowed to a canter, and they were deep into the Argent Forest, the birch trees unearthly in the dim light. Following Rane's advice, he stuck to the road. When the moon set, leaving only the stars to light his way, the shadows crept closer, taking on a sinister cast.

He focused on what came next, assuming he survived his foray into the fairy forest. Although Nevar had studied maps his entire life, he hadn't traveled outside of Teruelle. He had to rely on the princess's friends for now, but as soon as he devised a better plan, he'd disappear.

Before he could give the idea any more thought, a sparkling rainbow light floated through the starlit forest. He swung a leg over, ready to slide off the horse and fight. As the ball of light approached, Nevar made out a tiny human figure in it. He'd never seen a pixie before, but this must be one of the friends Rane had mentioned.

Rainbow sparks flew off the globe like miniature fireworks, and it grew in size until it was nearly as big as he was. With a flare, the bubble of light popped. Clad in skin-tight leathers and furs that contrasted with her pale skin, a lithe woman with iridescent dragonfly wings stood before him. The woman's corn-silk hair floated as though weightless, and a long, serrated blade hung from a hip. On the other was a silver dagger, its handle coated in red enamel reminiscent of fresh blood.

"The forest isn't safe at night, human."

Her voice was soft and raspy but not provocative. In the dim light, he saw dark marks around her throat. Two other balls of light floated in the distance, but neither came closer.

"Crown Princess Ranunculus of Lorea sent me."

His father imparted lessons on fairies not long before his illness struck. It was always best to be formal and polite with them.

"Has she need of our services?"

Nevar dismounted the horse and pulled out the folded slip of paper and the stone.

"I hope this explains."

The pixie took both items from his hand. After a quick glance at the stone, she replaced it in his palm. Unfolding the note, she gestured to her companions. They flew closer, casting enough light to read by. Her face scrunched in concentration, and her finger traced the lines as she read.

"You are Nevar, eldest son of the Baron of Otero and Ambassador from King Armel of Teruelle?"

"I am."

"And you are accused of murder?"

"Yes."

"Did you do it?" piped a high voice from a hovering pixie.

"No."

Hell, he wished he were as confident as he sounded. Nevar knew he hadn't killed the guard, but all the evidence pointed his way, even his flight tonight.

"We offer you sanctuary until Rane proves your innocence."

"Can we trust him?" A small voice rose from the darkness.

"Rane is our friend. If she believes he is innocent, I believe he is innocent." She bowed. "Welcome, Lord Nevar. I am Lark,

Eldest of the Seven Sisters of the Argent Forest. These are two of my sisters, Curlew and Wren."

The two balls of light flared at their names. Nevar bowed to them.

"Thank you. I will honor all rules of hospitality. Where are your other sisters?"

Lark smiled. Perhaps in the daylight she would look friendly. In the shadows cast by the trees in the starlight, she resembled nothing less than a predator with her eyes on her prey.

"Do you not have maps in Otero?

"Of course we do."

"Then you know how immense the Argent Forest is. There are only seven of us to patrol its interior. Depending on how long you stay, you may never meet all of us. Leave the horse. Curlew will escort him safely home. We have a long walk."

Nevar slid off Grunnin and reluctantly let go of the reins. The horse was his last tangible connection to Rane. With him gone, Nevar had nothing left except the memories of a few stolen kisses. It could have been so much more. His heart sunk and icy dread threatened to freeze him in place.

Curlew mounted Grunnin and headed back toward the castle, breaking the spell that had seemed to fall over him. Lark led the way off the road, and the other pixie flitted off, her sparks disappearing into the darkness before the dawn.

Chapter 13

Rane sprinted up the stairs. Maybe she could get back to Nevar's room before Alize awoke, move her, hide the body, something, anything to buy Nevar his needed time. By Idoya's sacred heart, she would give him as much of it as possible.

Piercing screams a moment later told her she was too late. Alize had awakened to what must seem like a nightmare to her. Rane hurried. Once they discovered the dead body, chaos would follow and someone would check on her. They'd better find her where she was supposed to be.

She burst through the hidden door, greeted by a happy Bash.

"Go lie down!" she ordered while she stripped her clothes off, even taking the time to fold them neatly.

Miren was no fool. She would know who had helped Nevar escape if she saw Rane in her current attire. Pulling on her chemise, a pang of loss struck her. This night should have had a much better ending, but she couldn't change the past. Her priority right now had to be keeping Miren from finding Nevar and proving Jocelyn had framed him.

Bash was curled up in front of the hearth in the sitting room, her ears perked and her eyes on Rane. The faint calls of guards drifted under the door as the hue and cry arose. Rane mussed the covers as much as she could. She crawled into her bed and closed her eyes, waiting for the other shoe to drop. It was going to be a very long day.

Pounding boots thundered in the hall, and unintelligible shouts echoed eerily. Her door crashed open, and Captain Jadran sprinted in, strangely calm in the midst of the chaos behind him.

Guards ran by, and a maid stood shivering by a statue. Jadran swept his gaze around the sitting room, keeping his sword at the ready.

"Your Highness?" His voice held a note of fear.

Rane leaped out of bed and grabbed the sword hanging by the door. "I'm here, Captain. What's going on?"

His shoulders relaxed at the sight of her, but he gently pushed her aside and swept the bedchamber.

"Clear!" he called out, voice echoing in the hall with many others saying the same. He focused on her. "There's been a murder. I'm not sure of much else."

"A murder?" She hoped her surprised reaction seemed authentic. Acting wasn't in her skill set.

"Yes. Dress, and I'll take you to your father."

Rane shut the door, sheathing her sword and dressing quickly.

Turmoil reigned. Guards and servants ran through the corridors with panic, fear, and anger written on their faces. Betony and Ebon joined her at the stairwell, escorted by their own guards. They hurried to the still-empty Council Chamber and sat in their customary places. The commotion in the halls didn't die down.

A guard wheeled in a teacart, proving how seriously Commander Miren took this. Rane rose and poured the tea, but the pot shook dangerously in her hand.

"Here, Rane, let me," Ebon said, taking the pot from her with worry further darkening his eyes.

She stumbled the few steps to the chairs and collapsed onto hers.

"What's wrong?" Bet asked quietly.

Rane merely shook her head. She hated lying to her sister, but she'd promised Nevar.

Ebon handed her a cup of tea. Rane wrapped her hands around it and inhaled the steam. The shaking stopped.

"Rane—"

He didn't get a chance to finish whatever he was going to say. Their parents walked in, shadowed by the steward and a few more guards. There were now more guards in this room than royals. The siblings rose, but instead of greeting them with his usual smile, the king's face was grim as he gestured them over to the table.

"You're sitting here today. We don't have enough time to

assemble the full Council. The more people I trust who know what's going on, the better."

In short order, the Minister of the Interior and the exchequer, Count Tahvo, joined them. The latter looked as though he hadn't slept a wink. The king gestured at Radclyffe to begin.

"Last night, Lord Nevar of Otero attacked Alize, Commander Miren's daughter, and killed one of his own men-at-arms when the man attempted to stop him," the steward said. "Other than her certainty Lord Nevar is the guilty party, Alize's memories are hazy. She woke in the ambassador's room next to a dead body. There is no sign of Lord Nevar, but the commander is leading the search."

Rane tugged on her braid and pushed away the guilt. She couldn't tell them the truth, but she could still try to help Nevar.

"Is that wise?" she asked.

The room hushed, and all eyes turned to her, shock in some, shrewd scrutiny in others. Until she attained her legal majority at twenty-one, she had no official voice on the Council and was expected to observe and only speak when spoken to. This suited her personal inclinations nicely. This wasn't official Council business, and she had a lordling in distress to protect.

"Why wouldn't it be?" Her father's voice was calm and authoritative.

Rane took some comfort in the king's words but licked her lips nervously. "The commander could be upset. Someone attacked her daughter and involved her in a murder. Should the same ever happen to any of my family, I doubt I would put justice over revenge. When she finds Lord Nevar, she may be disinclined to bring him back alive."

"The crown princess raises some good points. We would find bringing the commander to trial over a vengeance killing distasteful." Her father switched to the royal *we*. Though he hadn't called an official Council meeting, he was still making decisions on behalf of the kingdom, not his personal wishes. "Is justice the commander's only concern?"

"Commander Miren has served you for decades," said Count Tahvo. "Surely her record speaks for itself."

"Miren has never investigated an attack on her daughter before. We would like to discuss this further with her. Radclyffe, send a guard to inform the commander she must appoint someone to take over the search for Lord Nevar and have her report here."

The steward spoke quietly to the nearest guard, who saluted and left, his boots hitting the stone floor in an ever-increasing beat.

"Any other suggestions?" King Rowan asked.

"We should summon the baroness," Queen Beatrice said. "She could tell us more about Lord Nevar's character and perhaps where he might have run or if they have any friends in Lorea who might shelter him."

"Yes, that is an excellent idea." The king pointed at another guard. "Go fetch the baroness, please."

King Rowan's gaze tried to bore through the veneer of indifference Rane wore. She swallowed and pushed away her doubts and her guilt, allowing none of it to show on her face. He gave her brother and sister the same treatment.

"You three spent the most time with Lord Nevar. How do you judge his character?" After silence greeted his question, he turned those sharp eyes to her brother. "Ebon?"

Her brother swallowed and put on his scholar's expression. It differed slightly from his everyday one, blank, more disinterest in his eyes as he searched his memory for the details their father wanted.

"Lord Nevar is quiet and reserved, Your Majesty. Our interactions have been minimal, but there is nothing in any records or reports that would indicate he was capable of assaulting a woman or murdering a guard. Although he has a reputation with the ladies of the Teruellan court, they all seem to have been willing partners."

"Would you believe him capable of murder?"

Ebon tilted his head. "He does not seem quick to anger, and he doesn't have a propensity for violence. But Captain Jadran says anyone can kill under the right circumstances."

King Rowan grunted an acknowledgement. "True. Unhelpful, but true. Betony?"

Bet's bright green gaze darted toward her sister for an instant before she answered.

"I like him. He has a friendly laugh, and he is kind to the animals. Lady Hyssop didn't hate him."

Their father gravely considered this information. Similar to Bash, Betony had an instinct for people. Perhaps it was the fey part of them. The king turned his gaze to Rane.

"Ranunculus, you spent the most time with him at the feast. You even danced with the man. Your thoughts?"

She drummed her fingers on the table while she put her story together. Best to keep it as close to the truth as possible. Her mother had a keen sense when it came to lies.

"Bash likes him. That's always been enough for me."

"We are not deciding the fate of an accused murderer based on whether a dog likes him." Thunderous annoyance roiled in the king's eyes.

"Didn't stop you when that shitty bard was picking pockets at your birthday feast."

He slammed a fist on the table, causing everybody to jump. Everybody except Rane. It wasn't the first time she stood in the center of her father's anger and annoyance. It wouldn't be the last.

"Language. We are conducting official business, and you will be polite. And murder is a long way from theft."

Rane bent her head. "Sorry, Your Majesty. I will attempt to choose my words more wisely in the future."

Good, her plan had worked. Her simple dismissal of the possibility and her word choice distracted him, and he'd move on. The likelihood he'd catch on to her ruse was small; she'd always shown such disinterest in matters of state, it would take a lot more than her needling him to suspect she had ulterior motives. Even better, Commander Miren walked in, drawing all the attention.

"I am in the middle of hunting for the culprit. Couldn't this wait?"

King Rowan's lips pressed together. "Please, Commander, sit."

"I prefer to stand."

"As you wish. We are concerned your personal feelings will hinder a fair and complete investigation into the matter of your daughter's assault."

"Are you questioning my judgment?"

"Yes, we are." He switched to the personal. "Miren, if it was my child, nothing and no one could stop me from seeking retribution, whether or not I had proof. You love Alize, and you would do anything to protect her. We need to be sure we have the right culprit."

The commander's shoulders slumped in defeat.

"Once again, you prove wise, Your Majesty." She sat at the table, eyes bright with tears, color high on her cheeks.

"You have our assurance the criminal will be caught and brought to justice for both the assault on your daughter and the murder of the man-at-arms. You may run the search from the castle, but it is best for you to avoid a direct confrontation with the accused."

"I understand."

"Tell us what you have discovered so far, Commander."

"My daughter ran screaming out of the ambassador's quarters about an hour ago. A page fetched me." The commander sighed, her faced pinched and tired and sad. "The Oteran men-at-arms had secured the scene. Lord Nevar was nowhere to be found, and his dagger was still on the floor next to the dead man. It seems he packed a bag in a hurry and left."

A guard approached. "The baroness is here."

"Is there anything else you can tell us, Commander?" King Rowan asked.

"I ordered half of our guards to join the constabulary in their search of the city and the rest to search the castle. We will know soon should anyone have information about the murder or the whereabouts of Lord Nevar."

The king glanced around the table, meeting each person's eyes. Rane maintained a steady gaze, though her pulse raced.

"Any further questions for the commander? Or any information to aid her search?"

When no one else spoke, Rane cleared her throat. Her father's sharp eyes cut to her.

"Is there any evidence Lord Nevar did not assault Alize and murder the guard?"

The commander's eyes flashed, her anger palpable, but she answered calmly.

"No, Your Highness, unless you doubt my daughter's account." There was a hard edge to the commander's words. Rane shook her head. Alize was wrong, but she didn't have the evidence to prove it. "His dagger was the murder weapon, and except for a brief conversation with the steward, he seems to have been alone the entire evening."

Nevar had not been alone; he'd been with her. Nobody else was aware of the fact, and she didn't know if it would help or hurt his case at the moment. Seducing an ambassador was frowned upon. If she spoke up now, even to offer a partial alibi, it would only point Jocelyn in her direction. Rane had promised Nevar. Not a word. She wasn't sure she could live with the guilt if she was the reason his father and brother died, but it hurt to keep this to herself.

"Thank you, Commander," Rane said.

Queen Beatrice stared at her daughter a moment, as though trying to pierce the armor Rane had erected. Rane shoved the guilt down to join the sorrow and presented only worry. It didn't appear her mother bought it completely, but her father's voice interrupted their little face-off.

"Bring in the Baroness of Otero, please."

Jocelyn walked in, leaning heavily on the young page who escorted her. Radclyffe showed her to an unoccupied chair. She dabbed at her eyes with a handkerchief as the steward poured her tea. The cup trembled in her hands as she sipped, spilling tea into the saucer. If Rane hadn't known the baroness was acting the part, she would be fooled too. Goddess, she hoped they'd find something to nail her to the wall.

"My condolences for the loss of your guard, Baroness." The king patted her hand. "We will find the person who committed this crime. You have our word."

"Thank you, Your Majesty. I do not blame Lorea for this horrific act. Had I known what Nevar was capable of, I would have never allowed him to lead this diplomatic mission."

"What can you tell us about your son?"

"Stepson." The baroness had a lot to lose if she didn't put some distance in their relationship at once. Rane hated the woman for it. "Nevar was always a troublesome boy, lazy and self-indulgent. He's never taken an interest in politics until recently. When this mission arose, King Armel wanted to give him a chance to fulfill his father's legacy. I am beyond saddened to see he has not only failed, he has proven his true character is not worthy of Otero or Teruelle. You have my deepest apologies for my lack of judgment."

"It is difficult to believe the worst of family," Queen Beatrice said gravely, her eyes full of compassion.

Cold calculation crossed the baroness's face, and the woman's hand slid into her pocket, almost against her volition. Rane's stomach roiled with all the lies and insinuations, with the kindness her mother showed this woman. Her oath burned, the anger chasing away any lingering guilt, and she kept her mouth shut. The baroness might drop a clue among all the lies.

"Thank you, Your Majesty." Jocelyn dabbed her eyes again and added a pitiful snuffle on top. Rane rethought her earlier assessment. The baroness was better than many of the performers she'd seen at court.

Her father took out a folded slip of paper and handed it to Jocelyn. "Could you please tell us whose handwriting that is, Baroness?"

She gasped, and her eyes widened as she read it. "It is Nevar's."

Once again, Rane caught the false note in the baroness's flat tone as she named her stepson. She glanced at her mother. The queen peered intently at the other woman, but her face was neutral. If she had doubts about Jocelyn's statement, the queen kept it to herself.

"What does it say?" Ebon asked as the note passed back to their father.

"It is an invitation from Lord Nevar to Alize to join him after dinner," the king said.

This was horrible. If she hadn't been there, if she didn't trust Bash's instincts, she would believe he had attacked Alize and killed the guard. The only reason her family did was because she'd promised not to tell them what she knew. Jocelyn had given up nothing. She'd even provided a piece of evidence to use against him. The baroness was good at this game, and Rane was only a beginner. The guilt came crashing back.

"Thank you, my lady. We will keep you updated on the investigation. The guards will escort everyone to their rooms. Until Lord Nevar is caught or we are certain he is not in the castle, a guard will accompany you. Rane, Commander, please stay for a moment."

The room cleared out, leaving only the king, the queen, Rane, and the commander around the large table. The grim cast to her father's handsome features had only strengthened over the course of their discussion.

"If memory serves, Rane, you were particularly adept at finding hiding spots in the area surrounding the city not long ago," King Rowan said.

Her father's adroit diplomatic skills extended to his daughter, too. If there had been a place to hide away from her duties and obligations at court within a two-hour ride, Rane had found it. After all, it was how she'd made friends with the pixies.

"Yes, Your Majesty," she said, glimpsing where this conversation was heading and plotting how to use it to her advantage.

"Commander, you will coordinate all efforts from here. Appoint a captain to lead the search in the castle and another to work with the city constabulary. Rane will take Jadran and a few guards and begin a search of the surrounding countryside."

"Rane?" The commander scoffed. "She's just as likely to lose her escort as find the criminal."

For a moment, Rane believed her father would agree. If she was part of the search for Nevar, she couldn't ferret out clues and couldn't report anything to Nevar. However, if she went with them, she would know where they were and could keep them away from him. Either option presented difficulties, and it wasn't her choice.

"Who else worked out all the hidey-holes the way Rane did?" her mother asked. "I believe she evaded your guards much more frequently than we all care to admit."

A condemning quiet fell, and all eyes turned to Rane. She bit back a gloating reply. It wasn't the time or place.

"I will show you everything," she said. *Almost everything.*

Beatrice's darkling gaze caught hers. She suspected something. Rane suppressed any other thoughts and concentrated on the here and now. Nobody knew of her friendship with the pixies. As long as she kept them far from the cottage, Nevar would be safe.

"Fine," Miren relented, "but only because I doubt the ambassador is far. He is in unfamiliar territory, running for his life. If he's a halfway decent person, he'll be afraid, guilty, and panicking. I believe we'll find him in some abandoned building in the city or perhaps just outside."

Rane swallowed a triumphant grin.

"Good, it's settled. Rane, pick three guards and begin a search to the west," the king said. "If Lord Nevar is panicked, he will head toward familiar ground, toward home."

She bowed briefly before leaving. Her plan was working. Not only did they have no idea where he'd gone, they were concentrating their efforts in other directions. Now she had to figure out how to prove the baroness was behind all this while letting loose as many wild geese as possible.

Chapter 14

Nevar followed the glowing orb surrounding the pixie and questioned his sanity. He'd been taught to distrust magic and fairies, yet he'd placed his life into the hands of a pixie based on the word of a woman he'd known for mere days. If he didn't question his sanity, he'd definitely be in trouble.

His choices were *all* bad. Turn himself in and face the consequences of his stepmother's machinations. Run and all but prove his guilt. Or trust Rane, trust the pixies, and wait. Of all the choices, the last irritated him the most. He didn't like relying on others. Nevar wasn't even sure he knew how. This choice was the best of the worst, though, at least until he came up with something better.

Lark had taken Rane's admonition to protect him seriously. She sent her sister ahead to ensure nothing dangerous lay in wait, but breaks had still been few and far between. A few sips of watered wine and a bite or two from the travelers' bread in his satchel, then back to stumbling through the dark.

The legendary Argent Forest was a mystery to him. Fairies had blazed the shortest path possible through the forest from Teruelle to the Faerie capital when the armistice had been signed decades ago. Yet few made the trip. The stories of those who returned were eerie and dark, full of shadowy dangers and ill omens.

The forest seemed to whisper to him in the darkness, the birch trunks gleaming strangely in the starlight. Creaks and cracks from the branches above had him on edge, but the pixie didn't seem to mind. Distant howls filled the air. He touched his sword with every noise, hoping it would give him the sign of danger Rane had promised. Nothing.

Pale blue sky on the eastern horizon chased back the night, but the birds didn't stir. Lark lifted a fist. Nevar stopped and placed a hand on his sword once more. Cold lightning traveled up his arm and settled in his mind. He heard a faint snuffling and a rustle in the underbrush, maybe a few hundred paces away. Nevar pulled his sword free from the scabbard, and his breath turned icy, leaving small clouds in the air.

Lark glanced back, her eyes widening in surprise. She darted over and perched on his shoulder.

"What is it?" Nevar asked, all his senses focused in the direction of the noises. His nose detected a whiff of decay, and his eyes could almost see the faint motion of leaves disturbed by the creature.

"Nothing that will attack if we steer clear. This way."

Lark tugged on his ear until he broke the connection with whatever was out there. He turned to the right and proceeded with a light step. His blade warmed to the ambient temperature, and the peculiar focus eased.

"You can put away your blade now," Lark said. "Where did you come by fairy-wrought steel?"

"Rane." He slid the sword into the scabbard. "She said it would warn me of danger."

"It's a rare gift. She was wise to lend it to you." She flew off his shoulder, and the glow returned, though he almost didn't need it with the sun now rising. "We're almost there."

A few moments later, they stepped into a clearing. The other pixie buzzed excitedly, like a bee around a flower, but there was nothing special about this clearing.

"Where are we?"

The pixie named Wren giggled. "Our home, of course."

Nevar inspected his surroundings, confused. The silver-barked birch trees surrounded a clearing about a hundred paces across, not at all different from those they'd already passed through. The ferns and bushes of the undergrowth stopped abruptly at the edge, replaced by a small meadow of dried grass and fading wildflowers, the sweet scent filling his lungs. He stood next to a small circle of red-capped mushrooms. Birds twittered and a light breeze rustled the yellowing leaves. It was as bucolic as any storybook he could imagine. But there was no house, or cottage, or fort, or lean-to, or stable, or—

Did they expect him to sleep in the open? Perhaps, but it didn't matter. Nevar didn't plan on staying long.

"Silly human." Lark, now the size of a small woman, hooked her arm through his, patting it as one would a confused elder's. Wren flew to the opposite edge of the clearing and disappeared.

"What?" He blinked his eyes and took a step toward where he last saw her. "Where did she go?"

"Put the stone Rane gave you around your neck."

He fumbled it out of his pocket and did as she said. The cool touch of metal around his throat sent a shiver through him. It had absolutely nothing to do with who had worn this last, or so he told himself. When Nevar looked up, a moss-covered stone cottage stood across from him, as though a curtain had lifted.

Wren, in her human-sized form, held open the door. "Shelter," she giggled.

Nevar followed Lark to the cottage. Ivy clung to the rough-hewn stones, and the roof sagged. A worn door hung crookedly, and wavy greenish glass in the window distorted the interior. A cracked pane added to the dilapidation. Hoping the inside was more sound than the outside, he stepped through the open door.

A small, rough-hewn table stood in front of the hearth, a merry fire blazing. Four spindly chairs surrounded it, and a colorful quilt covered the bed in the corner, all human-sized. It was clean and cozy.

"Where do you sleep?" Nevar asked.

"There are pallets stowed under the bed. We don't use this place often. Usually only in the depths of the winter or to care for an injured sister. Occasionally we offer respite to lost or weary travelers. It will be yours alone while we fulfill the princess's debt."

Nevar dropped his satchel, walked to the bed, and flopped onto it, staring at the thatched roof. Exhaustion swept over him, his limbs and mind numb. The odd humming of the fairies' wings filled the air, and he fought off the urge to close his eyes and rest. It had been a long night, but there were still things he needed to know.

With a sigh, he sat up, startling the orange-winged fairy hovering nearby. Wren, again at her tiny, pixie size, skittered off and tugged on Lark's arm. The Eldest stalked over. From the fierce expression on her face to the weapons at her hips, everything about her screamed hunter.

"Wren thought you asleep, my lord," she said, a hint of disapproval in her voice. "What can we do for you?"

"I have questions."

"Humans always have questions," Wren trilled from somewhere above.

"Hush," Lark said. "You may ask your questions, Lord Nevar, but then you must rest. We have promised Rane to look after you. Do not make us go against our word."

He nodded. "Where are we?"

Lark smiled, a small, sly thing that vanished almost before he noticed it was there.

"A few miles from where we found you."

He blinked. "But we walked for hours!"

She waved a hand, batting away his objection. "We spread your scent throughout this part of the forest, so it will be harder to trace you. Today, my sisters will spread it even further. If those hunting you come close, they'll know you were in the forest, but they won't be able to tell where exactly."

Nevar realized he'd misjudged the pixies. Fairies were so disparaged in Teruelle, even after the armistice had been signed, he'd assumed they would be less than intelligent. He was wrong, and he would need to check his prejudices from here on out. They were only trying to help him.

"How did I not see the cottage earlier?"

"Magic, of course," trilled Wren.

She sat on the large table, eating a berry. Its purple juice adorably stained her face. He needed to stop thinking of them as cute. They'd already proved cunning, and he was only beginning to learn what they were capable of.

"The pendant you wear is a small piece of the house. It allows you to see and enter it. When you have rested, we will give you another so you may return that to Rane."

He shivered. It was time he got used to magic if he were to live with pixies.

"One last question before I pass out," he said. Lark nodded gravely. "You know what I'm accused of, yet you help me anyway. Why?"

All traces of mirth left her face and voice. "We owe Rane a debt. This is the first time she has ever called it in. We take our obligations seriously, Lord Nevar."

"Thank you, Lark. Please, drop the 'Lord.' You have more than earned it."

Another smile graced her face, and Lark bowed deeply.

"Sleep. You are safe here."

As though he couldn't refuse the suggestion, his eyes grew heavy. He pushed his satchel to the floor and burrowed under the cozy quilt. Before he could question whether Lark had used magic to ease him into rest, sleep claimed him.

The sunlight streaming through the window painted the floor golden when Nevar awoke sometime later. Orange and pink brushed the clouds he glimpsed through the window. It was late in the day. He stoked the fire with a couple of logs lying next to the hearth and put a kettle on to boil. Nevar rummaged through his satchel and pulled out the food he'd brought from the castle. Cheese, fruit, and a loaf of day-old bread. It would be enough for tonight and the morning. He poked through a few containers and found tea and a crude mug. It wasn't a dinner to be proud of, but it would do. Tomorrow would sort itself out.

The question remained, however, as to how. Did he plan on staying here until the princess solved his problems for him? Could he trust her? Sure, she'd sent him someplace safe, with guardians who seemed more than willing to protect him, but he'd never trusted anybody to have his best interests in mind before.

A whirring noise outside caught his attention. In short order, Lark darted through the front door and hovered. She flew to him and grew once more to human size.

"I did not expect you to awaken so soon," she said.

He offered her a hunk of cheese and a slice of bread. Her fingers deftly took them.

"So soon? I slept most of the day."

Lark shrugged and ate her morsels.

"I thought I had the house to myself," he continued when she held her silence.

"I am standing guard over you. I heard noises, and I came to investigate. You have the house, but do not assume you have privacy."

Good to know. "I thank you for the hospitality."

"You are welcome, but I do it for Rane, not for you. If something were to happen to you, it would hurt her. You are marked for her."

Marked for her? What was he, some sort of prize? Nevar snorted. He was no prize, not under these circumstances. A fugitive, a failed ambassador, a fool.

"Is that not true, Nevar?"

"I don't know what's true anymore."

She patted his hand. "That is a good place to start."

Enigmatic little pixie. He sighed and drank his tea.

"We must discuss some rules." Lark licked the crumbs off her fingers.

Of course they did. Even pixies living in the forest had rules, it seemed.

"If we must."

"First, be in the cottage by sundown. This is the Argent Forest. More than wolves, bears, and lynx hunt here at night. You are safe from them in the cottage."

Nevar shuddered, remembering the cold warning his sword gave him this morning. He knew how to handle mundane beasts of the forest. If she warned him against the fairy beasts, they were something to be feared.

Lark held up another finger. "Second, stay close. The beasts of day are more skittish but can be dangerous under the right circumstances. Should you encounter anything fairy, you will be safest if you can shelter here, at least until we can make sure you can handle them."

"Seems reasonable."

She held up a third finger. "Last, we will bring you food. Eat nothing we do not provide. There is much about the forest you do not yet know. Once we teach you, you can forage and hunt on your own. Do you understand?"

He replied with gravitas. "Yes, I understand."

Lark bowed, shifted into her tiny form, and flew out the door into the deepening twilight. It was too late to follow her, and he'd given his word. He brushed off the crumbs and lifted his satchel. Nevar pulled out the two tunics, the extra pair of breeches, and some stockings and placed them in the small trunk at the foot of the bed. The rest of the food went on the table with the flagon of wine. Thank god he had the foresight to bring it.

He lifted his belt with the sword and dagger and hung it on a hook next to the door. It would be ready should he need to defend himself. That was it. His new life took only a few moments to put away.

Exhaustion weighed him down, and he crawled back into bed. Instead of the sweet release of sleep, his mind turned over the events of last night. It had started out so promising. An excursion into the city with Rane, her lips on his, her body in his arms. It was everything he'd imagined and more. Then the horror of the following hours, the mad dash away from the castle, and the journey here.

Nevar rolled out of bed, still exhausted but any hope for rest banished. If only he had the sense to pack a book.

Chapter 15

Rane held tightly as Sunny flew over the sun-dappled road, her quick hooves growing the distance between them and the guards.

"Princess," Captain Jadran called.

She was far enough away to pretend she hadn't heard him.

They drew to the edge of the ancient apple orchard where she'd first met Nevar. This was the last and best of her hiding spots, and the twisted trees were old friends. Sadness and longing coiled around her heart. If she had known then… No, she wouldn't change how they'd met, but she would change what happened now. Looping Sunny's reins around a low-hanging branch, she continued her "search" on foot. The rest of the party thundered up, leaving their steeds in the care of a guard.

Rane wasn't trying to outrun Jadran; she was tired and grouchy after spending the last few days hunting wild geese. A part of her was sickly gleeful to be leading everyone in circles. Another part was growing frustrated by the whole endeavor. The longer they searched, the more likely any evidence pointing at Jocelyn as the true culprit would disappear, and her ability to save Nevar and his family diminished.

A final part of her, the strongest part, wanted to run to Nevar. She told herself it was to check on his wellbeing, but the truth was far more terrifying. She'd developed an infatuation for the young lord, but her fate did not lie in stolen kisses, or liquid bronze eyes, or in the fairy forest. Someday, she would rule Lorea with an appropriate consort at her side. Nevar defied any reasonable person's definition of "appropriate," especially after recent events.

Jadran finally caught up to her, the other two guards fast on his heels.

"Your Highness, we cannot protect you if you do not stay close."

"I don't fucking need your protection. I'm perfectly capable—"

"Lord Nevar is a murderer."

"Alleged," she muttered. He shot a dubious glance at her.

"Even if he isn't a fighter, he has more reach than you, more muscle, more mass. That is nothing to scoff at and could be the difference between winning and losing."

Rane clenched her jaw. She was in no danger from Nevar, but she couldn't tell Jadran. It would give far too much away. Instead, she ceded the point.

"Apologies. It has been a frustrating two days. We have covered all the hiding places I know in this region. This is the last."

He dipped his head, granting his forgiveness. He had little choice, true, but as the heir to the throne, she didn't need to apologize at all.

The breeze rushed through trees laden with apples, their rosy skins inviting. Birds chirped, and the soft ground swallowed their footsteps as they approached the first shed. Rane pulled her dagger, the leather-covered hilt warm in her hand. *Make this look good*.

She yanked the door open, and Jadran entered. The shed was empty except for a few tools and baskets for harvest. Dust sparkled in the light, and a musty scent filled the air. No one had been here in a long time.

"Two more," Rane said.

The other shed revealed similar results. Dust, must, and tools. Not a hair or a footprint showing anyone had been there in the past few days. Rane slid her dagger through her belt and slumped her shoulders.

"This is the last," she said. "I guess when I have children, you'll know the best places to search for them."

Jadran smiled. Now he had all her hiding places. Grief needled her. These had been her safe spaces to go when the burden of being crown princess grew too great, or she needed to escape her siblings. Acknowledging that time of her life would close in two months didn't make it hurt less.

"It's time to head back and regroup," Jadran said, leading the way.

Sullen murmurs joined the tweets in the air as they mounted up. At least it was over. She wouldn't need to pretend disappointment for much longer. The last few days had been miserable, eating travel rations of hardtack, dried fruit, and dried beef. To keep the fugitive from spotting them, no fires had been allowed at night, and somebody always had to be on watch. Between taking her fair share of watches and bedding down on the ground, Rane hadn't slept over four hours the past two nights. She couldn't wait to spend the night in her own bed and eat a proper meal.

Guilt twisted her belly. Her guards suffered the same, and she was the only one who knew they'd been out here for nothing. They had fulfilled their duties to the best of their abilities. Her father's voice in the back of her head reminded her the royal family was nothing without the people they served. She owed them more than a fool's errand. Rane vowed to the annoying voice they would get some sort of reward for their efforts. It was the least she owed them.

A quick but undemanding pace brought them to the gates of the Lorean capital shortly before sunset. The fatigue seeped deep in her bones, and she could barely keep upright. Rane handed the reins to a groom. Though she preferred to care for her horse herself, Sunny deserved proper attention tonight, and she was too tired to give it. A decorative metal vase clattered to the floor as she stumbled to her room. It didn't break, but the racket only cut off when she shut the door. Thank the goddess for small favors.

Rane dropped her sword belt on the floor, pulled off her tunic and breeches, and wiped her face and hands with tepid water someone had been kind enough to leave in the ewer. A bath would wait until the morning. She crawled into bed naked, the notion of locating her chemise causing a pinprick of pain behind her eyes. Her last conscious thought before she drifted off was whether Nevar was as tired of hiding as she was from searching.

"You've spent too much time at the Faerie court, Rane."

Her sister's melodious voice woke her. Darkness pressed around them, the only light a small ball of blue-green iridescence floating over Betony's hand. Idoya's tits, they needed to have a discussion about sending her to Faerie. And about privacy.

"You've spent too little." Rane sat up, wrapping the sheet around herself and rubbing her eyes. "What time is it?"

Bet rolled her eyes, and Rane snorted. Her sister's relationship with time was off, yet she was never late. Rane always had to know what time it was, usually because she was late for something.

"What is it, oh magical one?"

"I came for this." She dangled the invisibility charm from her fingers. "You've been up to something."

"Me?" She tried her most innocent voice.

"Rane." Bet didn't buy it, and disapproval dripped over her name. Tits. Did Bet *know* it or suspect it?

"Fine, but can I at least get dressed before being interrogated?"

Her sister smiled and tucked back an escaped cranberry-colored lock. "I have breakfast ready in the other room."

She skipped out and shut the door behind her to the sound of Rane's stomach rumbling. Breakfast. Fresh-baked bread. An egg, maybe. Oh goddess, something that didn't take her entire concentration to chew. Rane jumped out of bed and pulled out a fresh tunic and breeches. Before she could think better of it, she joined her sister, who was already slathering butter on a thick slice of sweet apple bread. The smell of cinnamon filled the room, and Rane's mouth watered.

"Holy Mother, you stink. You need to go to the baths as soon as you eat. I thought it was your clothes emitting such a stench."

"No, it was me," Rane said around large mouthfuls of melt-in-your-mouth deliciousness.

Betony poured the tea, adding a generous dollop of honey to Rane's. her sister regarded her shrewdly over the edge of her cup before putting it aside and folding her hands on the table.

"I was walking the castle wall the other night. I saw you come back from the city with Lord Nevar. Please tell me what happened. I'm worried about you."

The idea of unburdening herself from the secret of Jocelyn's guilt tempted her for a beat, but she'd made an oath. She couldn't endanger Nevar's family, and she certainly wouldn't endanger her own. If Jocelyn was capable of setting up her own stepson for murder merely to hold on to power, who knew what else she would do if her freedom or life were threatened.

Her sister wouldn't let this go, and she would rope Ebon in, too. Both her siblings would be in danger. She'd never understood the phrase "between a rock and a hard place" until now. Fuck.

"I can't tell you much," Rane said. Bet opened her mouth to protest. "I took an oath. I *can't* tell you everything. But I know Nevar didn't do what everyone believes he did."

"How?"

Rane shook her head. She'd said too much, confirming her belief in Nevar's innocence. Any more would jeopardize everything.

Understanding lit Bet's face. "You're in love with him."

"What? No. I just met the man."

"Mm-hmm." Her sister smiled, eyes glinting mischievously. "Why did you call him Nevar and blush when you spoke his name?"

"I did not—" Shit, she had called him Nevar.

"Maybe you're not in love, but you're definitely in lust. And you like him. Are you sure your feelings aren't clouding your judgment? There isn't another person you'd be willing to risk so much for."

It stung, having her own words about Miren thrown back at her, but she didn't blame Bet. If their positions were reversed, she'd be thinking the same thing.

"You and Ebon."

"Besides me and Ebon."

"Innocent lives are at stake, Bet. Please, don't push me. I can't!"

Tears spilled down her cheeks and the sobs she'd held back erupted like a long-dormant volcano. After days on the hunt, after sending away the man she was falling for, after witnessing the aftermath of a brutal crime, Rane had no walls left. If her sister asked again, she wasn't sure she'd be able to keep the secret.

"You are in it up to your neck," Betony said, a hardness in her tone rarely present. Rane wiped away the tears and clamped her mouth shut, silencing her sobs. "Lord Nevar has taken what little sense you have and wrapped it around his finger. I hope he's worth it."

Goddess, so did she. "What else can I do?"

"Let me help you."

Rane raised a disbelieving eyebrow. "How?"

"You were planning on seeing him today?" Bet guessed. Her sister was too clever.

"Yes."

"I'll be your alibi. Write your report. I'll tell them I checked on you and found you incomprehensible. You needed more rest, so I grabbed your written report for them."

"Why?"

"You're my sister. I don't need another reason."

Rane bit her lip. She had to protect Bet, too, even if it meant bending her oath.

"Don't trust the baroness, Bet. She is dangerous."

Her sister pursed her lips and considered Rane for a moment. "I assume you can find your way out of the castle?"

Rane rolled her eyes. "I've been sneaking out of the castle since before you learned to walk, sister-mine."

"I've heard the stories. It's a miracle Mother and Father didn't die of heart attacks before they had me. I'm still trying to figure out how a five-year-old managed to get all the way to the city gate."

"I'm special, I guess."

Bet laughed, a rich musical sound. As much of a pain-in-the-ass as she could be, Rane loved her with a ferocity that trumped her sense of duty to the kingdom. If it came to choosing between Lorea and her siblings, she would do anything to keep her family safe. Which was another reason she couldn't marry for love. If she felt this way about her siblings, imagine what fury she would unleash for a true love.

"May I offer one last piece of advice?" Bet held a serious expression for an instant before she broke into a wide grin. "By all that is holy, run a brush through your hair before you go."

Chapter 16

Nevar fought his imaginary opponent until it was dead several times over, the same way he had every morning since the pixies had taken him in. The sword was something else. Every day, it became more a part of him, a part of his soul. When he slid it back into the scabbard at the end of his practice, it was all he could do not to take it out again, waiting for it to sing for him some more.

The pixies had helped him develop a routine over the past two days. Mornings were for sword practice and laborious chores, chopping firewood, fixing furniture, or repairing the roof. Afternoons were for hunting and gathering. Wren had shown him the edible plants growing in the clearing and among the nearby trees, and Curlew had taken him fishing at the pond the previous day. He'd caught two lovely trout, which supplemented the remaining food he had brought with him. One apple sat lonely on the table.

He'd even met two more of the Sisters. Pipit had been extremely interested in his sword and let slip it had been a gift from the Queens of Faerie. He'd known the blade was special, but not that special. He shouldn't have accepted it. If Rane had given him something so valuable, perhaps she expected something in return. Most people would.

The little pixie with brown wings had stayed for a cup of tea and a lengthy discussion of the merits of various kinds of blades. Pipit pulled out five of her own, and damned if he knew where she hid them all.

Towhee had been more reticent. She dragged a couple of long-dead trees into the clearing, made eye contact, and left without saying a single word. Pixies must be stronger than their dainty forms suggested. Towhee was shorter than Rane yet seemed to handle the trees with little issue.

Those trees weren't going to cut themselves into firewood. Yanking the ax from the chopping block, he started in on the first tree, chopping it into manageable logs.

His routine kept him from utter boredom. The repetitive physical exertion calmed his mind, but nothing erased the events from the other night. Three days. He'd been here three days and still no word from Rane. Some part of him understood the possibility she could've visited any sooner was minuscule, but here he was, hiding in a cottage in the woods, waiting for someone else to solve his problems for him.

He'd been so close. He'd won his first concession during the early negotiations, and only minor obstacles seemed likely, nothing he couldn't handle. If his stepmother hadn't interfered—no, this was worse than mere interference. She'd killed a guard, placed an innocent young woman in jeopardy, and threatened his family. He'd let her, which galled him more than anything else. If only he'd trusted his instincts, he wouldn't be here now.

Nevar took his frustration out on the logs, splitting them into smaller pieces to fit the hearth inside. Though the days were still delightfully warm, the nights held an early chill.

How long did Rane expect him to wait? Days? Weeks? She'd sent him on his way without explaining much of anything, but he couldn't wait forever. He wasn't a sad, lonely man dependent upon the pixies and a princess for his wellbeing. He was Nevar of Otero, and he needed a backup plan in case Rane's didn't work.

If he was honest with himself, it probably wouldn't. His stepmother had fooled him, had fooled everybody around her, for years. She wouldn't be brought to justice easily.

The kernel of an idea tickled the back of his mind. It had something to do with an old story his nanny once told him about a band of rebels hiding in a forest and offering aid to any who fled a repressive king. Could he do something similar?

Nevar finished chopping wood as the midday sun beat down on his already sweat-soaked body. He peeled his tunic away from his skin and used the hem to wipe the stinging sweat from his eyes. His stomach rumbled, and he headed inside, snagging the last apple. Biting into it, he rummaged through his satchel and found the bar of cedar soap he always kept there. It did an adequate job of washing his clothes and his body. He'd be able to accomplish both at the pond today. Whistling all the way there, he soon recognized the tune as the song he'd danced to with Rane.

The pond shimmered in the sunlight, a million diamonds sparkling on the blue-green surface. Willow trees dipped their long branches into the water, and two ducks flew away as he approached. Nevar stripped off his breeches, folded them neatly, and placed them on a rock. Holding the soap, he waded into the cold, clear pond in his tunic, skin tingling with the sudden contrast of temperatures.

He scrubbed his tunic, removing a berry stain and salt from his sweat. After throwing the tunic over a sun-warmed boulder to dry, Nevar washed himself from head to toe. He dunked his head under the water and watched the suds swirl away. Once his body was used to it, he found the water refreshing and went for a swim.

Cracking branches and the snort of a horse caught his attention when he was halfway back from the far side of the pond. He made a beeline to a willow, taking shelter under its branches. If he stayed perfectly still and made no sound, perhaps the rider would move on without spotting him.

She appeared, standing there like a wood nymph out of a storybook. Rane. Her chestnut hair shone in the sun, the red highlights sparkling garnets come to life.

She led her horse to the water's edge, the fairy hound bounding next to her. Rane's eyes lit upon his breeches, neatly folded, and the tunic drying in the sun. A mischievous grin spread across her face, and she scanned the surface of the pond, finding him hiding under the willow. A frisson of desire quickened his breath.

"I hope you're up for some company," she said in a husky voice. "I'm afraid I didn't have a chance to bathe the past few days. The stench is unsuitable for polite company."

No harm in replying now she'd spotted him. "Who said I was polite company?"

Laughing, Rane undid her belt and unlaced her jerkin, tossing them both next to his breeches. Oh shit, she was serious about joining him. He turned his back as she grabbed the hem of her tunic to pull it over her head, glimpsing her belly. Despite the cold water, heat spread through his body.

"Stay, Bash. Watch Sunny."

The dog whined, but only Rane splashed into the water. Nevar imagined how she looked wading into the pond, the water beading on her skin, her dark hair floating around her. Did she transform from wood nymph to water nymph? He pushed away the thought. It wasn't helping anything.

"You can turn around now. I didn't mean to offend your sensibilities."

Her voice came from somewhere closer than he'd expected, still husky, still strumming the strings of desire connecting them.

"You didn't offend anything, Your Highness." His voice roughened.

"I didn't realize Oterans were modest." Closer now.

Nevar cleared his throat. "We aren't as a rule, but it is considered rude to watch a lady of your station undress unless invited to do so."

"Ah." If he reached out, he'd touch her on the other side of the branches. "Consider this an open invitation."

Oh, fuck.

Rane parted the branches, her wet hair flowing behind her, and her bare shoulders gleaming from the water. She swam to him and dropped her feet. If he looked down, he'd have a clear view of her nakedness. He kept his eyes on hers through a monumental effort of will.

"Hello, Nevar."

"Hello, Rane. What brings you out here on this fine day?"

"You."

"Me?"

"I'm supposed to be searching for you."

He gulped. "You found me. What will you do now?"

"I could be persuaded to forget that fact for a small price." She smiled with a hint of seduction, and her voice held a teasing note.

"Are you demanding a bribe, Your Highness?" His tone matched hers, guessing where this was going. It was, by any objective measure, a terrible idea for both of them, but he couldn't seem to help himself.

Her smile widened. "Only a kiss, my lord. Surely your freedom is worth a kiss."

He wanted to kiss her. It was the only thing he was sure of. Nevar snaked his hands into her wet hair and pulled her to him. The contact of their naked bodies under the cool water was intense, sending bolts of raging lust to every limb. Rane gasped, and he lowered his mouth to hers, swallowing the tiny sounds of desire she made. His world narrowed to this point of connection, all heat and longing. He swept his tongue across her lower lip. She shivered in response and pulled him closer, her full breasts crushed to his chest. Rane's tongue touched his, and he groaned with pleasure.

"I want you," she whispered hoarsely against his lips.

Her legs wrapped around him, and he could only think of what it would be like to lose himself in the feel of her soft flesh. He kissed her again, delving into her mouth, reveling in the taste of her. Oh, God, how he wanted her, but he pulled his head away and broke the kiss.

"I am an accused murderer and a lowly baron's son," he murmured. "No proper match for a future queen."

She laughed, a low throaty thing that sent another wave of desire crashing over him. "I never said I wanted you forever. I want you *now*. I know you want me."

Rane slid her hand between them and grazed her fingers against the hard length of him. Nevar pressed his lips together, but a groan escaped from deep inside.

"This isn't how it works, Highness." He shook his head in disappointment.

"It is for me. You're not my first. I'm not promising you tomorrow, Nevar. Only now."

He'd be a fool to reject her. Nevar opened his mouth to do just that.

Chapter 17

Rane placed a finger over his mouth. He was going to say no, and she didn't want to hear it. With a sigh, she dropped her legs. Nevar's warm, rough hands didn't release their grip on her body. She tingled from head to toe as his bronze eyes stared into hers.

"Only now?" His voice was as rough as his hands, sending more prickles of passion coursing through her veins.

"Yes." It was all she managed before he crushed his lips to hers.

Her legs wrapped around him again as he moved his lips down her neck. Small noises came from her mouth, urging him on. Instead, he stopped.

"This is a bad idea."

Oh, she knew it was a bad idea. The worst. Except… not taking this step made her insides freeze and her heart shrink. They only had this moment, and maybe a handful of others, before their destinies would tear them apart. Hers waited back at the castle, his was somewhere far from here.

"Yes."

"Just so we both know it. Hold tight," he muttered.

Nevar carried her to the grassy shore, splashing the cool water all around and drenching anything not yet damp. He laid her gently on the ground and knelt next to her, his eyes exploring the generous curves of her body. It wasn't enough. She placed his hand on her breast.

A wicked grin pulled up the edges of his mouth as he traced the outline of first one breast, then the other. Rane arched into his hand, and he slid his other under her. He pulled her close and fastened his lips around a nipple, circling the hard nub with his tongue. She let out a long sigh of pleasure. This, this is what she wanted, for as long as she could have it.

The water on their bodies vanished in the warm sun, and his rich brown skin gleamed. The shivers rippling through her now were entirely from lust. He switched breasts and trailed his other hand down her side until he cupped her ass. She wrapped her leg around him and lifted her hips off the ground, begging for more. His erection dug into the yielding rolls of her thigh.

Nevar groaned and traced the long scar on her hip, sending another round of shivers through her body. "You're so beautiful. You tempt me to do things I shouldn't."

"Like what?" she murmured thickly.

His fingers danced across her skin and dipped to the juncture of her thighs. He stroked the sensitive skin of her inner thigh with his thumb as one finger found the wetness of her slit. Rane moaned. This was what she'd wanted.

"I want to bury myself deep inside you, but you don't need to suffer the consequences."

She laughed, and shock froze his face. He tried to take away his hand, but she held it to her with her own.

"The blessings of having a fairy godmother are many," she said, still smiling. "But one of the best is a special tea she makes to remove those consequences if taken every day. I haven't missed a day in nearly five years."

"Oh." A hungry smile lit his face, and his eyes turned molten. "Oh."

Rane removed her hand from his and stretched her arms over her head. "Do what you will. Consequence free."

His thumb moved from her inner thigh to the nub between her legs. She arched her hips into his hand. His fingers dipped into her, filling her. Rane wanted more.

His tongue flicked her nipple, granting her wish. Lightning shot through her, and her hips bucked, driving his fingers deeper. Still, Rane wanted more.

He drew her nipple into his mouth and suckled. Wave after wave of pleasure washed through her and the pressure built. More. Goddess, more.

Nevar trailed kisses down her soft belly, nipping gently at her skin. Still further, placing a kiss above her mound. Another finger entered, stretching her. A heaviness settled low in her body, tipping so close to the edge, but not there yet.

"More," she moaned.

He worked his three fingers in and out in rhythm with her bucking hips. "Like this?"

"More."

A throaty chuckle greeted her demand, and his tongue found the nub, suckling it much the same as he'd suckled her breasts. Rane exploded, ecstasy rocking her body even harder against his hand, his mouth. She lost herself in the golden haze and pleasure.

His lips left her, and he withdrew his hand. Rane mewled in protest. "More."

"Hush, my princess, I'm not leaving." His voice was raspy with hunger.

The hard length of him pressed into her, filling her as her inner muscles still clenched rhythmically. It was exquisite torment. Nevar groaned with pleasure as he eased into her. Rane wrapped her legs around him and lifted her hips to take him in deeper with every thrust.

The length of him rubbed against her still sensitive flesh, sending whirls of bliss along every inch of her body. The pressure built again, their bodies crashing together in a dance as old as time. His thrusts increased their pace and grew frenzied. He let out a cry as he spilled into her. The warm rush of his release tipped her over the edge, and the next instant she came, too. He eased next to her, leaning on an elbow, gazing at her with his perfectly crooked half-smile. Rane snuggled in closer to him and relaxed for the first time in a long time. She was right where she belonged.

A distant bay and the whinny of a horse brought her back to reality.

"Aren't those your animals?" Nevar asked drowsily.

"They're fine." She pulled his head to her for a kiss, but he resisted.

"They sound far away."

Rane glanced over to find Sunny had wandered away and seemed too interested in something in the forest. Bash harried her, trying to get her to return. The horse whinnied again and stepped into the tree line.

"Shit!"

She let go of him and ran after the beasts. The sun warmed her naked body, and the gentle caress of Nevar's gaze followed her. Rane caught up to Sunny before her tail disappeared into the trees, and Bash woofed in satisfaction. She grabbed the reins and led Sunny back to the pond.

While she'd been occupied, Nevar had dressed and now perched on the rock where his shirt had dried to watch the end of the show. He couldn't keep his eyes off her, though. She'd take it as a win.

Rane tossed the reins at him, and Nevar caught them with a deft hand. She dressed as slowly as humanly possible, giving him a show she hoped he wouldn't soon forget. Slinging the jerkin and her sword belt over a shoulder, she led Sunny to the pixies' cottage. Bash trotted happily alongside, darting between Nevar and Rane, perfectly content to get attention from either.

Nevar followed. Rane swayed her hips and smiled to herself when a rough, masculine groan drifted through the trees. She tied the reins to a sturdy branch on an oak next to the cottage and pulled off the saddlebags.

"I have something of yours." In one heartbeat, he disappeared.

Rane hadn't seen it from this point of view before. It was eerie. One instant he was just… gone.

A moment later, he appeared as suddenly as he had vanished. Her necklace dangled from his hand. She reached for it, but he shook his head, a lazy smile lighting his face. Nevar stepped behind her. Rane lifted her hair, and he fastened the delicate chain around her neck, placing a kiss at the nape when he finished. The cottage popped into sight as soon as the stone touched her skin.

"I brought supplies," she said in a breathy voice, following him into the cottage. The bags made a satisfying thud on the table. "I remember what the pixies consider appropriate human food. This might make the next couple of days easier for you."

Rane pulled out a pot of honey, more apples, two loaves of bread, a sizable chunk of cheese, several hand pies, and the pièce de résistance, a flagon of red wine. His stomach gurgled.

"Hungry?" she asked.

A hint of wickedness burned in his eyes, igniting a flame in her. It was as though they hadn't spent the past hour satiating their lust.

"Yes, but first, how goes the investigation?"

Rane shook her head. "Not until you eat something." He opened his mouth to protest. "We can talk while you eat."

"Fine." He bit out the word with all the pent-up frustration she'd expected. He would feel better with some food in his belly.

She watched appreciatively as he moved about the cottage gathering plates and utensils. Gone was the pretense he was weak. His hard muscles moved with deliberate ease, and she longed to run her hands over them again. As though he could sense her gaze upon him, Nevar looked over his shoulder and gave her a slow once over. She darted her eyes away, afraid of showing how much she wanted him.

He sat, his plate laden with two hand pies and some of the cheese. "I'm eating. Start talking."

Rane sighed. "I haven't had much of a chance to do anything. Father sent me to search for you to the west. I only returned last night. I wanted to see you."

"How are we going to prove my innocence if you're off hunting me?"

She ran her fingers through her hair, tugging a strand in frustration. "I'll figure something out. Trust me. Perhaps I'll invite the baroness on my next outing. She might share something with me I can use."

Nevar winced. "Be careful. Jocelyn is shrewd. I knew she was devious but never imagined she would resort to murder. She'll turn on you in a heartbeat if she suspects you know where I am. She'll do anything to keep control of Otero."

"Is she such a bad ruler?"

That was an inane question. Anyone who would put their own power ahead of another's life wasn't fit to rule. It was why, as much as she joked with her siblings about abdication, she wouldn't. Bearing the burdens of rule was her fate, not theirs.

"It's hard for me to tell," he said carefully. "She has completely shut me out of all Oteran business. I don't know how we make our money, how we pay our people, if our people are well cared for, the relationships at court, nothing."

"What do you know?"

"Our family has plenty, and our guards and servants seem well-compensated for their labor, but since my father's illness, it seems more and more of my people are hurting. I noticed some odd things on our trip here. When I traveled with my father as a boy, there were always some people who came out to greet the carriage, usually with a wave and a smile, sometimes a cheer. This trip, many of the villages we passed through were abandoned, and the people I saw looked hungry and tired. Beggars were frequent, and Jocelyn wouldn't allow the guards to share our food with them. These aren't the people of a prosperous barony."

Rane poured him some wine to buy herself a bit of time to think. Nevar made appreciative noises.

"This is good. I didn't know Lorea had good wine."

"It's Oteran." She winked, and his belly laugh filled her with joy.

"Do you want some?" He held the mug out.

"It's all yours. There's plenty more where that came from." A flash of sadness crossed his face at the reminder she'd be leaving soon.

"What's the plan?"

"Keep everyone chasing their tails while I find something to prove Jocelyn's guilt. I spent the last two days searching for you in the countryside surrounding the castle."

"Why you?"

Rane bit her lip to keep from smiling. It wasn't funny, not really.

"Let's say when my parents decided I needed to step up to my duties as heir, I disagreed and became intimately familiar with all the hiding spots within a few miles of Avora."

It was how she'd found all the ways out of the castle and city. It was also how she'd met the pixies and saved them from a hobgoblin.

Nevar's bright smile made her feel seen. "But you've since accepted your role?"

A sour laugh escaped her lips. "Oh, I wouldn't say that. If I had, you'd be under lock and key right now."

"For that, I am grateful." He lifted his mug in salute and took another sip. "What happens when you don't find me?"

She twisted her hair around a finger, wanting desperately to know the answer.

"I'm not sure. Perhaps wanted posters, communication with

your king, more man hunts. We'll definitely work with the baroness on the mineral rights agreement."

"Which destroys my purpose for being here. A successful agreement was my way out from under her thumb. It would've shown I could conduct business on behalf of my father, my people, and the king. She's really fucked me over."

Rane held his hand. "I'll slow it if I can. If we can find proof she murdered the guard, any agreement she made would be void. We can still salvage this."

He snatched his hand away and stood. She hid her disappointment. It was nice holding his hand.

"How do you prove magic?"

"I don't know. I was hoping you'd let me tell Bet and Ebon. No one can navigate the library like my brother, and Bet is acquainted with magic."

"No, absolutely not. If Jocelyn finds out, my father and brother are as good as dead, and your siblings might join them. I won't risk it."

"Bet already knows something is up."

"You promised not to tell." His voice crackled with anger, and his fingers tightened around the mug. For a moment, she believed it would break.

"I didn't tell," Rane said evenly. "She guessed. My siblings aren't stupid, and they could be helpful."

Nevar sat stiffly on the edge of his chair. He ran a hand over his face and polished off the wine. Rane refilled the cup and rested a hand on his shoulder. He didn't shrug it off, but he didn't lean into her touch either. She jerked her hand away, but he grabbed it.

"I don't want to endanger anyone else. Please, Rane. Don't tell your siblings."

Rane squeezed his hand. "I won't, but I can't promise they won't figure it out on their own."

He pressed his lips together. "If they do, tell them to let it go. It's not worth their lives."

"But it's worth yours?" She would not allow Nevar to sacrifice himself on the altar of an oath. His life was as important as her siblings'.

"It's my life, so it's my call. Leave it be, Your Highness."

"You've seen me naked, now. You can stop calling me Your

Highness," Rane teased, trying to bring the conversation out of the dark hole it had found.

"That's probably not the best idea."

"At least when it's only us?"

Rane despised the pleading tone seeping into her words. None of her other lovers knew she was royalty. She was merely a person to them, not a princess. Nevar was special. With him, she felt equally both. Your Highness was as much of an endearment as her nickname coming from his lips, but she heard the first far more often from him.

"Hell. This is hell." He squeezed her hand hard, and she squeezed back, offering whatever comfort she could.

"Do you have any idea what kind of magic she used? Or who she learned it from?"

"Apparently, I'm not the only credible actor in Otero. I have no idea. I suspected her of using poison, not magic. My stepmother is a beautiful, powerful woman. For all I know, she convinced the poor, besotted fool of a guard to kill himself without using magic at all."

"There must be a way to trace magic buried in the library, but no one can trace poor, besotted fools."

"You found me easily enough." His shoulders released a little of the tension he'd held, and his lips quirked up at the corners.

Rane snorted. "You're not a fool."

Nevar pulled her into his lap. His lips hovered next to her ear. "So, you think I'm besotted?"

The words sent a thrill through her. "I don't know. Are you?"

He kissed her again, slow and deep, growing a fierce fire within. She wanted him again, as much as she ever had. More.

Nevar broke the kiss and held her eyes with his gaze. "Most definitely."

"Oh, I'm sorry," squeaked a tiny voice.

Rane looked up. A shimmery ball of light floated in the doorway. The smallest pixie stared at them, a sly grin on her tiny face.

"Hi, Wren," she said.

"Rane, it is good to see you."

She glanced out the door. The shadows were long and the light golden. It was past time for her to leave. If she didn't make it back for dinner, they'd send out a search party, defeating what few plans she held. Rane sighed and untangled herself from Nevar.

"Will you stay for dinner?" Wren asked.

"I have to go before I'm missed." She picked up the saddlebags and walked out of the cottage, Nevar right behind. She threw the bags over her horse and turned toward him. "Keep a bag packed, if you can, and extra food. I will keep them as far from here as possible. If the search party gets too close, the pixies will know."

Nevar pulled her close and kissed her gently.

"Be careful." He brushed a curl away from her cheek.

"You as well."

Rane swung herself on top of the horse.

"I still don't understand why you're doing all this for me," he called out as she rode off.

"You're not the only one who's besotted."

Chapter 18

Nevar leaned against the cottage and watched Rane leave. He was a wanted man who had slept with the Crown Princess of Lorea. Apparently, he had a death wish, indulging in matters of the heart instead of trying to find a way to fix the situation. Lives were on the line: his father's, his brother's, his own, and Rane's. Yet, here he was, pining after the one thing he could never have.

A shimmery ball of light burst forth from the forest, pulling him out of his head. Lark landed next to him, a brace of partridges slung over a shoulder.

"You just missed Rane," Nevar said.

"Ah, that explains the brooding."

He snorted. Yes, he supposed it did.

"Did she have answers for you?" Lark continued.

"No. She hasn't had a chance to search for answers, let alone find any."

Though Rane seemed confident she could find evidence to exonerate him and implicate Jocelyn, his stepmother was smart. The question remained, was she too smart to get caught? Nevar's gut told him yes. It had taken years for Nevar to suspect she'd poisoned his father, and he'd never guessed she dabbled in magic.

"Rane is driven toward justice. She will prove your innocence. I have seen how she looks at you."

"What do you mean?"

"It is obvious how she feels. Do you not feel the same?"

It didn't matter if he did. Even if Rane cleared his name, whatever was growing between them could never be more than an affair, no matter how good and true it seemed.

"I am a baron's son accused of murder. There is no path forward for us."

His father had taught him enough about royal politics. The heir to a throne couldn't consider matters of the heart in marriage. The needs of the kingdom outweighed anything else. Though they were in negotiations over mineral rights, it was a minor matter. If suddenly Otero had something of extraordinary value to offer, possibly; but as things stood now, Lorea would gain nothing long-term from a union with Otero.

"When she clears your name, there might be."

He pushed aside the flutter of elation at the thought. Even if his stepmother was no longer in the picture, someone had to run the barony. His father had been unable to for years, and Nevar didn't know if Leon would ever recover. His brother was only thirteen. It would be years before Orom was properly trained to assume the role of Baron. Too many ifs.

"No, there isn't. At best, I can be her lover."

"Would that be so bad?"

Nevar let his mind continue down the rosy path. Should everything turn his way—he'd never wager on those long odds—would he carry on an illicit long-distance affair with the crown princess of another kingdom? The logistics would be nigh impossible.

He pressed his lips together. Perhaps if he didn't have his own responsibilities at home, he could make a place for himself in her court, but he'd always be last on her list. First would come the kingdom, then her consort, and any children they may have. He would be left with crumbs of her time and attention. Could he live with that? Nevar shook his head.

"It wouldn't be enough."

The way Rane reacted to him was like nothing he'd experienced before. The mere memory of her firm muscles underneath silken skin and a buxom body set him afire. Nevar knew himself well. He wanted her in his bed every night, not on the rare occasions they could steal away from their duties. Against his better instincts, he wanted all of her, and he could never have that.

"Let us go inside, Nevar." Red-gold light painted the clearing in eerie shadows. Lark's wings vibrated faster than he could see, and little puffs of air tickled his neck. "It grows dark and strange creatures are afoot tonight."

"Will you join me for a meal? Rane brought some food, and I don't want to be alone."

Lark followed him in. She dressed the birds while he set out mugs and plates.

"You have doubts about Rane." She had made short work of plucking the birds, and the feathers lay in a neat pile by her feet.

"I do."

"Perhaps you are curious how we came to owe Rane a debt."

He smiled. "The question crossed my mind a time or two." Or twenty.

"I will share the story. Not much will stop the princess when she is determined to do something." Lark speared the birds onto a spit and lit the fire with a snap of her fingers. She turned the spit as she spoke. "Seven springs ago, a hobgoblin kept us prisoner here in the forest."

"How does that happen?"

She chuckled wryly. "I will not give you the means to imprison us again, but it involved magic as much as manipulation. Gwid forced us to steal from those passing through the forest. We led humans into bogs and ponds and took their horses, then all their food while they slept. When they would search for things to eat, all they found was poison. Many died, but we were powerless to stop it."

Nevar had never considered a fairy could be powerless. After all, they had magic, and magic was a powerful force in the world. Though having one kind of power did not always mean one couldn't feel powerless. He'd spent the last few years feeling powerless in his own home.

"I am sorry that happened to you."

Lark shrugged. "It was our past. Our present is much better because a young princess wandered into our forest."

He grinned at the picture of a fierce fourteen-year-old Rane marching through the trees as if she belonged, no matter what strange creatures roamed through the underbrush.

"We did not know she was a princess," Lark said with an answering smile. He hadn't known she was a princess either the first time they met. "Her clothes were plain, and she carried nothing of value with her, only a small bag with food, a slingshot, and a hunting knife. Yet our captor insisted on taking what she had and luring her into the swamp."

"Why?"

"Gwid was not one for explaining his reasoning to mere pixies. I never understood why he chose to steal from some and kill others. Rane turned out to be lucky. We approached her under cover of darkness, but Bash was at her side. The hound kept her safe, though my sisters stole her food and hunting equipment. She tracked us back to the cave. The hobgoblin was out, and she asked why we'd taken her things."

The princess had a history of treating people with compassion, even those who wronged her. She put justice over the law, even for those outside her jurisdiction. Rane may not believe it, may not want it, but she would make a fine queen someday.

"We told her, and she became angry. We did not understand she was angry for us, not at us. When the hobgoblin was angry, he hurt us, but Rane promised she would free us. She found a sword in the hoard Gwid kept and lay in wait for him. He returned near sunset but could tell something was amiss. Realizing she'd lost the element of surprise, Rane faced him anyway. It was a vicious fight. Perhaps you noticed a scar on her hip?"

The innocent expression Lark wore said she'd surmised they'd slept together. He brushed aside his embarrassment. She wouldn't tell anyone. He gave her no answer, and she continued her story.

"She won with a swift strike to his heart. His death broke the magical bond tethering us to him, and we were free. He'd killed our mother and several of our sisters. We brought her here, an old woodcutter's cottage long abandoned, and tended to her wounds."

The mouth-watering smell of roasting poultry filled the cottage. Nevar sliced the bread and broke off a couple of bits of cheese. He added two of the red apples to their plates.

Lark continued the story as they waited for the partridges to finish cooking. Without the magical protection of the hobgoblin, another dark denizen of the forest was likely to capture or kill the motherless pixies. Rane wrote a letter to the Queens of Faerie, petitioning them to employ the sisters into their service. Amused by the princess's audacity at the tender age of fourteen, they made the sisters guardians of the Argent Forest, answerable only to the Queens.

In return, the Sisters protected the trees and animals from human poachers. They escorted human parties through the forest, keeping them safe from the darker inhabitants. They helped lost humans, guiding them back to the road or giving them sanctuary at the cottage if injured or sick. From time to time, they spied on those who wished the Queens harm, be they fairies or human. Guides, medics, and spies, the Seven Sisters kept busy making up for their years helping the hobgoblin.

He understood, finally, why they loved Rane. She'd saved their lives and given them purpose. They owed her a debt they could never repay. If she told them to keep him safe, it was what they'd do, no matter the cost to themselves.

He understood more about Rane, too. She wouldn't give up on him. She would continue to search for the evidence to exonerate him, no matter the cost. The realization was both encouraging and horrifying. He couldn't allow her to sacrifice for his benefit.

Lark slid the birds off the spit and onto their plates. They ate in quiet contemplation.

"Thank you for the story and the company, Lark." He began clearing the table.

"It was my pleasure. Do not give up on Rane. She is a surprising creature for a human. Few can defeat a hobgoblin."

She bowed and left Nevar to his own thoughts. They spun too quickly for him to grasp onto a single idea, flitting by much like the pixies in their tiny forms. He couldn't stop dwelling on the princess who had dropped out of a damned tree. What did destiny mean, and how could he change his or change hers?

No answers came to mind, sadly. Nevar threw himself on the bed. He tossed and turned until falling into a restless sleep. Nightmares haunted him. Wolves chased him, rending his flesh. His stepmother slit his father's throat in front of him. Then Rane's. The last had him bolting upright in bed, unable to return to sleep.

Whatever else happened, he had to protect Rane from his stepmother. If Jocelyn believed she won, she would have no reason to hurt his family or Rane. He could disappear. With Nevar gone, Rane would be safe. He could make his way back to Otero and wait and watch, keep Orom safe. Maybe make life difficult for

Jocelyn. Bide his time until she was weak, until the peasants had enough, and take back his rightful place. Even a witch didn't live forever.

It could work, but he wasn't ready to let go of his princess yet. He would give Rane a little more time.

Chapter 19

Rane returned to the castle at sunset, and her mother waited at the stables, arms crossed, a frown highlighting the new creases appearing in her face.

"Your father wishes to speak with you," Queen Beatrice said, voice icy.

Rane handed Sunny to a stable hand and followed her mother through the castle. She kept her eyes down, trying her hardest to seem contrite. Doubtless, her mother wasn't fooled. No one could fool the Queen of Lorea for long, a lesson her children had learned early and often, but Rane had to hope her ruses would buy her enough time.

When her mother stopped at the door to her father's private study rather than the Council Chamber, Rane bit her lip. Her memories of the study were mostly unpleasant. The time Betony had fallen off a horse and the lecture she and Ebon had received on proper emergency protocol. The time Ebon faced consequences after gloating over beating a guard in hand-to-hand. Not for winning, but for the gloating. And when she'd run away five years ago instead of joining the caravan to the Faerie Court. The last time the king had summoned her had been to inform her of the negotiations with Teruelle.

Her mother lifted her hand to rap on the door and paused, examining Rane with her keen, darkling eyes.

"Rane, I don't know what you're doing." Rane opened her mouth to protest, but stopped when her mother lifted a hand, a tiny frown breaking the carefully controlled face of royalty. "I hope it is something constructive and not shirking your duties again.

What I want—no, what I need you to do is remember who you are, what you represent. You turn twenty-one soon and more responsibilities will fall to you. You've made it perfectly clear to both your father and me you have little interest in your birthright. Nevertheless, it is your birthright, and this kingdom will be yours someday, whether or not you are ready. We've given you latitude, but we need you to step up. This kingdom needs you to step up. Do you understand me, Ranunculus?"

Rane's tongue wouldn't work. She bobbed her head.

"Good." Queen Beatrice knocked gently, closing the conversation.

"Enter." King Rowan's muffled voice drifted out, and her mother left.

Rane opened the door, the heavy oak slab squealing on the ancient hinges. Her father sat at a large desk, a stack of papers on either side of him. He pulled a document off the pile to the left, skimmed it, scribbled something, and placed it on top of the pile to the right.

"Ah, Rane. Back from your ride?"

It was nearly impossible to keep a secret in this fucking castle. Hiding everything she did was pointless, and she was lucky she managed to keep one.

"Yes, Father."

"Sit, please. I have a couple things to discuss with you."

Rane settled on the chair facing her father. The wooden monstrosity was ridiculously uncomfortable, all angles, the seat still rough even though a thousand asses must have graced it.

He finished with the paper in front of him and put it aside. The king tented his fingers, leaned forward, and regarded his daughter, his green gaze holding hers in a long-practiced ritual. Hadn't she proved this particular stare would never get her to spill her guts?

"We're placing the search for Lord Nevar on hold. He is not in the castle or the city, and between you and the other patrols, we've found no trace of him in the area nearby. We'll find a more practical approach to the search, including wanted posters and small patrols. The Baroness of Otero has helped our artists come up with a sketch."

Of course she had. The sooner Nevar was captured and put on trial, the sooner Jocelyn could solidify her hold on Otero.

"If any further places the fugitive might hide come to mind, please inform Commander Miren at once."

"Yes, Father." She hoped he didn't sense the lie.

"I need you to stay here for now. No more unscheduled excursions. We put the negotiations on hold while we investigated and allowed time for King Armel to appoint a replacement. His letter came last night. Baroness Jocelyn of Otero is the new ambassador, and he withdrew diplomatic protection from Lord Nevar. I need everyone I can trust in the Council Chamber, and you must learn how to handle yourself during trade negotiations."

"Isn't there plenty of time for that? You're still healthy and spry." Her father snorted. It was true, though. He appeared ten years younger than his fifty-some-years, still able to ride and hunt and fight better than many men half his age. Having fairy ancestors, who lived many times as long as humans, blessed the royal family with extended lifespans.

"None of us know how long we have, not even with a fairy godmother to watch over us. And the more practice you have now, the fewer mistakes you will make when I am gone."

A ripple of sadness washed over her. Rane knew, had always known, the kingdom would only be hers once her father died, or was too ill or feeble to rule. She chose not to think of it too often.

"Is there anything else?"

He sighed. "There's something off about this entire mess. I need you to play nice and see if you can make friends with the baroness or any in her entourage. Report anything amiss to me immediately. Only to me. I worry the commander will take matters into her own hands. I wouldn't blame her, but the breach of diplomatic protocol will cause more trouble than her revenge is worth. Can you do that for me, Rane?"

Her father wasn't easy to fool, either. The whole situation stunk like an unmucked stable.

"Of course. Whatever I can do to help." This had played right into her plans, which did not happen nearly often enough. Perhaps her insistence that Nevar wasn't the murdering sort was being taken more seriously than she'd assumed.

"Excellent. I will see you in the Council Chamber immediately after breakfast."

She turned to leave.

"Oh, your mother wants you to wear a dress."

After being caught sneaking in, Rane didn't have any leverage to insist on her usual attire the next morning. She donned her favorite purple linen dress, which looked formal but moved with her body in a way she found comfortable. And it had pockets. She'd never tell her mother, but that was the other reason she preferred the jerkin and breeches. Besides not needing a corset, those items had pockets.

She was on time, properly dressed, and bored out of her mind, standing over a map. All this talk of ore and gems, workforces, horsepower, settlements, roads, supply lines, blah, blah, blah. Instead, she allowed her mind to wander back to the pond, and the water glinting like jewels on Nevar's skin.

"What do you think, Princess?" the baroness asked.

Shit, caught daydreaming. Rane studied the map, trying to piece together the bits of the conversation she missed. Either they were talking about the search for Nevar or the proposed mine. She closed her eyes, as though considering the question. She had a fifty-fifty chance of getting it right, and she needed to put him out of her mind.

Her finger snapped down on the mountains to the northwest, the site of the proposed mine.

"The terrain here is difficult to traverse, even by horseback. Mules might help, but you might be better off investing in infrastructure. I've heard King Armel has something called a funicular to help the citizens navigate his steep city."

Thank you, Ebon, for the juicy tidbit. Once she realized there was no getting out of her obligations today, she'd paid a call on her brother. He had a few suggestions.

"My daughter raises an excellent point." Pride beamed on King Rowan's face.

Her mother peered at her through slit eyes, suspicion writ large. Rane smiled sweetly, but it didn't work. Her mother crossed her arms over her chest and kept a closer eye on her daughter. A queen's sharp elbow to the ribs would do what this dull discussion couldn't.

"Yes," the baroness said. "A funicular might work. We can put it into the agreement. Perhaps Teruelle could provide the technology and operators for a further percentage of the mine's profits."

"Oh, it's not that easy, my lady. The technology, yes, but we can provide operators if they can receive training."

Rane's attention wandered again, as she planned her subterfuge. Maybe she could invite Jocelyn on a picnic, a way of getting acquainted with the new ambassador.

Her father's least favorite laugh brought her back. The hearty but insincere guffaw told her he had enough for one day. She'd heard it often enough growing up, especially after being hauled back from an unapproved excursion.

"We've made excellent progress, but we all deserve a rest. We can toast to a good day's work at supper after sunset."

Oh, thank the goddess. Rane gathered the few things she'd brought and made to follow the others out of the Council Chamber.

"A moment, please, Rane," her mother said firmly.

They waited for the others to depart. Her mother turned to her, onyx eyes flashing in annoyance.

"You weren't paying nearly as much attention as your father believed."

"Mother—"

"Is it Lord Nevar?"

Rane's heart raced. Had her mother guessed? No, she would have no problem calling her to task for such foolishness.

"Why would you say that?"

Her mother's voice was compassionate. "I saw how the two of you looked at each other at the feast. The young man couldn't take his eyes off you, and I've never seen you blush so much."

"It doesn't matter, does it? He's been accused of something horrible, even though something doesn't seem right."

"You're allowing your feelings to cloud your judgment. As queen, you will need to keep a clear head."

"You've been telling me that for the past ten years. If my head were any clearer, it would be glass!"

"Rane—" The queen's voice was reproachful, but Rane couldn't stop herself.

"I don't expect a happily ever after, Mother, but don't I deserve a happy for now?"

"Oh, my sweet buttercup." Her mother's arms enfolded her

and held her close.

Rane sniffed and wiped her face on her sleeve. The best she could hope for was what her parents had. Their marriage wasn't without compassion and tenderness, but it was about strengthening the kingdom, not passion for each other. The only love they shared was for their children.

"You and Father have a strong partnership," Rane said. "And I noticed how you made sure he had a chance to *be* a father, to be something, someone other than the king. I just want something more."

"Shh." Mother handed her a kerchief from somewhere. She always had one when needed.

Rane blew her nose loudly and dabbed at her eyes. She tucked the kerchief into her own pocket. Her mother held her hand.

"There is a lot going on right now, but when we settle these mineral rights, when we find Lord Nevar, and when your birthday has passed, we will talk about what's next. You read too many romances and not enough history. Royalty must marry for the betterment of the kingdom, but that doesn't mean love can't follow. Your father and I do care for each other, and I wouldn't change the life we've built for anything."

"But I can't marry only for love," Rane said in resignation.

"No, child, you can't. It is your sacrifice for the kingdom. I promise you, we will find a suitable match for you, so your sacrifice will be as painless as possible."

She threw her arms around her mother once again, taking comfort in her warmth and strength. Firm hands stroked her hair. After a few moments, she broke away.

"Thank you."

"I love you, Ranunculus."

"I would've preferred Buttercup."

"Me, too. Fairies have a strange sense of humor." Her mother's warm laughter filled the Council Chamber as Rane walked out the door.

She needed to walk this off and get her mind straight before approaching the baroness. From everything Nevar told her, from what she'd observed, the woman was shrewd and dangerous. She'd wrested control of a barony from its ruling family and framed the heir for murder. By the goddess, Rane hated politics.

The heavy door slammed shut behind her, caught by the breeze. Rane's quick strides carried her on the path through the castle grounds. *Speak her name...*

Jocelyn sat on a stone bench at the apex of the path's loop, staring at a small, golden hand mirror. Was she truly vain enough to carry around a mirror everywhere she went, or was the mirror something more? Rane slowed her steps, but too late. The crunch of her feet on the gravel announced Rane's presence before she could get close enough to see what might be looking back from the reflection.

Hyssop once told her why fairies rarely used mirrors. Most often, the mirror reflected what everyone else could see. Every once in a while, the mirror revealed the essence of the person to anyone who glimpsed it in the right instant. Fairies prided themselves on the tight illusions they created: power, beauty, truth, and wisdom. A simple trick of light off a silver-backed glass could snap those illusions. Rane had never seen it firsthand, but she trusted her godmother.

The baroness rose in greeting. She tucked the mirror into a pocket, the same one she'd touched when brought in for questioning shortly after the murder. Rane's fingers itched to hold it and discover its secrets.

"Please sit, my lady," Rane said. "May I join you?"

Jocelyn arched a brow and gestured for Rane to join her. Maybe acknowledging the difficulties would placate the baroness. She'd known more than a handful of ladies in the Lorean court who would open up when offered commiseration.

"I am sorry for the trouble these negotiations have caused you, both personally and as a representative of the king," Rane continued.

"Thank you for the sentiment, but it is I who must apologize. I have known the boy since he small enough to ride a pony and should have seen through his pretense. I suspected Nevar was incapable of fulfilling his duties as ambassador, but I never believed he would resort to murder on foreign soil." Jocelyn sounded properly bewildered and shamed. No wonder her parents only vaguely suspected something was off, instead of sensing the lie. The woman was an excellent liar.

"The king must be grateful he sent you along." Another

attempt to stroke her ego.

The baroness kept her face carefully neutral, her hazel eyes narrowed in uncertainty. Tits, it didn't work. Jocelyn was too wary by far.

"Yes, well, he would be a fool to send an untested boy alone to conduct negotiations for something so profitable. And King Armel is no fool."

"We are glad to have such an…experienced representative." The petty part of her soul enjoyed making the baroness blink as she hinted at her age, a small revenge for calling Nevar a boy.

"How goes the search for my stepson?" Although her expression hadn't changed, the sharpness of her question rubbed Rane the wrong way.

"Not well. We are changing strategies as it doesn't appear he poses an immediate threat to the kingdom. It's possible he outpaced our search parties and is on his way someplace he believes safe. Commander Miren would appreciate any suggestions where such a place might be."

Jocelyn's lips thinned and her hand fluttered to her pocket as though seeking reassurance from the object within. "I do not know where he would go under these circumstances. I'm sorry I cannot be of help."

"There is nothing to be sorry about." Rane plastered on her best fake smile. Once again, she couldn't tell what went through Jocelyn's mind. Would she prefer they found Nevar or not? Rane supposed as long as he didn't accuse the baroness, Jocelyn didn't care. And he wouldn't with her threat hanging over his family. "The guards will find him. The commander is very thorough. But that's not why I sought you out. I would be most honored if you joined me tomorrow for a picnic luncheon. I know the perfect spot not far from the city."

Jocelyn blinked. This hadn't been what she'd expected. Good, let her be caught off guard for once.

"Is it safe, with my stepson still on the loose?"

"The guards have completed a thorough search of the castle, the city, and the areas immediately around us. Anything within a few miles should be secure. We'll have a full contingent of Lorean guards, and you may bring as many of your own as you wish to ensure your safety."

A cautious smile planted itself on Jocelyn's face. "Then, by all means, I'd be delighted to join you."

"I look forward to it," Rane lied.

Chapter 20

The repetitive activity of chopping firewood cleared Nevar's mind and solidified his desire to leave this place. Caught between wanting to stay and needing to go, he was a man without purpose, waiting only for his lover to return. The next time he saw Rane, he would tell her to stop fighting the inevitable. He'd tell her he was leaving. It was the only thing he could do to keep her safe. When he'd burned away the frustration, Nevar headed to the pond for a quick swim to wash away the sweat left behind.

Of course, since Rane's visit, it was no longer a peaceful part of his day. Visions of her still sparkling with water droplets as her muscled legs carried her quickly away haunted him. She'd been a wood nymph in her natural habitat. It was glorious and damned distracting, causing frustration of another sort entirely.

He was pulling his breeches back on when a low baying froze him in his tracks. Nevar grabbed the rest of his clothes and his shoes and ran for the cottage. The baying came closer, the paws rustling the leaf litter. No matter how fast he ran, the dog would catch him. Nevar skidded to a stop. Before he could turn to face the oncoming hound, it ran into him full force from behind and knocked him onto his hands and knees. The bays turned into happy whines, and a warm, wet tongue licked his face.

Bash.

"Gah. Dog slobber," he protested. It did no good. The creature wouldn't stop licking his face.

Giving in, he scratched behind her ears. She flopped on the ground in front of him, tail wagging, and presented her belly for rubs.

Rane burst forth from the forest, hair flying wildly behind her. Leaves and twigs dotted her locks and clung to the blue dress she wore. As lovely as she looked in breeches, Rane in a dress took his breath away.

"What are you doing?" she snapped. "Run, fool!"

She grabbed his arm and hauled him to his feet.

"What's going on?"

"No time." She dragged him away from the pond, picking up the pace with every step.

"I—"

"You can run and have the option to question me later, or you can face the squad of men-at-arms that will be here before I can answer any of them. Your choice, *my lord*."

Nevar ran, Bash and Rane at his heels. She didn't have to be snippy about it.

As they approached the cottage, Lark stepped out from the underbrush.

"Rane. It is good to see you—"

"Sorry, Lark. I'm not alone. Get him inside and keep his mouth shut. I'll explain later if I can."

The pixie grabbed him by the arm and pulled him toward the door.

"Come, Bash." Rane smacked her thigh with her hand.

The dog walked over and watched Rane with adoring eyes, and they walked away. Did he look the same when gazing at the princess? It wouldn't surprise him. The memory of how she'd felt in his arms, her soft curves fitting into his hard muscles, flooded his body with heat. Rane froze and rushed back, as though drawn to the same heat. He tingled in anticipation.

"Do you know anything about the mirror your stepmother carries with her?"

He opened and closed his mouth twice before finding words to answer her unexpected question. "Her mirror?"

"Yes, the mirror. Is there anything odd about it?"

"I don't think so, but I always found its constant presence strange."

"She takes it everywhere?"

"Yes."

Sounds in the distance brought them back to themselves. More dogs barked, more people tromped through the forest. Voices called out for the princess.

Rane placed a gentle kiss on his cheek. "Thank you. Get inside. I'll distract them."

She put on her crown princess mask and smoothed her features, and she walked sedately away. Bash gave him a forlorn glance before following Rane, ears flopping and white-tipped tail held high. Rane picked a stray twig out of her hair and tossed it into the trees. Her hands smoothed her gown, and her transformation was complete.

Lark pulled him into the cottage and shut the door with a quick click. He pulled a chair over to the window and settled in to watch.

"They can't see the cottage, right?" he asked.

"No. Only you and Rane have the ability."

Good.

A dozen guards emerged from the forest and formed a rough perimeter around the clearing. Half wore the brown and emerald green of Lorea, and half wore the blue and silver of Otero. Two guards handled the horses, and the rest faced the forest, eyes scanning for trouble.

Nevar resisted the urge to duck below the window. Nobody could spot him, but it didn't feel that way. The rumble of men's voices layered on top of the clinking of chain mail and snorting of horses. The lighter, sweeter voices of the women twined through them, making it harder to make out what anyone said.

Prince Ebon unloaded the saddlebags while Princess Betony unfolded a large, colorful blanket and spread it on the grass. Rane chatted with his stepmother, keeping her gaze away from the cottage, though the others' eyes sometimes stared through the spot. His life was in her hands, and her skills as a spy were piss poor. Ah, the sweet irony of trusting a privileged princess in a foreign land. Of course, he had no choice.

Rane and her siblings sat on the blanket, the women's skirts billowing around them. Rane's knocked over a basket of fruit and a flagon of wine, creating a flurry of activity as the others rushed around to clean it up.

Jocelyn graced the blanket with a sour face. Never a fan of frivolity, she wouldn't sacrifice her dignity for a picnic at home. Only an invitation from a social better would have her here.

There was no way for him to tell what Rane was playing at. Not until he talked with her again. Why in the world would she bring his stepmother and the guards so close to the cottage?

"Is there any way to hear better?" he whispered to Lark.

"Shh."

The pixie sat at the table and seemed unconcerned about the activity going on outside the door. Nevar pressed his ear to the windowpane. He could watch them and not know what they said, or he could listen. He chose to listen.

"Again, I am sorry Bash ran off," Rane said at her sweetest. He heard something deeper, but his stepmother didn't. "She gets a whiff of rabbit and…"

"You should have trained that out of her by now," Jocelyn snapped, her voice dripping with the disdain she usually reserved for Nevar.

"Bash is a fairy hound," Ebon said, his voice sharp. Nevar looked up at this, needing to see Jocelyn's reaction. She eyed the dog with wariness now, instead of contempt. "They have minds of their own."

Bash barked happily at this, not giving a fuck what the baroness thought of her. She licked Betony's hand in contentment. They had cleaned the mess Rane created to the best of everyone's abilities, and the small party passed around the food and ate.

An uncomfortable silence hung over the clearing. Rane cleared her throat.

"I wondered, Baroness, if you had your lovely little mirror with you today. I would like a closer look, if I may."

What was it about the damned mirror?

"Oh, I left it back at the castle today, Your Highness. I didn't want it to break on our excursion."

"Pity. May I ask where you found such a remarkable treasure? The markings were unusual."

"It's only a bauble handed down to me by my grandmother. It's not worth anything other than sentiment."

Nevar heard the lie in her voice. The way she spoke those words so smoothly gave her away. And he knew for a fact she loathed her grandmother. On the rare occasions she referred to the woman at all, it had been with derision.

Rane couldn't know that, and she let the matter drop.

"What do you think of the Argent Forest?" she inquired after another few moments of awkward silence. "I have to admit, it surprised me when you wanted to see it. I assumed magical things made you nervous."

Now there was an interesting fact. Jocelyn had insisted on coming here.

"A forest isn't magical in anything but a metaphorical way."

Nevar bit his cheek to stop himself from laughing, and bit harder as he pictured his stepmother's face if the pixies came flying out of the woods.

"We'll have to agree to disagree," Rane said.

"I'm glad Prince Ebon suggested this place."

"It's close, and the pond might be nice if we stay longer," the prince said.

"And you're positive Nevar isn't here?" Jocelyn asked.

Rane's gaze darted to the invisible cottage, and she pressed her lips together.

"If he was in the forest, he wouldn't be any longer," Ebon said. "The forest has many mysteries and doesn't take kindly to strangers. Most who stray from the main road are never seen again."

A faint gasp left his stepmother's mouth.

"Don't worry, we're not most people," Betony said dreamily.

"Perhaps it is the best justice I can hope for. I would hate to tell the baron his son was executed for murder."

She would revel in informing his father of that, if he ever recovered enough. Of course, Nevar guessed his father might never hear of his alleged crime. Once he was out of the way, his father would be next, and Jocelyn would rule Otero until Orom came of age. By then, she would have an ironclad grip on the barony, and Orom would be little more than a puppet.

It would be more than foolish to run out and confront her. The Lorean and Oteran guards who surrounded her were on high alert. They had three royals to protect, a murderer on the loose, and fairies on the prowl. He wouldn't last a minute, let alone deal his stepmother a fatal blow. Even if he did, he'd be a murderer in truth instead of fiction.

Just wait. Someday soon, she would pay for her actions.

Chapter 21

For the first time in her life, Rane's tendency to create chaos played right into her hands.

Chasing after Bash, a common occurrence, had given her an opportunity to warn Nevar and get him to safety. Knocking over the fruit basket and the wine had provided a needed distraction. She had noticed Jocelyn looking around with her characteristic shrewdness. Did she suspect Nevar was nearby? Rane would give a pinky finger to know how that was possible.

"Perhaps it is a kindness of sorts," Rane said noncommittally.

Her carefully laid plans had gone to hell in a handbasket as soon as they set out that morning. Rane had planned to have the picnic in the middle of the old apple orchard, as far from Nevar as she could get. The countess had resisted, saying she'd never seen the Argent Forest. Ebon had been his usual helpful self, and Rane couldn't find a way to refuse.

In the midst of the chaos and fear of being discovered, Nevar's presence left her trembling with need. She wanted to run her hands over his body, feel his lips on hers. Forget the fact the woman who wanted him dead, or at least imprisoned, was right behind her. Forget the fact he was a fugitive and forget whatever they had between them couldn't last. Rane wanted him with every breath, every heartbeat.

Their chaste kiss would have to suffice. The stubble on his face was rough against her lips, and she'd fought off the temptation to move them to softer things. She'd thought it was a good thing the cottage had been close, but now she wasn't sure.

The baroness was coldly cruel, and Rane had to grind her teeth to keep from an ill-considered response. After all, an Oteran guard had been murdered in their castle. Keeping the peace was more important than defending her dog. Or Nevar. If she spoke a single polite word about him, it would raise too many suspicions.

The smile she gave the baroness did not touch her eyes. They finished lunch in relative silence, remarking on the weather, the wildflowers, and the birds twittering in the trees. Nice, polite conversation to avoid causing offense or catching any fugitives.

Ebon offered a hand to the baroness after lunch. While he was busy helping her corral her docile mare and everyone else was packing things away, Rane tucked some food under a bush near the cottage. She didn't know when she'd make it back, and this would keep Nevar fed for another day or two.

Before long, all the supplies had been repacked and loaded onto the horses. A tap on her shoulder stopped her from mounting her horse.

Jocelyn stood behind her. "I am sorry for insulting your pet, Your Highness."

Her contempt for Bash dripped off her words. It was as though the baroness saw things, and likely people too, only for their usefulness.

"No insult taken. Bash could use more training." Rane struggled to keep her voice calm and her face pleasingly blank.

Jocelyn brushed a hair out of Rane's face, tucking it behind her ear. "There, now you look the proper princess."

Rane was a proper fucking princess, but she held her tongue. She'd always found the politics of her life difficult, but maybe these games Jocelyn played would teach her what many hours of her parents' lecturing couldn't. With innocent lives at stake, with Nevar's life at stake, failure to play the game would cost her more than she was willing to pay.

Instead, she said, "Thank you."

Jocelyn smiled, and a fingernail scratched Rane's neck as she drew back her hand.

"Oh, I am so sorry, my dear." Her apology rang false.

Bash appeared, as if by magic, and stood between the two women. A low growl rumbled in her chest, and Jocelyn backed away. Rane suppressed a smile. If she hadn't guessed the woman was up to something, Bash's reaction would have pointed it out.

Magic. With her blood. There was nothing she could do without drawing attention to the situation, and that wouldn't end well for Nevar's family.

"Accidents happen. It's only a scratch."

The baroness curtsied and walked to her horse. As Rane pulled out a white napkin from her saddlebag, Jocelyn pulled out the mirror she had claimed not to carry. Rane pretended not to notice. What could she do anyway? She blotted her neck, and a few drops of bright red blood stained the linen. She tucked the napkin away in a safe place and mounted Sunny.

Betony rode up next to her and slowed, allowing the baroness and most of the guards to pull ahead.

"That was close."

"What was close?"

Bet eyed her, and a sly smile turned up her lips. Her brilliant green eyes flashed in amusement.

"Cottage." She kicked her horse forward before Rane could reply.

It was especially hard to form a wisecrack with her mouth hanging open. The cottage should have been invisible to everyone, normal human, fey, or fairy alike. Sometimes her sister's abilities were a royal pain in the ass.

Ebon drew next to her, concern on his brow. "What was that all about?"

"None of your fucking business." Rane kicked Sunny and joined the rest of the party. One nosy sibling was plenty, thank you very much.

Ebon caught up to her, mumbling to himself and darting angry glares her way.

"You're keeping something from me, Rane. I hope it doesn't bite you in the ass." He pulled ahead and rode beside Jadran to lead the way.

Upon their return, Betony and Ebon took charge of the horses. Rane and Jocelyn needed to be in the Council Chamber as soon as possible. In the chaos, Rane lost sight of the baroness until she spotted a figure with long, black hair on the steps leading into the castle. Too late. If she ran now, it would look suspicious.

Rane followed Jocelyn into the Council Chamber for the afternoon session of negotiations. She slowed her steps when she spotted her father and Commander Miren speaking in low voices. They were too good at this, no hints of words escaping their conversation. Rane joined the others at the table, including Jocelyn, who stared in rapt concentration at her mirror.

What did she see there? Rane craned her neck, hoping she could catch a glimpse, but the movement caught the baroness's attention. She snapped the mirror shut and tucked it into her pocket.

The discussion continued for a moment more, and the commander marched away. Her father stood near his seat at the table, a pensive frown on his lips, until the steward cleared his throat. King Rowan blinked, returning his attention to the matter at hand.

"Commander Miren informs me of a possible sighting of Lord Nevar to the south of here. She is taking a full company of guards to hunt him. Baroness, would you like any of your men-at-arms to accompany them?"

"An excellent idea, Your Majesty. My captain can suggest a couple candidates."

The king gestured to a nearby page and instructed her to pass along the message. He clapped his hands together once.

"Now, let's get back to business."

Her father's face lit up in a glee he reserved for these types of negotiations. He loved it when both parties profited from a joint venture, reasoning those were the relationships least likely to fall apart. The afternoon passed in a flurry of maps, the scratching of quills, and the quibbles of the Teruellan mining administrator and her father's exchequer. Rane quickly lost track of who said what to whom, and where the damn mine was going to be. She would read a draft of the proposal before her father signed the final version. They were still a few days away from that happening, based on what she'd been able to discern today.

Alize walked in, pushing the teacart. Thank the goddess the day was almost over.

The young woman served the king and queen. This was the first time Rane had seen her since the incident. She appeared unfazed until she stood next to the baroness. The teapot shook in her hand, and as she poured, tea splashed onto the baroness.

"Idiot cow," Jocelyn snarled, snatching at Alize's apron to pat her dress dry. Her venomous glare and pinched lips sent the maid running from the chamber.

"We do not speak to the servants in such a manner here, Baroness." Queen Beatrice's voice was firm with disapproval.

Jocelyn's face went positively gray. "I apologize, Your Majesty. The tea was hot, and I was surprised."

Beatrice inspected the woman across from her. Rane knew the look. Her mother sensed a falsehood, and there wasn't much that bothered the queen more than a lie. Rane waited with glee for what would come next.

The queen shook her head and rose. "I will check on the poor dear. I hoped getting her back into her routines would help after the incident." She left, her skirts swirling around her ankles in her haste to chase after Alize.

Her mother never passed up the opportunity to call out a lie with her children. Was her ability failing, or had she chosen not to confront the baroness? If so, why? Mere politics, or did her mother play a deeper game?

Negotiations continued for another hour. Her father invited the baroness to join the royal couple for a quiet supper. Rane let out a sigh and barely kept herself from smiling. The last thing she wanted tonight was an official summons of any kind. She had one thing on her mind, and supper with her parents wasn't it. Her hunger ran to other things.

As soon as Rane turned the corner and nobody could see her from the Council Chamber, she ran, her skirts billowing behind her. Her first stop was the kitchen.

"I'll take my supper in my room," she informed Cook. "Could you include a small flagon of your best ale? I have some reading to do."

She took the stairs to her room two at a time and was already trying to slip out of the dress before the door closed behind her. When the knock sounded, her arms were stuck in her tunic.

"Just leave it outside." She yanked the stupid garment down.

The door flew open instead. Ebon stood there, accompanied by Bash.

"Where are you going?" he demanded.

"Fresh air, once I've eaten."

"Liar."

"Prove it."

Ebon kicked the door shut behind him, his lips pressed into a thin line. He dropped the tray with a clatter onto the desk and leaned on the door with his arms crossed.

"You're not leaving here until I know what you're up to."

Rane laughed. Her little brother assumed he could stop her?

"I'm not kidding, Rane. I can beat you in a fair fight."

"Not every time."

"Often enough. And I outweigh you, so I'd like to see you make me move."

"Bash could make you move."

He glanced at the hound. "You wouldn't."

It was a statement of fact. Her brother knew her well, and he knew she wouldn't lift her sword to force him from the door.

"Fine." She crooked her finger, and Ebon followed her into the bedchamber. Rane sat on the bed, and he leaned against the closed door. "Promise to keep this to yourself."

"No, it doesn't work that way. You tell me, then I decide who else needs to know. We aren't children anymore, and you're not the boss of me."

"Well…"

"Not yet."

She wanted to tell her brother. He was the smartest of the three of them. If anyone could figure this out, Ebon could, but she had made a promise and breaking it would both betray the trust Nevar had placed in her and put her brother in danger. Everything she'd observed Jocelyn do today confirmed she wouldn't hesitate to follow through on her threat. The baroness would stop at nothing, including murder, to get what she wanted.

"I can't tell you everything, but innocent lives hang in the balance."

He snorted.

"I'm not exaggerating. All I can tell you is I *know* Nevar didn't attack or murder anyone."

"How would you know?"

She bit her lip. "I was there."

"I don't believe you."

"Have I ever lied to you?"

Ebon held up a finger. "You told me Hyssop would steal my

teeth when I was five." He held up another finger. "You told me the apples on the tree in the kitchen garden were poisonous." Another finger. "You—"

"Have I lied about anything important?"

He glowered. "No."

"Trust me, please. I can't prove his innocence without you."

"This is bad, Rane." He collapsed onto the stool in front of her dressing table. "You must tell Father."

"Tell him what? If I said I was in Nevar's bedchamber that night, he would call it a conflict of interest and dismiss anything I have to say."

"Tell *me* what happened," Ebon pleaded, his darkling gaze trying to see past the walls she built to keep this secret.

"I can't, Eb. If you know, you'll be in danger."

"I'm willing to take the risk."

"I'm not, and it's not only you. Other people, including a child, will be in danger. You have to trust me."

"I hate this." He braced his elbows on his knees and hung his head.

"Me, too."

He dragged a hand through his hair. "What can I do to help?"

"Is there a way to trace magic?"

"Are you telling me magic was involved in the guard's death?"

Rane stared straight at her brother, lips pressed tight and giving nothing away.

"If it's magic, we need to tell Hyssop," Ebon pressed.

"I promised to say nothing." This was already breaking her promise, but Ebon wouldn't let it go without a good reason. She was desperately trying to give one.

"What about your boon? A simple wish and this would all go away."

He wasn't wrong, but what if something even more dire were to occur? With lives at stake, she needed to keep her boon to protect the innocent, and that included Nevar.

"Not yet. I promise I'll use it if I have to, but I haven't exhausted all other options."

"You've lost your damned mind."

"Probably."

"Is he worth it?"

Nevar made her feel like a normal person and a princess all at once. He set her skin afire, and her heart thumped at the sight of him. His determination to protect his family at all costs reminded her of her own.

"Yes."

"Every time you visit him, you risk someone finding out."

"I can't seem to help myself. He's gotten under my skin."

"You're in l—"

"Don't fucking say it." If he said it, it would be real, and she couldn't deal with that. Not yet.

"I won't, as long as you know it." Ebon rose from the chair and gave Rane a hug. "If you need me, I'll be in the library with the magic books."

"You'll help me?"

"Of course. If you say he's innocent, he's innocent."

"Thanks, Eb."

He kissed her on the forehead and left. Rane pulled on her boots, packed the food and flagon of ale, and used the secret passage to make her way to her lover.

Chapter 22

"Stay here," Lark hissed at Nevar. The pixie changed into her tiny form but without the light show, and darted out of the cottage, taking off after the royal picnic party.

The fuck I will.

That was too close. What the hell had Rane been thinking?

He'd told himself from the beginning this arrangement would only be until a better plan presented itself. Nevar still had nothing, but today's little escapade proved he had run out of time. The pixies had taught him a lot over the last few days, and hopefully, it would be enough to survive until he reached his destination. Wherever that was.

He shoved his tunics and breeches into his satchel. In no time at all, he packed his meager possessions.

Nevar had no other option but to run. If he stayed, he'd get caught, and then he'd have to choose between himself and his family. This time, he'd been lucky, and Rane had acted quickly. What about next time? He had no doubt there would be a next time, and trusting in sheer luck was not in his nature.

The pixies would be in danger, too, and he'd be damned if he allowed any harm to come to them for helping him. It wouldn't take long for others to connect the dots and figure out who had aided his escape. His stepmother's machinations could bring down Rane and the entire Lorean royal family. The last was a bit of a stretch, but even if the possibility was remote, he wouldn't allow it.

He had no friends. Jocelyn had kept him isolated since her marriage to his father, claiming she couldn't stand it if the baron lost another member of his family. The Argent Forest was no place for a human long term. Odd whispers and cries seeped through the door and windows at night, setting his teeth on edge.

Nevar wasn't sure how long he would survive in the forest without the pixies, but he would have to try. Trekking through the Argent was the fastest way by foot to Otero. Though the terrain of most of the barony consisted of grassy plains, there were plenty of places to hide in the mountains on the border, the same mountains under contention in the negotiations that had brought him to Lorea in the first place. He could disappear, leave Lord Nevar of Otero behind, and become something else. Exactly what escaped him. He didn't have many skills besides riding, swordplay, and pretending he was more stupid and lazy than he actually was.

Slinging the satchel over his shoulder, he picked up the last apple and bit into its crisp flesh. The taste reminded him of home. It reminded him of Rane. Everything did, but he would only bring woe to her now. This was the best move.

He snagged his sword belt on the way out the door, hanging the magic talisman in its place. Nevar stepped through the door, and the cottage vanished. The sun shone in his eyes, lower on the horizon. He would need to make good time to reach a safe spot before nightfall.

Whatever may come, he had a plan that wouldn't risk anyone else. He kept to the deer paths and streams and headed west. He'd find the main road and follow it north to where it joined the route to Otero. His stomach rumbled, but he pushed on. The more distance he put between himself and the cottage, the better.

Another rumble joined the first. Nevar froze. That wasn't his stomach. The sword at his side radiated bitter cold. A warning.

The low growl sent fear snaking through him. He pulled his borrowed sword from its scabbard. It vibrated in greeting as his hand closed around the hilt, and a puff of frosty air issued from his mouth. The sword both unnerved and thrilled him, the perfectly balanced blade seeming to anticipate his moves. It was more than a weapon. It was an extension of his body.

The stench of rotten meat assailed his nose. Nevar turned toward the foul odor. A green-scaled beast larger than the warhorse Rane had "borrowed" to steal him away skulked in a clearing a hundred paces to his right. Gobbets of meat dropped from its gaping mouth, which was wide enough to tear off a horse's head in one bite.

A marraco. His nanny had scared him with stories when he was a child. Nevar believed that was all they were, stories, and yet, here was the wide-mouthed dragon, the symbol of the Teruellan royal family, alive and well in the Argent Forest.

Nevar didn't look too closely at what the creature ate. He didn't want to know, only hoped it wasn't a pixie. The creature devoured its meal as Nevar slipped away. He exhaled as the distance grew between them.

A roar echoed through the forest, far too close, and Nevar ran. Another of the creatures burst out of the glen up ahead, charging straight for him. The thundering steps of the beast behind him approached. He was trapped.

Tossing aside his satchel, the icy fingers of the sword's magic nestled in his mind and focused his senses. The first creature leaped at him. The sword seemed to do all the thinking for him, his body merely an extension of the deadly steel. Slicing through the air with an otherworldly whistle, it hit the tough hide of the beast. A screech of metal on metal rang out.

Fuck. There was no way he could best a beast with scales made of metal.

The creature cried out in pain as the blade parted the scales and thick, crimson blood poured out of the wound. It swung a great, clawed foot at him. Nevar ducked, the air of the blow passing directly above his head. The beast beat its wings, and Nevar toppled to the ground from the rush of wind.

The other marraco sped toward him. With his years of training, Nevar quickly found his feet and put his back to a great pine tree. At least this way, he'd see his death coming for him.

A small ball of light streaked by him, followed by another, and another. A loud, ululating cry came from above. Lark dropped out of the sky, her wings tucked neatly against her back and both her blades drawn. The beasts stepped back in surprise.

Nevar held his blade at the ready. The four human-sized pixies fanned out behind the pair of marracos.

"He is not prey," Lark said.

The uninjured dragon to his right growled. Its foul breath washed over him and made him want to empty his stomach. He padded toward it. It growled again, and its companion joined in. At the sound, all the hair on his arms stood at attention.

A movement in the underbrush drew Nevar's attention. A crooked figure emerged, a head shorter than Lark. Its skin was like the bark of an alligator pine, its hair like the moss hanging from the trees in the swamps near the Teruellan capital. In its right hand, it wielded a blade as black as coal.

"His kind are not welcome here, pixie, and neither are you. I made that clear the last time you trespassed here," the figure said, its voice rough and sneering.

"We are the guardians of the forest, Gita, not you. We cannot trespass. Call off your pets, and we will leave."

The fairy glared at Nevar and the four pixies and… smiled was the best word Nevar had for its expression, but exposing those razor-sharp teeth was a threat, not a friendly gesture.

Faster than Nevar could react, the fairy cast himself forward. As though the movement was a silent signal, the marracos charged the pixies. He would face his opponent alone. The pixies had much bigger foes to contend with. The black blade sliced at Nevar's belly. He parried the blow, and orange sparks flew off their swords, dying before they hit the forest floor. His opponent's eyes widened as Nevar thrust his sword. The fairy blocked it easily, but now they had the measure of each other. Trading blows back and forth, the two circled around the trees, trampling the grass and flowers into the dirt.

"You do not deserve such a blade," the fairy said, swinging wildly.

Nevar didn't have the wind to answer him. He concentrated on finding an opening to end this. The pixies kept the dragons busy but did not seem in any hurry to end their fight. They led the creatures away and into the glen, leaving him to fend off the forest fairy.

The fairy pressed the attack, forcing Nevar to defend himself. Soon, sweat dripped down his face and stung the many scratches Gita had inflicted on his skin. Nevar tripped on a gnarled tree root, landing on his back. Before he could leap up, the fairy's black blade pricked his throat. A trickle of blood wet his collar.

Another wicked baring of the teeth. "You are pathetic, human. It will be my great pleasure to rid the world of another of your kind."

Nevar kicked out as hard as he could with both feet at one of the fairy's knees. It crunched as it broke, and the creature howled in pain. Nevar leaped up and swept his sword outward, disarming his attacker. The black blade skittered across the forest floor and the fairy fell. Nevar held the tip of his sword to the fairy's heart.

It scowled at him and muttered something. The fairy disappeared in a flash of green light, and the roars of the dragons in the glen ceased. Nevar propped himself against a tree, sliding his sword back into its scabbard with trembling hands. He wiped the sweat and blood from his face. Fortunately, the worst of the damage was the nick on his neck, which had stopped bleeding, and a few bruises.

Something hit him in the shoulder, like a river rock shot from a sling. "Ow."

Another hit to his other shoulder, this one pushing him to the side. His foot sunk into a small hole in the forest floor. Nevar windmilled his arms to keep upright, to no avail. He fell to his knees. Three balls of light surrounded him, tiny, squeaky voices shouting rude things at him.

He raised his arms. "Fine, I give up."

The squeaking stopped, and the sisters hovered around his head. Lark emerged from the undergrowth and tweaked his ear.

"Ow," he said again.

"Serves you right, fighting a hobgoblin. I told you not to wander the forest alone. I also told you to stay at the cottage."

"I wasn't wandering. I was leaving." She tweaked his ear again. "Stop it."

"As soon as you talk sense, I will. There is no leaving. Rane said you would stay with us until she fixed things. Things aren't fixed, yet, are they?"

"No, but—"

"Then you stay," chirped Wren, crossing her tiny arms.

"You don't understand. My stepmother is too good at what she does. She'll kill my family if I don't have ironclad evidence she's the guilty party, and Rane hasn't been able to make any progress. It's best I leave now before they find out Rane helped me. Before they find out *you* helped me."

"No, it is you who does not understand. We owe Rane our

freedom and our lives. Until we pay back the debt we owe, or she releases us from it, we will do as she says. If you leave the forest, we go with." Lark gave his ear one last tweak before stepping back and joining her sisters.

"Wouldn't you get in trouble with the Queens?"

A tiny shrug. If they weren't so fierce, it would be cute.

"They would recognize our obligation," said Curlew. "After all, it is a time-honored tradition of the Faerie. They wouldn't be pleased, but there would be nothing they could do."

Rane had earned their loyalty by risking her life for theirs. She'd done the same for him.

"Come back to the cottage. Give Rane more time. She will fix this," Lark said, not unkindly. Out of all the pixies, she was around the most and saw how hard he worked to keep busy, how hard it was for him to do nothing while others gambled with his life.

"Fine. I'll return to the cottage with you."

It was a bad idea to leave this late in the day. Even now, the forest darkened. Maybe he'd leave first thing in the morning to have the entire day to travel.

"He ran once. He could do so again, and we do not have the numbers to watch him and perform our duties," said a pixie he hadn't met yet.

"Robin has a point," said Lark. "I need your word, Nevar, that you won't run again."

His word was his bond. It was one of the few things he knew about dealing with fairies. The consequences for breaking your word would be dire. Everything from a duel to indentured servitude to death was on the table.

He had little choice. They would come with him and leave the forest unprotected if he didn't, leaving other trailers without aid, and the pixies wouldn't be welcome in Otero.

"You have my word. I will not leave without your permission again."

Little Wren dropped the silver-wrapped stone in his hand. He fastened it around his neck and trudged back to the cottage.

The moon had risen by the time he threw himself on the bed, exhausted after the fight. He stripped down to nothing and crawled under the covers, asleep before he could form any other thoughts.

A butterfly-wing tickle along his temple woke Nevar. He raised a hand to brush away whatever annoying bug had flown into the cottage. Instead of a tiny insect, Nevar encountered warm, calloused fingers. He opened his eyes. Rane sat on the edge of the bed, her face glowing in the light cast by the fairy lantern near his bed. She seemed almost as fey as her sister, the garnet undertones in her chestnut hair gleaming darkly.

"Hello," she said, voice low and thrumming.

He must be dreaming. After fighting dragons and a hobgoblin, his mind was playing tricks, conjuring the one thing he wanted more than anything. He stretched his arms over his head, interlacing his fingers. Might as well enjoy this while he could.

Rane cupped his cheek, and a shock of desire heated his skin. This was no dream. She was here, in the flesh, and her gentle touch made him crave more.

"What happened to you?" She brushed her fingers next to the small wound on his neck.

"Hobgoblin," he said nonchalantly.

She smiled and pulled out the ribbon holding her hair back, dropping it to the floor. "Nasty things. At least your scar will be smaller than mine."

A waterfall of thick, silky hair fell forward as she bent down, curtaining them in a sweetly scented world of their own. He opened his mouth to respond, but she brushed her lips against his, just as soft as her butterfly caresses of a moment ago. Nevar forgot whatever he was going to say. He didn't want soft. One hand unclasped from behind his head and clutched the back of hers, pressing her lips firmly into his.

With a moan, Rane opened her mouth, inviting him in. He didn't take her up on her offer. Instead, he trailed kisses over her chin, her neck, and the outline of her collarbone before running his tongue along the line of her tunic.

She raised her hands to the buttons on her jerkin. He caught them, hesitating. Should they even be doing this? Rane whimpered in protest. God help him, he wanted her, needed her. Whatever he had promised the pixies, their time together was limited. He couldn't bring himself to reject the gift she offered.

"Let me," he growled.

She smiled and dropped her hands. Nevar made quick work of

the buttons and pushed the jerkin off her shoulders. It landed noiselessly on the floor. He slid his hand under her tunic, the skin of her belly velvety under his sword-roughened hands. Rane gasped.

The gasps became pants as his thumb found the hard nub of her nipple. His other hand rested on her hip, this thumb making slow, small circles above the line of her breeches. Nevar smiled as he pulled the tunic over her head. Her skin was golden in the low light and her eyes were half-closed in pleasure. Glorious.

Nevar fastened his lips around the other nipple. Her back arched, and another moan escaped her. Rane's hands threaded through his hair, holding him to her. He gave her nipple a lick and leaned back on his elbows.

"Take off your breeches," he said.

She stood and undid the buttons ever so slowly. He wanted to push her hands out of the way and finish the job, in a hurry to see her naked, in a hurry to bury himself in her sweet smell. The breeches joined the tunic and jerkin in a heap. Rane crawled onto the bed and straddled him, bending her head so her lips rested next to his ear.

"Is this what you wanted?" she asked, teasing.

He turned his head and caught her lips with his own. She tasted of herbs and berries, smelled slightly of the earthiness of horses and hay. He trailed kisses over her jaw and the side of her neck, nibbling on her earlobe, breathing in her sighs and moans.

"Sit up. I want to see you," he said.

She did as he asked, her rounded body radiant. He cupped her breasts and thumbed her nipples. She moaned in pleasure, arching her back and closing her eyes.

"You like that?"

"Yes."

He did it again and got the same result. Nevar let one hand drift down her body, skimming over her curves, caressing as much of her satiny skin as he could. His fingers drifted across her thigh and brushed the dark triangle of hair. He found the nub in her folds and stroked. Rane hissed, and he put more pressure there, setting a rhythm. Her wetness coated his fingers, and her moans became deeper and more insistent.

"Please, Nevar," she whispered, her legs trembling.

His name on her lips almost broke him. "You're the one in control, Rane. You can ride me whenever you want."

Her eyes opened, and she bit her bottom lip before a wicked grin took over. She grasped his hard length. It was his turn to tremble with need.

"You like that?" she asked.

He could only moan. She lowered herself over him, taking him inch by sweet, sensuous inch. Her long, low moan sent a shiver of pure need along his spine. His hips bucked, and she hissed in another breath. He kept the pressure on the nub as she rose and fell over him. He met her stroke for stroke, glorying in this beautiful creature losing control above him.

Rane's movements became more erratic, and her breaths became pants. She let out a long, echoing sob as she broke, her muscles clenching around him. The bliss of it shattered him, and he spilled into her with a final thrust, his groan mingling with hers. She collapsed on top of him. When he could finally see straight again, he rolled to the side and pulled her into his embrace.

A hush blanketed the cottage, and only the wind in the trees outside broke the silence. A chuckle started in Rane's chest, and a gentle smile formed on her rosy lips.

"I'd say I didn't mean to wake you, but clearly I'd be lying," she said.

"Clearly." He looked around the cottage, as though searching for something. "No Bash, tonight?"

"No. Bash has her uses, but she isn't subtle. It's hard to sneak out of the castle with an exuberant hound at your heels."

"We can't do this again, Rane. It's too dangerous." It broke his heart to say it, but one of them had to be realistic. A deep sadness enveloped him. Beautiful, intelligent, loving, Rane brightened his world when she was here, and the loss of her dulled it, like the sun disappearing behind a cloud. How had this happened in a handful of days?

Nevar tore his eyes away in a desperate attempt to make it hurt less. It failed.

She stretched out a hand toward his face, hesitant. He caught it in his own, holding it in place a hairsbreadth above his cheek. She snatched it back.

"How else am I supposed to look after you?"

"I'm not some hidden paramour you're supposed to look after. I'm the heir to a prosperous barony, and I'm perfectly capable of looking out for myself. Something you need to assure your friends I can do."

"I'm trying to help."

"By bringing the woman who threatened my family, who wouldn't hesitate to kill me herself, so close to my hiding place? Big help."

Rane put some distance between them. She looked a goddess herself in the golden light of the lamp. *Why am I telling her no?*

"I've never investigated a murder before, Nevar. I know she's guilty, you know she's guilty, but we can't prove it. I just need a little more—"

That was why. Murder, vindictive stepmothers, and duty. "We're out of time."

"No, we're not. We can't be."

"Have you found anything, anything at all?"

A calculating expression found a home on her face. "Maybe. Alize delivered tea this afternoon, and she seemed frightened of Jocelyn. Maybe she remembered something."

Hope flickered to life in his chest. If Alize remembered something important, it could solve all their problems. Except if she didn't remember the right things, the gambit would fail and give Jocelyn the opportunity to follow through on her threat. Alize would face the consequences of his stepmother's actions, and his father and brother would die. Jocelyn had used Alize as she would use a sword or a poison.

"Did she say she remembered?"

"No, but if I can—"

"Let it go, Rane. It's done. There's no rewriting history." Cold truth crushed the spark of hope.

Rane sighed. "This is hard."

"Try being in my boots." His voice was bitter. To have hope bloom and fade so quickly gave him a headache. "You didn't bring anything to drink, did you? Something stronger than tea?"

She pointed at the saddlebags on the table. "Good Lorean ale."

He pulled on his breeches. The air in the cottage was cool on his skin as he walked over and dug through the bags. He found the flagon and pulled the cork out. Nevar sipped it first. The Loreans didn't know good wine from sweet tea, but damn, did they make some fine ale. He drank a gulp and brought it over to Rane, holding it out.

She shook her head. "For you."

Rane pulled her tunic over her head and joined him at the table. This was his second favorite way to see her, only surpassed by the vision of her completely naked. But with her legs exposed, the tunic barely covering her ass, and a shoulder peeking out of the unlaced opening, she was nearly as alluring. Maybe more so, as the tunic begged to be thrown to the floor again.

"Thanks. Tea only gets me so far. Too bad there was no Oteran brandy." The brandy would make what he had to do next less painful. Maybe. Ale would have to do.

"I can look."

"That's not necessary." He took another swig. Rane was brave, loyal, and stubborn. He would have to push her hard, but there was no other choice. The longer he stayed here, the higher the chance he would be found, even with pixie magic hiding the cottage. He couldn't stay inside all the time. And it would only get harder to leave the more times she visited. It was nigh impossible to leave now, and they'd only known each other a few days. "In fact, it's best if you didn't come back at all."

She froze, eyes wide. "What?"

"You're playing a dangerous game, and you don't even know the rules. And my family will pay the price if you lose."

A flush of rage climbed her neck and settled in her cheeks. It made her even more lovely.

"I'm sorry I'm not as good a liar as you."

Oh, that was rich.

"So you told every man you slept with you were the Crown Princess of Lorea?" He hated those words as soon as they were out of his mouth, but he had to hit her where it hurt. It was the only way she would let go.

"That's different. You've spent the last few years wearing a mask, letting people believe you're something you're not. Every fucking day."

"While you chose not to tell your bedfellows an important piece of information, one which might change their minds if they knew the truth. Like you did the first time we met."

"You didn't complain."

That wasn't the point. The point was to make her mad enough she would be happy to see him on his way. "You're in over your head, Rane. We should acknowledge it and move on."

She stood and stalked over to him, poking a finger into his chest. Holy hell, she looked mad enough to run him through, yet his body reacted as though she were the only woman in the entire world.

"We are *not* out of time!" She crossed her arms over her chest.

"Listen to yourself, Rane. You sound like a child living in a fantasy, not a crown princess. You've lived so long in a world where the rules don't apply to you, where you always get what you want in the end. In my world, the real world, I will never be yours and you will never be mine. Tell the pixies their debt is paid so I can leave. I gave them my word I wouldn't leave without your permission. Act like an adult for once in your life."

He saw it then, the crack in her heart. The crack he put there with his words. Maybe they were true, a little, and she knew it, but he'd said them in a way that did the most damage. He hated himself for it, but right now, he needed her to let him go. For his good, yes, but mostly for hers. Should her involvement in his escape be discovered, she would face serious consequences for helping him. As the heir to the throne, those consequences would be dire for her entire kingdom. If she didn't see that, he had to make the choice easy for her.

Rane straightened her shoulders. "We can pick up this conversation later. If I'm not back by dawn, I will have to answer questions I'd prefer not to."

Wait, that wasn't how this was supposed to go. She was supposed to give in, tell the pixies to let him go, and good riddance.

"Let me go," he pleaded.

She pulled on the rest of her clothes, ignoring him. Anger replaced the sorrow he'd been trying to deny. Rane couldn't keep him here against his will when she knew what it could cost him.

She caught his gaze, but he turned away. "I'm doing all I can, I promise. I *will* clear your name."

"Don't treat me as a pawn in your game with my stepmother," he growled. "If you can't see I'm worth more than that, you shouldn't come back."

She glanced at him sadly. "You're not a pawn, Nevar, and

you'll never be just a paramour to me. I can't lose you. Stay here. Stay safe. And if you think of anything helpful, send a pixie to find me."

Rane disappeared into the night without another word. He hadn't expected her to be this obstinate. Where had he gone wrong?

Chapter 23

Rane fell asleep angry. Angry at Nevar, angry at Jocelyn, angry at herself most of all. She woke angry, too.

A staccato knock drew her from a disturbing dream where Nevar was trapped in a silver cage. Rane needed no soothsayer to interpret for her. Guilt ripped through her. Why wouldn't she let Nevar go?

"Crown Princess Ranunculus, your presence is required in the Council Chamber." Captain Jadran's voice carried through the door, carefully controlled.

She rubbed the sleep out of her eyes. Why was Jadran summoning her? Rane threw off the covers and stumbled to the door. Two hard rides, of different sorts, left her sore in interesting ways. Rane opened the door. Jadran stood in full livery, odd for this time in the morning. She blinked at him, her mouth and brain still not connected.

"You're late, Your Highness."

"Late? But I told the maid…"

"Apparently, the maids received a note saying they were not to disturb you this morning."

"Fuck."

"The council began some time ago. The queen sent me to ensure you came posthaste."

Her mother was going to kill her.

"She didn't say that."

"No. She said, 'Rane had better be dead.'"

"Fuck," she said again.

"Indeed." Jadran wore a wry grin on his face. Well-acquainted with her propensity to use colorful language, as well as her mother's wrath, he took all this in stride. "Get dressed. There's tea in the Council Chamber."

"Thank Idoya."

She slammed the door. This was a complication she didn't need. It was bad enough Nevar wanted to leave. She believed he cared about her, at least enough to give her time to save him. His words had been cruel to himself as much as to her. He was right. That's what made her so angry last night she couldn't sleep. He'd called out her horseshit. She was behaving like a child, and he deserved to be more than her paramour. She must prove his innocence.

Rane's best bet to survive the day was to be on top of her game. She needed to give her mother no other reason to criticize her. Pulling on an actual corset without anyone nagging her was a good start. She covered it with a sedate brown linen dress embroidered with golden leaves and twisted her hair up as best she could. Rane rushed through the corridors and paused outside the Council Chamber. She smoothed her skirt and pushed open the door, bracing herself for the repercussions.

All eyes turned to her. The king's face was blank, and a smug smirk on the baroness's face told Rane exactly who had written the note for the maid. Her mother was flushed with contained anger, her darkling eyes sparking enough to light the candles scattered around the room.

She dipped a deep curtsy. "I apologize for my lateness. It won't happen again."

Excuses would anger her mother more. Apologize and learn. Both her parents had drilled the mantra into her since childhood.

Her father inclined his head, and the baroness seemed to dismiss her, snapping her mirror closed and tucking it away. What was it with that mirror?

The queen, however, frowned deeply and didn't take her eyes off her daughter. Grabbing a cup of tea from the cart nearby, Rane stood next to her mother and focused on the discussions. There was only one sticking point left: what to do with the waste from the extensive mining operation. Neither kingdom wanted a bunch of slag on their side of the border, but it had to go somewhere. Rane kept her mouth shut as each side proposed a disposal site, only to have the other dismiss it out of hand.

Tempers flared after a few rounds of this. Her mother stood when Count Tahvo called the Teruellan mining administrator a squeaking toad.

"We should break for the day," the queen said, more calmly than Rane would have. She still had much to learn from her mother. "Some time away from this will allow a more productive conversation tomorrow, perhaps with some fresh ideas."

Everybody ceased bickering. Her mother's calm authority when everything fell apart around her was legendary.

"As you wish, my lady," her father said, a twinkle of amusement in his eyes, though the rest of his face betrayed nothing.

"Of course, Your Majesty," Jocelyn said. "You are correct. We should discuss this when cooler heads will prevail."

It didn't take long for the clerks to finish and everybody to leave. The king, the queen, and Rane stayed. The great, stony weight of the queen's attention pressed down on Rane, slumping her shoulders and bringing a flush of shame to her cheeks.

"I am sorry," Rane said before her mother could utter one word. "Truly. I didn't mean to oversleep."

"When you are up to all hours of the night, despite important business, what you mean counts for nothing." Though the queen's comment was calm, her eyes still snapped with displeasure. "We've had this discussion before, Ranunculus. Too many times. You reach your majority in two months. I expect better from you."

"The Lorean nobility takes their cues from us," her father said in a voice like velvet over steel. "We respect others, take their needs and desires into consideration with every decision we make. That way, the nobles do the same for the ordinary people of our kingdom. Should we falter in this, the nobles will see it as their prerogative to exploit others, make them wait, discount their needs. It's a road we don't wish to travel in this kingdom."

"I apologized, but I can't be perfect. I'm only human."

"No, you are not. You are the crown princess and will someday be queen. You must be better than human," her mother said.

"But—"

"Enough." A rare flash of anger from her father. "Rane, I am confining you to the castle and its grounds for the duration of the Teruellan delegation's visit. Am I clear?"

She bowed her head. "Yes, Your Majesty."

"Good." He held her hand. "Being a sovereign isn't about you. It's about your people, all of them. Respect their time, their talents, and their rights."

"I know. I'll do better."

King Rowan regarded her somberly, searching for the truth in her words, and left. Her mother examined Rane with her sharp eyes.

"Do you want to tell me what's really going on?"

This was a chance for her to come clean. Rane was tempted to tell her mother everything. The Queen of Lorea could fix it. At worst, she would insist on calling for Hyssop. Rane's promise to Nevar, and the possible consequence of breaking that promise, kept her lips pressed together.

"The baroness is up to something, but I can't help you if you won't tell me what it is." The last of the queen's anger bled away, replaced by motherly concern.

Rane bit her lip. Her mother's Idoya-blessed fairy intuition led her close to the truth. The stakes were too high. She shook her head.

Beatrice straightened and held her daughter's gaze with her own. "Your kingdom needs you, Rane. Your father needs you. Whatever is going on, it must stop. We require your attention here and now."

"Yes, Mother." Rane pressed her lips together to keep from saying anything else she'd regret later.

Queen Beatrice's skirt whirled around her as she left the chamber like a storm blowing out. Rane let out a sigh of relief and regret. Confinement to the castle made her task all the harder. She didn't even have a way of telling Nevar she couldn't leave.

She dragged her ass back to her room and flopped into a chair, not bothering to close the door. Rane stared at the ceiling for a long time, trying to solve the mess she'd made of everything. She should have let Nevar go. It was unreasonable to keep him when he didn't want to be here, but reason left her whenever she thought of him. Is this what love was? If so, no wonder her parents had settled for a good political match.

A small voice clearing her throat brought Rane back from her mental wanderings. Alize stood in the doorway, holding a lunch tray. The bare beginnings of an idea flared in her mind. Rane plastered on a wide smile.

"Please come in, Alize," she said, getting out of her chair.

The woman dropped a small curtsy and carried the tray over to the desk. "Cook mentioned you'd be taking your lunch in here today."

Rane nodded absently. All the better to check on her. Her mother was clever. "Thank you. Would you mind staying for a bit? I've taken too many meals alone lately." Almost a lie.

"Oh, I couldn't. Cook and the steward will be upset."

"Tell them the princess insisted." Rane waved her hand. "I'm lonely and would enjoy talking to my old friend."

Alize smiled at this. Rane remembered before the stubborn head of hierarchy raised itself, dividing up the easy friendships of the castle children into nobles, royalty, and those who serve them both. She had told Alize everything when they were young. The cute stable boys she had crushes on, the lordlings who asked her to dance at the feasts, the puppies and kittens in the kennels and stables. They planted gardens together and picked berries in the summer and apples in the fall. They helped decorate the harvest table and dusted the winter cakes with sugar.

Then one day, it all ended. Alize trained with various departments to see where her talents led. Rane regularly attended Council meetings, dropped in sporadically to tutoring sessions with various lords and ladies, and spent months at the Faerie Court.

"Please, sit." Rane poured tea for both of them.

Alize gave her another shy smile and sat, taking a teacup. "What can I do for the Crown Princess of Lorea?"

"I wanted to check in with you after the incident with Lord Nevar. You must have been frightened."

Alize's face paled, and the cup rattled in her hands. She placed it on the small table between them. A pang of remorse struck Rane's gut. She hated causing the other woman pain, but if Alize remembered something, anything, it could end this for all of them.

"To be honest, I remember little of it. It's like if I drew back a curtain, it would all be clear. Maybe that's good? From what everyone says, it's a blessing from Idoya I don't remember it."

"What do you remember?" Rane kept her voice calm, taking a

page from her mother's book.

"Just the poor guard with a surprised look on his face. And blood. There was too much blood."

The last was a whisper, and her friend's face changed from pale to green. Rane patted Alize's hand. The pang of remorse turned into a sharp blade. Alize didn't deserve to suffer for Jocelyn, or Nevar, or Rane. Her father's admonition came back to her. Respect her people's time, talents, and rights. Alize had the right to forget something so horrible.

"You're right. It's for the best you don't remember."

Rane changed the subject to happier matters, like the new stable hands and the upcoming preparations for her own investiture. A big holiday would guarantee some time off for most of the servants after the event and a few extra gold pieces for the time it would take to prepare everything. Not to mention visiting servants and guards would allow Alize a broader array of beaus than usual. It would be a good time for her, and perhaps she'd never have to remember.

There had to be some other way of unmasking Jocelyn's guilt.

Chapter 24

It had been three days since his lips had tasted Rane. Three days since they argued. Three long, lonely, miserable days. What a foolhardy thing to do, falling for a princess.

Nevar wavered between anger that she wouldn't let him go and grief because he didn't want to leave, but leave he must. He would do no one any good here, waiting for something that would never happen. Jocelyn had won, and the sooner they both accepted it, the sooner they could move on.

Practicing his forms brought Nevar no joy. All he could do was imagine an enemy keeping him from his princess. The intense new ferocity terrified him. If he was willing to battle imaginary opponents to a brutal death, what would happen should Rane ever be in real danger? What would he sacrifice to keep her? His barony? His father? His brother?

As it was, he would never see his family again. His people would be at the whims of his stepmother until Orom came of age, perhaps longer if she kept control in her hands. In Orom's desire to please his mother, he may never insist on taking over, and Jocelyn might decide to kill him anyway. Someone willing to kill a guard in order to frame the rightful heir would do anything to hold on to power.

Nevar couldn't stay in the cottage for the rest of his life, a kept man, his only purpose to wait on the princess who would one day become queen. He needed more out of life, especially once she married for the good of her kingdom and started a family he'd never be part of. His barony would need him. Orom needed him.

The few days away from Rane's intoxicating presence cleared

the cobwebs, and the cogs of his mind turned. If he couldn't prove his innocence, he needed to do something to protect his people from the vagaries of his stepmother. That long-forgotten story tickled his memory again; tales of a band of brigands in the mountains of Otero in his great-grandfather's time.

He went for an afternoon swim, the autumn air nipping at his fingers and toes before he dove in. Nevar pulled the long-forgotten stories out of the dusty wardrobe he'd put them in. They hadn't been ordinary thieves. Instead, the people celebrated them for giving away much of what they stole. Maybe, just maybe, he could try the same.

Nevar would live off the land and take from his stepmother whenever he could, in whatever way he could. He would give the wealth to his people: the overtaxed villagers, the mistreated miners, and the overworked farmers. It was doable. His life was already forfeit. If—no, *when*—she caught up to him, at least he would know he'd helped as many of his people as he could before the executioner took his head. He'd be an example to his brother and all those who opposed his stepmother's rule.

Perhaps, if God smiled upon him, he could find his way back to the cottage from time to time and lose himself in Rane's embrace. It wasn't the life he had prepared for, but it would be a good life for as long as it lasted. He needed paper, ink, and a quill.

"Lark!" he called out on his way back to the cottage, his black hair beaded with water. She was always close.

Lark darted out from the woods a few moments later.

"Yes, Nevar?"

"I need writing materials."

Suspicion clouded her face. "Why?"

"Rane hasn't been here in days. I need to leave soon. If you would accept a letter from her to release you from your debt, I could write her."

"Why do you wish to leave? You love her. It is obvious to any creature with eyes."

It didn't matter that he loved her. They'd fooled themselves into believing this would ever work permanently. He had a duty to his people, and she had a duty to hers. Love didn't factor into it. In fact, love would only make it harder.

"You should be happy to see me go," he said, not answering

the pixie's question. The simple answer, of course, was he didn't *want* to leave, but he had no better choice.

Lark grinned mischievously. "You're growing on me."

He laughed, startling the birds in the trees. "This arrangement was only meant to be temporary. I can't stay here for the rest of my life. Please, can you find me writing supplies?"

She gave him a stern look. "Do you promise to stay in the cottage and not leave for any reason while I acquire these things for you?"

Nevar placed a hand over his heart and gave her a deep bow. "You have my word. I will not leave the cottage while you are away."

The pixie watched as he entered the cottage and flew away. He busied himself with lunch, a mixture of leftover meat from the night prior, fruit, and tea. The ale was long gone.

The sun was still bright, but the shadows were longer by the time she returned with two of her sisters. A heavy item weighed down each pixie and slowed their progress across the room. Lark, being the largest, held an inkpot. Wren held a quill and Robin a few small pieces of paper. They landed on the table and carefully deposited their burdens. Wren and Robin flopped onto the table dramatically, spreading out their arms and legs, and giggled. Lark shook her head with a smile on her face.

Nevar rose from the bed and bowed to the pixies. "Thank you, gentle Sisters, for your aid in this matter. I did not mean to tax you so. Your sacrifice is noble."

The two younger pixies giggled merrily. Lark turned her smiling face on him and returned the bow.

"You are most welcome, noble lord."

Now he was leaving, he realized what a treasure the friendship of the pixies was. The bittersweet thought dimmed his answering smile but not his gratitude. He sat and arranged the materials to his liking.

"What will you write?" Wren asked, staring intently at the scraps of blank paper.

"I have to leave, and Rane needs to know why. I also need to explain myself to my brother. He deserves nothing less."

"Leave?" she squeaked.

"He's right, and he's telling Rane so she can release us from our promise to keep him safe," Lark said.

The pixies left the cottage, returning to their normal duties.

He tackled the letter to his brother first. He wouldn't mention Jocelyn's involvement, not yet. It would wait until he had more time and paper.

> *Dear Orom,*
> *By now, you've heard the accusations against me. They aren't true. I killed no one, nor did I attack the young woman in question. I was merely in the wrong place at the wrong time. I will stay in exile, helping our people to the best of my abilities with all the resources I have available. As the new heir, I hope you do the same. I love you, my brother, and know you will grow into a fine baron someday. Remember to act with kindness and compassion. It is more important to be a good man than a strict ruler.*
> *With my deepest regards,*
> *Nevar*

He set the letter aside to dry. Nevar gripped the quill in his fingers, and it quivered under the pressure. He made himself set it gently aside. After all, he only had the one. It wouldn't do to break it. He stared at the blank pages left to him.

Putting it off until tomorrow was a fair option. No one was forcing his hand here. He was safe at the cottage for as long as he wanted to be here, but delaying pain had never been his way. If he was going to take a punch to the gut or a stave to the head, it was best to get it over with. He picked up the quill, dipped it in the ink, and scratched a missive to the woman who had changed his life. The woman he loved, even though it was never meant to be.

Chapter 25

This late in the day, the Council Chamber was stuffy. The scribes wouldn't let Rane open the windows for fear of a stiff breeze ruining their work. She understood this, but the constant scritch-scratch of quills on parchment was getting on her nerves.

Rane had been on her very best behavior since she'd been late to negotiations the other day. She arrived early and stayed late, in a dress with her hair done. She paid attention. The thought of sneaking out to visit Nevar only crossed her mind once. Or twice. An hour. Fine, every fucking moment of the day.

The delegations had resolved the remaining points of contention in the morning. All that was left was for the scribes to put everything into a single document and make a few copies. Queen Beatrice busied the staff with planning an official signing ceremony and a celebratory feast in three days. That was all the time Rane had to figure out how to prove Nevar's innocence without upsetting the entire agreement.

The Teruellan delegation had returned to their rooms, and Rane stayed to ensure the scribes had everything they needed before they began the formal transcription. Hours later, as the sun set, the scribes blotted the parchment once more. They packed away their tools and papers, and she could finally leave.

Rane's feet carried her through the halls and out into the castle grounds. She breathed in the cool, fresh air, the scent of dirt, grass, and pine chasing away the odor of stale tea, ink, and sweat. The scrabble of paws on the gravel path gave her an instant's warning before her faithful hound lived up to her name. Bash bowled into her at half speed.

Rane knelt in the gravel and gave her dog some much needed attention. With everything going on, the poor creature was much neglected. One could tell by the shininess of her coat and how well fed she seemed. Rane received a happy whine in response to her vigorous attention, scratching every inch of Bash she could.

Footsteps brought her head up. The Baroness of Otero approached on the path, looking down her nose at the two of them cavorting. Well, the wicked stepmother could take a long walk off a short cliff.

"Good evening, Your Highness," she said with a sniff.

"Good evening, Baroness. Getting some air?"

It was an obvious remark, but perhaps by engaging her in conversation, she could get something, anything, to help her. Just because it had failed every day since the incident didn't mean it was going to fail today.

Rane had done everything in her power to find some shred of evidence to implicate Jocelyn. She'd invited the baroness to her rooms after negotiations one evening. She'd served her best Teruellan red. The baroness had a single glass before excusing herself.

Rane tried to bribe a maid to snoop the next time she was in Jocelyn's room. The steward overheard and nixed that plan immediately. Time after time, Rane had tried to get a good look at the little mirror the baroness had with her everywhere. Some instinct screamed its importance at her, but the closest she'd come was watching Jocelyn putting it away as she walked into a room.

"Yes." Jocelyn's assumed arrogance clipped her words. "You have lovely gardens."

"Thank you. Mother oversees them herself. Even Hyssop is impressed, and she's a plant fairy. How are your gardens in Otero?"

"Otero is on a dry plain. Our gardens are well adapted to the climate, but not as green or varied as yours. Fewer trees, more shrubs, but large swaths of wildflowers."

"It sounds breathtaking. I'd love to see them."

The baroness opened her mouth to speak, but a strange buzzing caught their attention. A ball of light zipped low to the ground, heading straight for Rane. Her stomach dropped. Something must be wrong for a pixie to approach in broad daylight. She shot a glance at the baroness, whose gaze focused on the pixie with fear and longing vying for dominance on her face.

As the pixie approached, her wings beating fast enough to be nearly invisible, she grew in size. By the time she landed next to Rane, she was a little shorter than an average human woman. Wren bowed and handed a small, folded piece of paper to Rane.

"Lark said to wait for your reply," Wren announced, glancing nervously at the baroness. Her wings slowed and folded against her back.

"What is *that*?" the baroness asked with an equal mixture of awe and revulsion.

"*She* is a pixie and my friend. Her name is Wren."

Jocelyn pressed her hands to her stomach and opened her mouth, her lips curled and her nose wrinkled. Whatever the baroness wanted to say would be nasty. Rane stood her ground, raising an eyebrow like her mother sometimes did when she wished her children to reconsider whatever it was they were about to say. The baroness slowly closed her mouth.

Rane glanced at the note addressed to her in careful script. She itched to open it. The only person it could be from was Nevar, so opening it in front of Jocelyn was daft. Instead, she tucked it into the pocket of her dress.

"Don't let me stop you from reading your correspondence."

Rane hesitated. If she pulled out the note, his stepmother would recognize his handwriting. If she didn't, it would draw unwanted attention to the note. Attention which could further complicate an already tangled situation.

"I don't want to keep you."

The barest smile twitched up the corners of the baroness's red lips. Shit. Her gambit had failed, but surprisingly, Jocelyn didn't push.

"Very well. I will see you tomorrow." She curtsied and headed inside, pulling out her Idoya-cursed mirror. Rane desperately wanted to get her hands on it.

"Come on." Rane led Wren to her favorite spot by the crumbling fountain, far away from any potential eavesdroppers. "Is everything okay?"

Wren looked at the note, her eyes welling with tears. "Read the note. Nevar made me promise."

Rane opened it.

R—
You are no closer to proving my stepmother's guilt. I can't stay here any longer. She said run or turn myself in. I am doing neither of those things. She will kill my family, and she may hurt you and yours. I could never live with myself if that happened. Please, tell your friends their debt is paid and to let me go. I wish things were different, in so many ways, but we must accept how things are in order to see how to make them better. I will hold you forever in my heart.
N

No. No, she wasn't ready to let go. Not yet. There was still time. Goddess, please let there be more time.

She paced around the fountain, clutching the note to her chest. She had to go see him. Fuck the consequences. She could persuade him to stay, to give them a little more time together. He couldn't leave until she granted him permission. He'd given the pixies his word.

A niggling arrow of guilt buried itself in her heart. It was her fault he was trapped. She could have released the pixies' debt the last time she was there, but then they would be out of time.

"I know that look. What are you up to?" Wren asked.

She strode with purpose back to the castle, tugging at her braid. There was only one way out where nobody would spot her and only one horse that could carry her swiftly enough to return before anybody realized she was missing.

"I'm coming with you."

"Oh, what a wonderful idea!" Wren clapped her hands and hopped.

"Shh, keep your voice down. I'm not supposed to leave." Rane stepped into the castle.

"You got it. Sneaky is my middle name." The pixie's voice bounced off the walls. Fantastic.

Wren shrunk to the size of a hummingbird and kept her comments to herself all the way through the castle until they came to the kitchen. Some good food might remind Nevar of the luxuries he would forego, and a full stomach always made her more amenable to listening.

The bustling room was quiet tonight, only a single scullery maid scrubbing pots. With the weekly exception of family dinners and the occasional feast, the royal family ate most meals alone or in small groups. Rane often ate with her brother and sister, but Ebon was off searching for Nevar to the south, and Betony hadn't shown up tonight. It was a good thing, considering the circumstances.

The maid turned in surprise when Rane entered and splashed water everywhere as she tried to curtsy. Cook would have Rane's head for disturbing one of her workers.

"Your—Your Highness?"

"Where is everyone?"

"Um, the queen gave everyone the night off so they can prepare for the feast. I drew the short straw."

"I'm sorry."

"Thank you, but I won't have to do it next time. Cook is fair."

"Well, I'm a little hungry. Please continue and act like I'm not here. I'll be out of your hair before you know it."

Another curtsy and another splash. "Yes, Your Highness."

Rane grabbed a loaf of leftover bread along with a sizable chunk of cheese. She found dried fruit and dried meat in the larder and shoved it into her pockets. On her way out, she grabbed two apples from the barrel kept there.

Rane came through the kitchen often to scrounge a quick supper before heading off to the stables, or the courtyard to train with Jadran or Ebon, or out for a walk. It was unlikely anyone would remark upon her stop tonight, especially since she doubted anyone other than her parents, siblings, and possibly the steward knew she'd been restricted to the castle. The king and queen preferred not to have family matters aired before the servants.

Once in her room, Rane dumped everything on the little table in her sitting room. She pulled out her saddlebags and tossed them onto the desk next to the tea tray someone had left while she was in the Council Chamber.

"Pack as much of the food as you can into this," she ordered Wren.

The pixie grew larger and placed her fists on her hips. "We've been feeding him well."

Rane turned and allowed a small smile to flit across her face. "I have no doubt, but I haven't been to the cottage in a few days. He might miss non-pixie food."

"Oh, I didn't consider that."

Wren wrapped the small treats in a napkin and placed them in the bags. Rane stripped off her dress and put on her usual attire but couldn't stop herself from picking out her nicest jerkin, the one with embossed vines crawling over it and leaf-shaped silver buttons. She helped the pixie pack away the rest of the food.

A gentle but insistent rap brought up Rane's head. "Go hide in the bedroom. Not a sound."

The pixie scurried into the room and hid in the wardrobe.

Rane opened the door, and Jocelyn lowered her hand.

"Good evening again, Your Highness."

Dammit. Of all the people who could have knocked on her door tonight, it had to be her. Rane did not get out of the way or open the door any wider than she had to.

"Is there something I can do for you, Baroness?" She hoped her clipped tone would give Jocelyn the hint to go away.

The baroness peered around Rane, ignoring her bad manners. "Where is your little friend? I wanted to apologize. I'm afraid her sudden appearance was a bit… disconcerting. We don't have fairies in Otero, and my experience with magic is practically nothing."

"I'm sorry, she left. She delivered the note and was off again."

"All is well, I hope?"

"Yes, very. If that is all?" Rane tried to close the door, but the baroness pushed against it lightly with her hand.

"May I come in?"

Rane clenched her jaw. There was no way she could say no without divulging the dangerous game she played. If Jocelyn suspected Rane knew what she had done, Nevar's family was as good as dead. She held in her exasperated sigh and opened the door wide.

"Of course."

The baroness's gaze roamed the room, alighting on the packed saddlebags. Fuck.

"Are you going somewhere, Your Highness?"

It was beyond obvious the bags were stuffed near to bursting. So, she had to lie. She hated lying when she didn't have the chance to get her story straight.

"No. Still unpacking from my last trip."

She'd smack her own forehead if she didn't have an audience.

"That was a few days ago, was it not?"

Was Jocelyn monitoring her movements?

"Yes, but we've been busy. I'm so tired at night I just collapse into bed. Come in and sit for a moment."

"Thank you." Jocelyn crossed the small room with a flourish of skirts, passing right by the saddlebags to sit in a chair facing the fireplace. Rane joined her, sinking into its matching companion.

"I'm sorry Wren had to leave. I'm sure she would have accepted your apology. Is there something else on your mind?"

"You have been so kind to me. I wanted to express my thanks before I leave. You have a friend in Otero should you ever need one."

A friend who would stab her in the back at the first opportunity. A friend who had taken the rightful place of the man she'd fallen for. A friend who wasn't at all friendly.

"Thank you, Baroness," Rane said, imbuing sincerity in every word. "It means the world to me."

Jocelyn pulled out a small, silver flask from her pocket, one with the Oteran coat of arms engraved on it. "Care to toast? I brought Oteran brandy. This vintage is from the year I married the baron."

"That sounds lovely." It did not. The baroness was poisoning her husband, but would she have the guts to poison the Crown Princess of Lorea? What would she have to gain by doing so? Only one way to be certain. "Please, let me get some glasses, and you can pour some for both of us."

Rane dashed into her bedroom, where she kept the glasses and picked out two. The wardrobe creaked open, and she glimpsed Wren's face. She shook her head, and the door closed again.

"Here we are." Rane returned to the sitting room.

Jocelyn stood next to the desk, admiring the tapestry on the wall. "This is fine work."

"I'll pass the compliment to Betony."

Rane put the glasses on the desk and flicked her gaze over the saddlebags. They seemed undisturbed.

"Your sister made this?" The baroness tipped a little brandy into each glass.

Rane picked up a glass and Jocelyn the other before sitting back in the chairs.

"She is talented with a needle and thread. I, alas, am not."

"To new friendships." Jocelyn raised her glass.

Instead of the woman in front of her, she imagined Nevar's perfect face, complete with his imperfect smile, floating through her vision. "To new friendships."

Rane watched the brandy touch Jocelyn's lips before she allowed it past her own. The liquor's sweet heat tickled her tongue and throat before it settled in a calm, glowing ball in her stomach. She closed her eyes and enjoyed the languor spreading through her body.

She forced her eyes open. For an instant, a spiteful smile graced Jocelyn's lips, and a cruel glint shone in her eyes. Her features smoothed.

"Do you like it?" Jocelyn asked.

"It is sublime. Father often keeps some in reserve, but it's gone. I believe someone mentioned an insufficient harvest a couple of years ago."

"Oh, if you are out, I will be happy to leave what we have brought with us. A small token of thanks for a well-negotiated agreement."

"Father will be thrilled." Rane yawned widely. Though she hadn't been out late in days, she still didn't sleep well. Too many failed attempts at gathering evidence and too many self-recriminations.

"You are tired, indeed, if a single glass of brandy overtaxes you. I will see you on the morrow." The baroness dropped a polite curtsy and left.

As much as she wished she could crawl into bed and sleep, she didn't have time to give into fatigue. She had a hasty ride and another unpleasant argument ahead of her before she could sleep. Rane rubbed her eyes and lurched out of the chair.

"Come on, Wren. It's time to go."

The door to the wardrobe burst open. "About time. When was the last time you aired this out?"

"I've been busy. Get the saddlebags."

The old bridle still hung on the wall where she'd left it after helping Nevar escape. She hadn't found the time to fix it, but there was no other choice. Rane grabbed it, walked over to the secret passageway, and pressed the brick. Once again, the door slid open. She and Wren made their way into the bowels of the castle and came out in the moonlit night.

Grunnin would get her to the cottage swiftly. Her ass wouldn't thank her, but time was of the essence. She pulled out a sugar cube and whistled for the horse. By the light Wren gave off, she fit the bridle in his mouth and tossed a riding blanket over him before settling her saddlebags over his withers. Giving him another treat, she mounted up and led him into the forest. She gave Grunnin his head and dug in her heels.

Wren stayed close behind them as they careened through the forest, Grunnin's long legs devouring the miles. Perhaps it was the protective magic of her godmother or plain luck, but she didn't run into anything or anyone. Soon enough, they arrived at the clearing. The bright moon washed out the greens and reds and browns into blues and grays. A light shone from the cottage windows.

Rane dismounted and tied the reins to a low branch. If Grunnin got it in his mind to pull away, it wouldn't stop him, but it was better than nothing. Wren settled onto the saddle blanket.

"I'll make sure he stays," the pixie said.

Rane pushed open the door without knocking. Nevar leaped from his chair, reaching for the sword lying on the table.

"I come in peace." Rane held out her hands.

Once Nevar picked up his jaw from the floor, a deep frown furrowed his brows. His eyes reflected the dim light of the cottage and seemed flattened with misery.

"Don't go." Rane failed to keep the desperation out of her words. She moved closer.

"I can't stay, Rane." Nevar stepped back. His words were bitter, but not from anger. He refused to meet her gaze, and his hands were in tight fists at his side. It hurt him to say this to her.

"Why?"

"You know why. If I'm caught, I will die."

"Lorea rarely executes its prisoners."

"Do you think King Armel will allow me to face Lorean justice? He isn't as kind as your father. You tried, but you failed. I can't risk my brother's life, or my father's, over your delusion that you can find something to prove my stepmother killed the guard. I can't help my people from here. They will need me more than ever with Jocelyn in charge. I won't put aside my duty to be your paramour."

"I never asked you to!" Anger rushed through her at his accusation.

"You say stay. Staying would mean all of that, if not more. I won't do it, not even for you."

"I—I—"

Rane had no suitable answer for him. Dammit, he was right. If he stayed, he would stay only for her. And she couldn't even give him all of her. He would always come last. Nevar deserved better, and she couldn't give it to him. The best she could offer him was his freedom.

"You have responsibilities, too. I won't keep you from them. You will make a great queen one day, and the last thing you need is a scandalous past. Too many great rulers have been brought low, their regimes tainted by far smaller scandals than sleeping with a fugitive."

She sagged against the wall, all the determination to make him stay, make him bend to her whim, gone.

"You're right." A tear fell down her cheek.

"I'm sorry." He stepped toward her. Nevar stopped when she raised a hand.

"You're right," she said again, louder this time, meaning it. She straightened and pushed away from the wall. "You deserve more than what I can offer, and you have important work to do. I won't keep you from it. I guess I wanted to see you one last time."

"Rane—"

Nevar walked toward her. She turned away. If she wanted to leave, she couldn't allow him to touch her. Rane doubted she would have the strength to go if he did.

"I have something for you. Wait here." She ducked out the door before he could say anything else and fetched the supplies from Grunnin. Rane dropped the saddlebag on the table and refused to meet his eyes. It landed with a surprising thunk. Wren had been overzealous in her packing. "It should last a few days, enough for you to clear the Argent Forest. The pixies will escort you, protect you while you're in the forest."

"Thank you."

Rane sighed and lifted her head. Her gaze found his, and a frisson of desire coursed through her. She was letting him go. It was the most painful thing she'd ever had to do.

"If there is anything I can do for you, all you have to do is ask."

"I am forever in your debt, my lady," he said, bowing.

Rane walked toward the door. Nevar's hand grabbed her, and he pulled her into his arms. His hands framed her face, and he lowered his lips to hers. Her need flared into a bonfire, consuming her as his lips worked desperately against hers. The sorrow, the yearning, the pain drifted between them, wrapping their wires around their hearts, tying them together for all eternity.

Pulling herself away before she was swept up with him and deserted her own destiny, Rane raised a hand to his cheek.

"Safe journey, Nevar of Otero."

She ran out of the cottage before he could say anything else. Rane hurried to Grunnin and addressed Wren, still standing guard.

"The Sisters of the Argent Forest have paid their debt. Nevar is free to go, and you owe me nothing else."

Untying the reins, she led Grunnin across the clearing. Rane paused at the edge, Nevar's gaze boring into her back, but she refused to look back, not even for a second. She stepped into the forest and left him in her past.

Chapter 26

Look back. Please, for God's sake, look back.

Rane did not look back. She disappeared into the forest, taking Nevar's heart with her.

He stood in the cottage's doorway and stared at the last spot he'd seen her, getting used to the new hole in his chest. Just because something was the right thing to do didn't mean it didn't feel like the fiery bowels of hell. Nevar waited. He knew without a doubt it was in vain, but he waited.

A small hand rested on his shoulder.

"Go inside, Nevar," Lark said. "You have a long journey in the morning. It would be best to get some rest."

He blinked and gave in to the inevitable. He pushed the door closed and walked to the table. The lumpy saddlebag sat there, filled to bursting. Nevar opened it. Bread, cheese, and other provisions. This would last him a few days, enough to make it back to the Oteran side of the mountains. His hand closed on a plain, silver flask. He twisted off top, and a familiar smell greeted him. The sweetness of apples balanced out the sharpness of the liquor. Oteran apple brandy. Rane must have found some stashed away, bless her.

Nevar poured a scant helping into one of the misshapen mugs. The golden liquor swirled over his tongue and melted down his throat. Some exceptional Oteran brandy.

After everything, he was alone, drinking brandy by the fire. He had embarked on the journey with a worthy plan to negotiate a treaty on behalf of King Armel and take his proper place as his father's heir. Now it was all shit.

Nevar may never see his father or his brother again. Jocelyn might kill them out of spite, but he had time to figure out a way to save Orom. Dear God, his brother would hate him after Jocelyn got through with him. He hoped the note he'd sent would help, but with how his luck had turned, it was difficult to find optimism right now.

The new plan started tomorrow. If God smiled upon him, he'd still be able to help his people. Saving even a few people from misery, from poverty, from death would be worth it. At least he didn't have to worry about his heart anymore. It was safe in Rane's hands, and he would never give it to another.

A relationship wouldn't have worked, anyway. Maybe in another life, one where his father was hale and hearty and had many good years left to him, the Crown Princess of Lorea could wed the Oteran heir. The barony could easily pass to Orom, and Nevar would become Rane's consort, but it wasn't the life he had. He had lost whatever status might make that scenario possible, and he'd become a fugitive. Nevar had nothing to offer other than his heart and devotion. Those would never be enough for a fucking crown princess. His chances of spending his life with her were now less than a fire in a rainstorm.

If only he was still in charge of negotiations. He could have won over King Rowan with his skills or his knowledge of mining or his winning personality. He could have shown the king how dear Rane was to him. Maybe his daughter's happiness would have been enough.

If only never served him well. If only his mother had lived. If only his father had chosen a better woman to wed. If only the baron was healthy. If only Nevar hadn't fallen in love. All *if only* did was cause regret and sorrow.

Nevar polished off the brandy in his mug. He wanted to pour more but stopped himself. The stuff would be difficult to find in his circumstances. Best to conserve it. A little brandy in the evenings could offer a touch of warmth when sleeping rough. He packed it back into the saddlebag.

No, he had to face reality. Unless or until proof came his way, he would be an outlaw. The best he could hope for was to be an outlaw with a purpose, to mitigate any harm the baroness might do in his father's or his brother's name, and to protect his people with his life.

Nevar would leave at first light to clear the Argent Forest before nightfall and avoid all the beasties that would make his life short, miserable, or both. There wasn't much to pack, and within a few days, it would appear he'd never been here. He hoped he'd made more of an impression on Rane than he had on the cottage.

He put everything he owned into his satchel. Checking under the bed to ensure he left nothing behind, he found the emerald green ribbon Rane had worn in her hair a few nights ago. Dizziness washed over him, and his heart clenched as he remembered that night. It didn't let up. He stumbled to the table and placed a hand on it to steady himself. *Drank the brandy too damn fast.*

His hand grazed his sword, and ice traveled up his arm and down his spine. *Danger.* Nevar tried to breathe deeply, but he couldn't pull in enough air. His vision blurred at the edges as he staggered toward the bed, panting and unable to call for help.

He almost made it. His legs collapsed beneath him a step away from the bed. His hands and arms were numb and unresponsive to his commands. The world grayed as he tried desperately to pull in a full breath. Hell, any breath. The pounding of his heart filled his ears, and stars danced across his vision. The last thing he saw before his world faded to black was the green ribbon fluttering away from him.

Chapter 27

Rane spent the night slouched in a chair in her sitting room watching the fire die and did not sleep a single wink. The thought of how foolish she'd been to fall in love with someone she couldn't be with rolled around in her head all the way home, all the way up the stairs, and for the rest of the night.

She washed her face and changed into clean clothes, folding what she wore last night and placing the outfit into the wardrobe. Her tunic still smelled of Nevar. She wouldn't allow anyone to wash it any time soon.

Walking through the halls in a daze, Rane ran a hand along the wall to keep her from bumping into too many things. Her steps led her to the kitchen garden. Betony sat at the table, surrounded by her animals. Rane joined her.

"Aren't you going to eat?" her sister asked after a while. Rane had no idea how long it had been. Time seemed wobbly at the moment, with instants passing like hours and hours like mere moments.

She blinked at the cup of tea Bet had poured, picked it up, and sipped it. It was cold. Rane put the cup to the side.

"I'm not hungry."

"Is everything okay, Rane?"

She pressed her lips together to hold back her tears.

"No, but there's nothing I can do about it." Her voice cracked despite her efforts, and a tear trailed a wet track down her cheek.

Betony took her hand and squeezed it, the same way Rane had done many times in their younger years.

"Maybe there's something I can do."

Rane shook her head. "Thanks, but there's no help for it anymore."

"If you change your mind…"

She gave her sister a weak smile. Bet was a good listener. Once able to talk about it, Rane would visit her first.

Ebon strode out, book in hand.

"When did you get home?" Rane hadn't expected him back for another day or two.

His eyes widened. "Late last night. Don't you have a meeting with Father in his study?"

"Oh, shit!" She nearly upended the teapot as she shot out of her chair and raced to the study.

Arriving winded at the heavy, gilded door, Rane straightened her skirt and tucked an errant strand of hair behind her ear. The guard standing outside spared her a tight smile. She knocked and hoped the king wouldn't notice she was a little late.

"Enter." He looked up at her from parchment he was scribbling on. "Have a seat, Rane."

She sat, folding her hands and waiting, mirroring her father's exact gesture. He considered her for a moment before letting out a deep sigh.

"You have been uncharacteristically quiet the past several days," he said.

"I think I was on Mother's last nerve. I didn't want to push my luck."

He chuckled. "Wise beyond your years, at least sometimes. That's one reason I wanted to talk to you."

Rane raised her eyebrows, but her father said nothing else for a moment. Patience. He'd get around to it.

"What do you make of the Baroness of Otero? Can she be trusted?"

She bit her lip and held back the first answer to come to her. Of course, the baroness couldn't be trusted, but the king would demand reasons, and she had none she could share with him. Rane tugged on a lock of hair. Time to see if all her work over the past week had been for naught.

"I believe she has negotiated the mineral rights agreement in good faith, but she can't be trusted any further. I believe the baroness always has plans within plans. It doesn't mean she wishes us ill, or she would act in a way to jeopardize Lorea. But there is more to her than meets the eye."

A grin flitted across her father's face.

"That is my take as well. You have good instincts."

Another twinge of guilt stabbed at her. She should tell him it was more than instincts, and the woman would sacrifice her own family in order to secure her power. She opened her mouth.

"You can't go in there," the guard called out.

"Rane!" a tiny voice cried from the crack under the door. Wren squeezed through, and she flew to Rane's shoulder. "Thank the goddess you are here. You must come with me."

The pixie looked carefully at the king and back to Rane. Wren leaned in close to her ear.

"Something is wrong with Nevar," she whispered.

Rane stood suddenly, and Wren almost toppled from her shoulder.

"I have to go, Father."

"We are not finished here, Rane."

"I must go!"

She turned and ran, her father's voice bouncing off the walls behind her. Servants and guards scrambled out of her way as she rushed through the halls like a gale-force wind. Rane ran all the way to the stables. She whistled for Bash before darting inside. A high-pitched bark from the kennels next door acknowledged the summons.

"Saddle Sunny," she ordered the head groom.

He crossed his arms over his chest and shook his head. "I can't let you go, Princess. Your parents—"

She turned to Wren. "A little help, please."

The pixie flew over to the stable master. He tried to bat her away, but she snuck under his waving arms and placed a tiny hand on his temple. In the old fairy tongue, she muttered, "Codladh." *Sleep.*

Rane caught the man before he hit the ground and dragged him out of the way. She pulled a bridle off the hooks and marched straight to Sunny's stall. She didn't have time to get a faster horse, but Sunny was hers. Trust would make up for what she might lose in speed. Nevar needed her.

So much for letting go.

With Wren's help, she had Sunny saddled and bridled quicker than even the best stable hand. She led the mare out of the stall and mounted up. Bash bounded over and sniffed the air. The hound settled in next to the horse, matching her pace.

"You're not going anywhere, Ranunculus."

Her mother stood in front of the open gate, hands on her hips.

"Sorry, Mother. I have to."

"You are still restricted to the castle grounds from your recent misjudgments."

"Get out of the way."

"What, or you'll run me over?"

"I made a promise to protect someone. A princess doesn't break her promises. I may not be the perfect example of royalty, but I know that much. I will accept the consequences of my actions, but I have to go now. Please get out of the way."

Her mother peered at her, darkling eyes lit from within. The tiniest hint of a smile curved the corners of her mouth, and she stepped out of the way.

"I would never stand between a future queen and her word, nor a woman and her heart. Go."

Rane aimed the mare at the gate and dug in her heels. Sunny tore off down the road, Bash right behind. They raced through the city, sped through the countryside, and barely slowed when they reached the forest. Wren had threaded her arms through Rane's hair and held on so tight she was afraid she'd have chunks missing. They crashed into the clearing. Rane jumped from the saddle and ran to the cottage, Bash at her heels. The door stood wide open.

Three pixies surrounded a limp form on the floor. Rane dashed over, and two of the pixies changed into their small forms, little balls of light rising to the ceiling. She knelt and took Nevar's cold and clammy hand in hers, his usually burnished brown skin ashen. Bash crawled over on her belly and whined at the unconscious man.

"Wake up, Nevar." She put as much royal authority as she could in those three words. *Oh, please wake up.*

Nothing. No movement at all, except the all-too-slow and shallow rise of his chest. His pulse was thready and weak under her fingers, and his skin was cold, as though he'd been out in a snow storm.

"We tried that, Rane," Lark said. She had remained on the floor with Nevar while the others flew off.

"Nevar!" Rane shook his shoulders, and Bash licked his fingers.

No response. His head flopped in the same way as the solstice goose Cook prepared for the holiday feast. *No, no, no.*

"What happened?" she demanded.

Lark clapped her hand on Rane's shoulder. "I don't know. Wren swears he was well when she left last night, sitting at the table and drinking from the flask you brought."

"Flask?"

She didn't remember a flask. She reluctantly let go of Nevar's hand and walked over to the table. In the middle sat the saddlebag she'd brought last night, and a plain silver flask stuck out from it. Rane picked it up; the cap was tight, but a shake confirmed a small measure was missing.

She unscrewed the lid of the nearly full vessel and sniffed. The potent scent of apple brandy greeted her. A low growl rumbled from her hound. According to Cook, there was no Oteran brandy left in the entire castle. Rane had found Jocelyn standing close to the saddlebags after she fetched the cups for a toast. The baroness must have known—she would bet her kingdom it had something to do with her mirror—that Rane was off to visit Nevar. Son of a bitch, she'd poisoned her own stepson and used Rane to do it.

Rane replaced the cap and wrapped the bottle in Nevar's extra tunics. He wouldn't need them right now. Her gaze met Lark's, and the somber pixie toyed with the blades at her hips.

"Whatever you need, Rane."

"Send someone to inform Hyssop." Her promise didn't matter if he was dead.

"I'll go," Wren chirped.

"Thank you. Tell her it's an emergency. Tell her I'm collecting my boon."

The pixie left, making a beeline for the fairy capital. If Hyssop wasn't there, they would find her.

"What can we do?" Lark asked.

"Gather reeds and long, thin branches. I'm making a travois."

Rane fetched the axe from the chopping block and attacked the first sapling she found.

Chapter 28

By the time Rane returned to the castle, the rich velvet of night had blanketed the kingdom. A cranky Sunny pulled the travois with Nevar strapped to it. He hadn't moved at all during the hours-long return journey, barely even breathing, but their slow pace was necessary. Bash kept her nose to the ground, only looking up occasionally to sniff the night air for hints of danger. Pulling a travois took far longer than the mad dash out. Jadran waited for her at the castle gate, a dour frown creasing his brow.

"Your mother—"

"I am familiar with my mother's temper, Captain, but I come bearing a gift." She swept an arm toward the travois, and Jadran's eyes widened.

"Are you all right, milady?"

"I'm fine. Please inform my parents and the commander I have found Lord Nevar, and I will meet them in the Council Chamber. Under no circumstances is the Baroness of Otero to hear of this."

She'd spent the entire journey working on a plan, and surprise was the only card in her hand worth playing.

Rane didn't wait for a response and tugged on Sunny's bridle. The horse followed in resigned indignation. Jadran snapped an order to the nearest guard before taking a position on the other side of Sunny, who snorted in agitation.

"Shh." Rane absently ran a hand along the mare's neck.

"Are you going to tell me how you defeated a vicious murderer?" the captain asked in a quiet voice, reminding Rane he was her friend. He'd taught her everything she knew about fighting.

She still couldn't tell him. The mere thought of it closed her throat. Rane swallowed, forcing her guilt away.

"Alleged murderer," she said, finding her voice. "And I'd prefer to tell the story exactly once. If the commander has no objection to your presence, you're welcome to stay."

They walked the rest of the way to the stables with only the clip-clops of Sunny's hooves and her occasional snort to break the silence. Rane glanced behind, hoping to see some sign of life in Nevar. He was as still as he had been throughout the journey. Her plan didn't require his survival, but her heart did, Idoya help her.

A stable hand took Sunny's reins.

"Where's the head groom?" she asked.

"Still asleep," Jadran replied with only a bare hint of reproach in his voice.

Rane winced. It was a mean trick, but she hadn't had the time to persuade him. She'd apologize when this was all over and offer a payment in recompense. Rane detached the travois, and Jadran had three guards carry it.

"Take him to the Council Chamber and put him on the table," Rane ordered. The guards' eyes grew overly large. "Do it. Bash, stay with Nevar."

Her icy authority mirrored her mother's, and they obeyed with no further delay, Bash trotting alongside dutifully.

"You're getting good at that," Jadran said.

She carried the saddlebag holding her evidence as carefully as she handled the ancient porcelain teacups her mother used.

"I have to. I will be queen someday, as everyone is fond of reminding me."

He stopped talking. They walked into the chamber as the guards carrying Nevar departed, leaving the young lord on the table, eerily still in the flickering lamplight. Bash stood guard at the head of the table, eyes alert and ears up.

"Is he dead?" Jadran approached the form with trepidation.

"Not yet. He breathes, barely."

Voices echoing in the hall cut off whatever else she was going to say. It was time to face the consequences of her actions. This wouldn't be fun by any stretch of the imagination.

Her mother entered first, her skirt swirling around her feet as her quick steps carried her into the room. Queen Beatrice was so focused on ensuring her daughter's well-being she didn't notice the form lying on the table.

"Are you ready to tell us what's been going on, Ranunculus?"

"Holy shit, Rane, what did you do to him?" Ebon's voice cut across her mother's, earning him a sharp glare from the queen.

"Ebon," Beatrice warned.

"The table, Mother," Betony said, her shocked tone finally drawing the queen's attention to the center of the room.

For once, Rane rendered her mother speechless. The queen glanced at the table. Her father had noticed the still form as soon as he'd entered and waited for his wife's attention to focus where needed rather than at the object of her exasperation. Once the room hushed, the king turned his attention to his eldest daughter.

"Now that I have your attention," Rane said, only to be interrupted by the last invited guest, Commander Miren.

"What in the name of the goddess is going on? Why was I summoned from my dinner—"

The commander caught sight of the royal family gathered around the body on the table and broke off her complaint. She, too, turned her attention to Rane.

"Jadran, shut and bar the door," Rane ordered. "I only want to say what I have to say once, and any further interruptions will spoil my plans."

"Plans?" Her mother's voice was half an octave higher than usual. "What plans? You come back with a dead ambassador, you owe us explanations, Rane."

"He's not dead, Mother."

"Looks dead to me," Ebon said. Betony thwacked him on the arm. "Ow."

"Shut up, Ebon."

"Shut up, all of you," Rane said, exasperated. "Save your questions, comments, diatribes, and lectures to the end."

Her father provided the example all the others followed. He pulled out a chair and sat, focusing his quiet attention on Rane. Once the others followed his lead, she told her story. The commander opened her mouth when she explained Alize's involvement in the original crime.

"She didn't kill the guard, Commander. Alize wasn't herself.

She was under the magical control of the Baroness of Otero."

A ripple of denial went through her small audience. Rane silenced them with a raised hand. She was getting good at this authority thing.

"I wanted to tell you, but I promised Nevar I wouldn't. She threatened his father and brother."

They allowed her to finish the story without further interruptions. Rane told them everything. Well, not quite everything. She left out the bits where she and Nevar were naked. Betony raised an eyebrow at one point. She couldn't fool her sister.

Rane closed her eyes before she got to the last part, the part where she'd found him unresponsive on the floor of the cottage. She steeled herself. In a voice devoid of emotion, she finished the tale, ripping out her heart with her own hands.

Silence filled the room like a great, quiet beast. She waited for somebody to say something, to send the unease running for the hills.

"How did Lord Nevar end up near death?" King Rowan asked, surprising her with his gentleness. He had every right to be as upset as her mother, but he wasn't.

She pulled out the flask of apple brandy from the saddlebag on her shoulder. "The baroness poisoned him with this."

"Do you have proof?" the commander snapped.

Rane ignored the commander for a moment. "Ebon, have you found any way to trace magic?"

He shook his head. "If I had known the whole story, it might have been more of a priority."

That's what she'd been afraid of. Rane turned her attention back to the commander. The color had risen in the woman's face. She wasn't used to being ignored. "I can get proof if you'll play along for a bit more."

"You've lied to us, snuck out of the castle, and harbored a criminal. You've been acting the silly girl in love, not the heir to the throne. Why should we give you any more leeway?" The queen's icy words bit into Rane. Every single accusation was true, but a softness in her mother's gaze suggested she had a reason for pressing Rane like this.

"Do you want to take the chance of making a lasting agreement with a murderer? If I'm wrong, I will apologize, and take whatever consequences you see fit. By the Mother of All, I'll even marry the first appropriate suitor you find."

It wouldn't matter, anyway. If Nevar died, there was no one else for her. She might as well make her mother happy, for she would never be happy again.

"I'll hold you to it." Queen Beatrice folded her arms over her chest, but she seemed more gratified than displeased.

"What do we have to do?" Ebon asked.

"Play along," she said. "And fetch the note Nevar supposedly sent Alize."

"That doesn't sound like much of a plan," the commander said.

"You're not wrong, but it's all I have."

Commander Miren snorted, a wry grin and a gleam of determination in her eyes. "I've done more with less. I'll do it. For Alize."

"I'll help, too," Ebon said dryly. "Idoya knows you need all the help you can get."

"I like Nevar. I'll do what I can," Bet said.

"When this is over, you and I need to have a chat," her father said. "But I trust your instincts in this, Rane."

Her mother merely nodded her head once in acquiescence.

Rane turned to Jadran, standing quietly in the shadows near the door.

"Please send for the baroness. Tell her we have reason to celebrate. And have a servant bring in glasses." She picked up the flask of brandy. "After all, what kind of celebration would it be without a toast?"

Chapter 29

The Baroness of Otero strode in, head high, the sumptuous gown of golden silk clinging to her slender body. Rane had to hand it to her. The woman barely paused when her glance fell upon her stepson, still lying on the table. If Rane hadn't been staring at Jocelyn, she would have missed the ever so slight upturn of her lips and the triumphant gleam in her eyes.

The flask of brandy was back in the saddlebags. Seven cut crystal goblets reflected the lamplight in the room, sparkling like gemstones. Jocelyn curtsied to those seated around the table. Bash lifted her lip and an eerie snarl wove its way through the room. The baroness's expression of smug satisfaction disappeared along with some of the color in her cheeks.

"Enough, Bash," Rane ordered. The snarl ceased, but the dog didn't take her eyes off Jocelyn. *Good girl.*

"Please, Baroness, join us. We have reason to celebrate," King Rowan said.

"I see you have found my stepson." The golden fabric swirled around her as she sat. "Is he dead?"

There was no emotion, not even satisfaction, in her voice. Nevar could have been a stranger. A rage as deep as the ocean swelled in Rane's chest. At some point, it would escape, and woe to the Baroness of Otero when it did. For now, she fought it down. She still had work to do.

"Yes," Rane lied. Nevar breathed so little it was imperceptible in the low light.

"I suppose it's for the best. A formal execution would be socially difficult for all of us, but I believe justice has been served. It's truly a pity. I tried to correct his laziness and other undesirable tendencies when I first married his father," Jocelyn said in the same dispassionate voice.

Rane dug her fingernails into her palms to keep herself from wrapping her hands around the woman's neck. She would pay for every lie, every insult, every moment she made Nevar feel less than.

"How did you find him?" the baroness asked.

"On my ride tonight, he came staggering out of the forest and fell dead at the feet of my horse," Rane said with forced indifference. "Truly, as though your god or our goddess had a hand in his fate. Although I wish he could stand trial for his crime, his death is worthy of celebration, is it not?"

The tension ebbed from the woman and a flash of a smile creased Jocelyn's face, vanishing before anyone else caught it. Rane noticed and added one more thing the baroness would pay for to her list.

"Of course, Your Highness."

Rane pulled the flask of apple brandy from the saddlebag at her feet, opened it, and sniffed. "I found this among his possessions. I believe it's Oteran brandy."

Jocelyn's eyes narrowed as Rane poured a small measure into each of the seven glasses. Everyone around the table raised a glass in salute. Everyone, that is, except the Baroness of Otero. She eyed her glass as she would a viper.

"Do you not like brandy?" Miren asked quietly with a small, friendly smile that didn't ring true.

"Well, um..." Jocelyn said.

"Then please, join us in a toast to celebrate the end of a murderer," King Rowan said.

"This is ridiculous." She glared at Rane, hatred oozing off her in a slick, sickening flood. Jocelyn folded her hands in her lap and focused on them.

"Why won't you drink, Baroness?" Rane's voice was frigid and anger seeped out, equal to Jocelyn's hatred. No, stronger. "Is it because you poisoned this flask?"

"Anyone could have put it in the saddlebag."

"That's not true. Father finished the last of the Oteran brandy the day you arrived. You told me yourself you brought some, but Cook said you had not given her any. You were the only person in my room last night other than me. As I recall, you were alone with these saddlebags for a moment or two, long enough to slip in a flask."

"You accuse me of poisoning my stepson, but you knew where he was. You were hiding him from justice. Why am I in this chair, and you are not?"

"A valid question," King Rowan said. "And my daughter will answer for her actions, but the question of murder, not once but twice now, is more important than aiding a fugitive."

"I am the duly appointed ambassador of King Armel. You can't question me like this."

"Actually, we can." Ebon jumped into the conversation. "According to the Treaty of Somora, magical crimes committed by Teruellans in Lorea fall under Lorean jurisdiction, as Teruelle has few measures in place to deal with magic."

"Poisoning isn't a magical crime," the baroness protested.

"No, but enchanting someone to commit a crime for you is. Bring in the witness," Rane ordered the commander. Perhaps confronting the baroness with her actions would loosen her tongue. A confession would spare Alize. Though Rane had her own testimony to add, her actions after the event tainted it.

"Your Highness, I must protest," the commander said, standing. "Alize is too fragile for this."

Rane stood, too, and faced Miren, who stood several inches taller than her. She pulled her shoulders back and thought about what her mother would do. And her father. She was both, and neither, of her parents. In the end, she was herself. She would succeed as queen only if she continued to be Rane.

"Miren," she said, using only the commander's given name for the first time. She pushed away the twinge of doubt, and her voice held compassion and strength. "Alize is a witness to a serious crime. The alleged perpetrator sits among us and has worked hard to ensure she doesn't face the consequences of her actions. Justice is more important than your daughter's sensibilities. Besides, Alize is stronger than you realize. This is not a request. It is an order."

The commander opened and closed her mouth for a moment before bowing her head.

"Yes, Your Highness. I will fetch her." She saluted and turned smartly on her heels.

They waited in the quiet, all eyes on the baroness, as though she might run at any moment... or turn into a chicken. Who knew? The commander returned quickly, her daughter in tow. The young woman dipped a curtsy and stood next to Rane.

Rane kept her voice low and looked her childhood friend in the eye. "Alize, please tell us what happened on the night you discovered the dead guard."

A shiver raced through Alize's body, and tears pooled at the corners of her eyes.

"I had night duty. When Lord Nevar pulled the cord, I went to see what he needed. Everything is fuzzy after. The next thing I remember, I woke on the floor next to the guard's body." In a hushed tone, she added, "There was so much blood."

"You didn't receive a note inviting you to his chambers?" Rane asked.

"I only remember the bell ringing."

Rane pulled out the note Jocelyn had identified as written in Nevar's handwriting immediately after the incident.

"Have you seen this before?"

Alize read it and shook her head, handing it back. Rane handed it to her father, along with the letter Nevar had sent via pixie.

"You can see that the writing isn't the same. Lord Nevar did not write the note used to condemn him. Alize, did you see the baroness that night?" Rane gestured at Jocelyn.

"I don't remember anything after the bell rang. I don't believe so."

"Then why do you avoid looking at her?"

"I don't know what you mean."

"Every time you could look at the baroness, you don't. You find somewhere else to put your gaze. Why Alize?"

"I...I have a bad feeling about her ladyship. Begging your pardon."

"She doesn't remember," the commander said.

Tits, Rane needed Alize's testimony. The brandy thing was a good bit of theater to show she wasn't making things up or being paranoid, and the mismatched handwriting was a clue suggesting Nevar had been framed. In order to convince everyone Jocelyn was the guilty party, she needed Alize to remember.

"You have nothing," Jocelyn said, addressing King Rowan. "All the evidence points to my stepson. Even if the handwriting doesn't match, he has proven himself intelligent enough to alter his writing. Your heir aided and abetted him in his escape from justice. I am a baroness and have been making decisions on behalf of Otero for years. My husband is an invalid, and with Nevar dead, I will continue to do so until my son comes of age. I demand you release me immediately."

"Alize wasn't the only witness, Baroness." Rane didn't want to reveal this to Jocelyn, hoping to save it for the trial, but if Alize couldn't remember, Rane must. "I was there that night, too. I heard you tell Nevar to run, and I heard you threaten Baron Leon and your own son."

A sly gleam sparked on Jocelyn's face. "Are you certain, Your Highness? You heard those words in my voice?"

The bitch had a point. Though something had been off about Alize's voice, the maid had spoken those words. Sure, Jocelyn had controlled her, but without Nevar's testimony, without Alize's, all Rane had was the brandy and the notes. Worse, her testimony would implicate the maid. She needed to send Jocelyn to the deepest, darkest cell in the most isolated prison, not condemn an innocent.

The Baroness of Otero stood and brushed off her skirts. "I am done playing along with this farce. I will lodge a complaint with King Armel. You should know better than to treat diplomats with such callousness."

She strode toward the chamber door, and a loud clap of thunder sounded. The corners of Rane's mouth twitched up. Shit was about to get serious.

The door blew open, and Hyssop stood in all her glory, a wind no one else felt blowing her yellow hair and roiling the skirt of her blue dress. She stalked in, a hunter with a predatory gleam in her amethyst eyes.

"Hello, darlings. What did I miss?"

Chapter 30

Jocelyn stepped back from Hyssop, the blood leaving her haughty face as the elegant fairy strode into the chamber.

"Don't let her leave, Godmother," Rane said.

Like a striking snake, Hyssop grabbed hold of Jocelyn's arm and dragged her back to the table with ease, despite the baroness's attempts to extricate herself from the fairy's grasp.

"What do we have here?" Hyssop raised pale eyebrows at Nevar lying immobile on the table. "What happened to the poor lordling, Ranunculus?"

"He's a murderer, not—" Jocelyn began.

Hyssop whirled on the baroness, pressing a finger on the underside of Jocelyn's jaw to hold her mouth shut.

"I was speaking to my goddaughter, treacherous old bat," the fairy hissed, eyes flashing between impatience and malice.

"She poisoned him," Rane said. Fairies preferred direct answers from humans. It rarely worked the other way, but that was the price of dealing with a fairy.

Hyssop's eyes found hers, and they softened for a moment. "Truly? She would poison a member of her own family?"

"Yes."

The fairy turned her now venomous gaze back to the baroness. "Is this true? Answer honestly. I can sense lies, human."

She removed the finger from under Jocelyn's chin. The woman gulped and opened her mouth to answer, her gaze darting from Hyssop to Rane to Nevar. The baroness closed her mouth, pressing her lips in a fine line, white around the edges, and shook her head. Hyssop drew back her hand as though to slap the answer out of the baroness.

"No, Godmother, it's against our laws to strike a prisoner," Rane said.

The fairy sighed. "You humans and your rules. Fine. I will abide by your laws. What proof have you?"

"She refused to drink the brandy she provided to Nevar."

"That is all?"

"A forged note she claimed was in Lord Nevar's handwriting. She also used magic to kill a guard."

"And what proof do you have?" Hyssop asked, vexed.

"I caught the end of the conversation, the other witness can't remember, and you see what condition Nevar is in."

"Sweet child, you did not learn the lessons you needed from the fairy court."

"I learned enough to spot treachery. Not enough to be an expert in it."

"Well, tis better than naught. Hand me the brandy."

Rane handed a glass to her godmother. A small smile spread over the fairy's lips when she swirled the liquid around and sniffed it. She dipped a finger into the brandy and allowed a single drop to fall upon her tongue. Hyssop closed her eyes for a moment and blew out a breath. Smoke curled up from her nostrils, and she glared pointedly at Jocelyn.

"Clever witch," she said. "Valerian, seed of the poppy, and shadow viper venom, brewed at dusk in rainwater collected from a grave. A spoonful of the Living Death in a bottle of brandy is enough to cause extreme fatigue and a wasting, unpleasant death. This brandy has much more. If the lordling had consumed another sip, I could do nothing for him."

"You cannot prove I had anything to do with that bottle, fairy bitch."

Before anyone could blink, Hyssop held a leaf-bladed silver dagger to the baroness's throat. She dug in the tip and a single drop of crimson blood dripped down the woman's neck.

"Show some respect."

Jocelyn gulped once more and held her tongue.

Rane's heart fluttered. Had she heard Hyssop correctly?

"Godmother, does that mean you *can* do something for Nevar?"

"Perhaps," Hyssop said. "He still breathes, and he should continue to do so for long enough to get the truth from his wicked, wicked stepmother. She will have the answers you seek."

Without even looking, the fairy found Captain Jadran standing in the shadows and crooked a finger at him. Almost against his will, his feet carried him toward her.

"Escort the baroness to the fountain in the middle of the castle grounds. My magic is strongest when surrounded by the elements, not cooped up in stone, metal, and glass."

Jadran grabbed one of Jocelyn's elbows, and Commander Miren grabbed the other. Jadran looked at her with surprise.

"She killed someone in this castle. Her fate is my responsibility. Not to mention the trauma she caused my daughter," Miren said.

"You cannot do this," Jocelyn said, struggling against their firm holds. "You have already determined my guilt. This is not a trial."

"Shut up." Hyssop turned her cold eyes on the baroness and waved a hand. Jocelyn's mouth moved soundlessly. The blood drained from her face, and her body sagged in the grasp of her two escorts as they dragged her out of the room. The royal family followed, a macabre parade out into the night. Rane carried a lantern and brought up the rear.

The fairy's dress glowed a luminous blue in the dark as she led them into the center of the castle grounds, to the fountain where Nevar had almost kissed her. The only thing brighter was the nearly full moon bathing the gathering in ominous silver light.

"Hold her there." Hyssop pointed at a spot equidistant from the fountain and the tree line. She kicked off her shoes, delicate sandals that appeared to be made of spider silk.

Jocelyn flailed her feet wildly and tried to pull her arms away. Commander Miren and Captain Jadran were well versed in escorting those who didn't appreciate the courtesy. The baroness only managed a few glancing blows, neither slowing nor bothering her two guards.

"Come here, Ranunculus."

Rane approached, careful to keep out of Jocelyn's way. Hyssop held out a hand, and Rane stopped an arm's length from her.

"Raise the flame as high as it will go," Hyssop said.

With a satisfied smile on her lips, the fairy turned up her hands, opened her mouth, and sang. Later, Rane couldn't describe the song, but it was the most beautiful one she'd ever heard. Hyssop's voice wove its way through the air, around the fountain, and into the ground. The flame of Rane's lantern pulsed in time to the song, and the vibrations traveled through her body, changing the rhythm of her heart. Betony swayed in time to the music with eyes closed, and her hands mimicked the fairy's.

Golden motes of light appeared in the air and swirled around them. Green sparks joined them from the ground, red from her lantern, and blue from the fountain, a veritable fireworks show of a fairy's natural magic, drawn from the four elements. They spiraled around Hyssop, a cyclone of color and power. She lifted her arms to the heavens, and the colored particles funneled into her body. The fairy's skin glowed, an opalescent shimmer in the night.

"Bring forth the witness," Hyssop said in an otherworldly voice.

Betony escorted a trembling Alize to the fairy.

"This will not hurt, child." Hyssop held a finger to the young woman's temples. She muttered a word that sounded like a song, and Alize's eyes flared in the dim light.

"I remember," Alize said dreamily. "I remember the bell for the ambassador's room rang. When I arrived, the baroness stood next to a guard. She handed me a drink. I became dizzy, and the next thing I remember is waking up next to the guard."

"Was Nevar there?" Rane asked.

"No."

"Thank you, Alize," Hyssop said.

The strange light left the young woman's eyes, and she slumped into Bet. The princess escorted the maid to the side and helped her sit on the ground.

Hyssop stepped close to the baroness and placed her hands on the woman's temples.

"Now, Jocelyn, Baroness of Otero, you will speak true." Her voice roared with constrained power.

The baroness stopped struggling, and her body went still as a statue.

"Who poisoned the young lordling?" A great power threaded through Hyssop's words and lodged itself deep in Rane's belly.

"I did," Jocelyn said in a flat tone. No emotion showed on her face or in her words.

"Who else did you give the Living Death?"

"My husband."

A collective gasp went through the small audience. Nevar had been right. His stepmother had wanted the power for herself and would do anything to keep it.

"Did you kill the guard?"

"No."

"Did you arrange his death?"

"Yes."

A long finger tapped her godmother's pursed lips. Rane opened her mouth to demand how, but Hyssop raised a hand to her, as though following her line of thought.

"Did you pay someone to kill him?"

"No."

"Did you spell someone to kill him?"

"Yes."

"Who?"

"The maid."

Commander Miren's grip tightened on the baroness, who showed no sign of registering the pain. Had she been free to do so, the commander would have slit the woman's throat.

"How did you enchant the maid?"

"A potion and my mirror."

Hyssop's eyebrows furrowed in confusion. "A mirror?"

"She has a small hand mirror she's never without. Perhaps she has it in a pocket," Rane said.

The fairy gestured to Jadran. He pulled out a small, round object from the baroness's pocket. At a look from Hyssop, he handed it to Rane. Slightly smaller than her palm, the gold case was etched in an intricate design of entwined flowers with dark enamel berries. She'd recognize belladonna anywhere. One of her first lessons in woodcraft had been on the deadly beauty with a poisonous berry that would kill painfully.

"Open it, child," Hyssop said, "and tell us what you see."

Rane did as she was bid. The case opened easily, revealing a small mirror on one side, but instead of reflecting her face, the mirror showed her an entirely different scene.

After a moment of shock, she described to the others what she saw. "I see Nevar's body on the table in the Council Chamber.

Bash still stands guard."

"A Spy Glass. Interesting." Hyssop frowned.

"What's a Spy Glass?" Rane asked.

"With a drop of blood, the user can spy on a person. Combine that with a sleeping potion, and you can take control of someone's body. Wherever did you find it?" Hyssop asked the baroness.

"A tinker passing through Otero."

"His name?"

"I never asked."

"Something to pass along to the Queens." Hyssop tapped her fingers together and changed tack. "Who taught you magic?"

"An old crone who lived outside Castle Otero."

"Who else have you spied upon while in Avora?" Rane asked. Jocelyn remained silent.

"Answer the question," Hyssop ordered.

"My husband. My stepson. And the crown princess."

"Why?" Rane asked. Hyssop repeated her question.

"I ensured my husband remained bed bound, and I never trusted Nevar was as lazy and uninterested in politics as he let on. I suspected the crown princess was working with Nevar."

"I only have another moment before this rotten excuse for a woman fights off the spell I have wrought," Hyssop said.

Her father nodded and allowed the fairy to proceed.

"Where is the antidote?"

"In my workroom in Otero."

"Dammit," Hyssop muttered.

"What is the antidote?" Rane asked, unable to keep her mouth shut or desperation out of her voice.

"The antidote takes weeks to prepare, child. Your Nevar doesn't have weeks."

"Fuck."

"Indeed."

"Language, Rane!" her mother admonished.

"Mother, if ever there was a time for swearing, now is it," Ebon said, coming to his sister's defense.

Queen Beatrice wasn't pleased, but kept her mouth closed, tacitly acknowledging Ebon's point.

The light on Hyssop's skin faded, barely perceptible. Jocelyn twitched in another attempt to pull away from her captors.

"Our time is up, I see," the fairy said. "You have damned yourself, Baroness. Your fate is now in the hands of the King of Lorea."

"No. You forced the words out of me," Jocelyn said, eyes wild.

"I only forced you to tell the truth. Not one lie came from your lips."

"Magic is not evidence." Spittle flew from her mouth, and she fought the restraining hands even harder, to no avail.

"Perhaps not in Teruelle, but the laws of Lorea allow for magical testimony," King Rowan said. "Between Alize's testimony, the forged note, your mirror, and your own confession, we have enough for a trial. I have the authority to detain you until we can make arrangements with King Armel."

"No!" Jocelyn lost it as Jadran and Miren dragged her back toward the castle. "You bitch! You wanton, stuck up hellion. When I get out—"

With a cold glare, Commander Miren slapped the baroness across the face.

"I thought you did not strike your captives," Hyssop whispered in Rane's ear.

"Father will give her a warning, but there are extenuating circumstances. Perhaps it's not legal, but it is understandable," she explained.

"You humans and your rules. There's always an exception." Hyssop shook her head.

"Is there no other antidote?" The words fell from Rane's trembling lips.

"There is not."

"Then I claim my boon, Godmother. Restore Lord Nevar to health."

Hyssop placed a finger on her bottom lip and studied Rane. "I will do so if you answer me truly. Do you love him?"

Rane glanced around, but no one paid them any mind. Jocelyn's indignant screams carried through the castle grounds, and her family huddled near the fountain, discussing who knew what.

"What does it matter if I do? I can't be with him."

"Oh, child, love always matters. In fact, it is the only thing that truly does."

Licking her lips, she admitted the one thing she'd kept buried deep inside, knowing it would only cause her pain.

"I do. I love him."

"I will grant your boon." Her godmother smiled her first genuine smile of the evening. For an instant, the fairy's skin glowed in a rainbow of sparkles again. The magic flowed over her and condensed at the end of one fingertip. Hyssop raised the finger and traced Rane's lips. "Go. The magic fades quickly."

"Thank you, Hyssop."

Without a look back, Rane sprinted back to the castle as though chased by the all the monsters in the Argent Forest.

Chapter 31

Death was surprisingly verdant. And noisy.

Many voices washed over Nevar as he floated through the afterlife. Since childhood, he'd been told God would judge him at death. If found wanting, all that was left was a quick trip to the fiery bowels of hell. If he met God's expectations, his reward would be peace and bliss in heaven.

At peace, his cares dissolving into the verdant haze, Nevar assumed this must be heaven. He'd laugh if he could. Since he couldn't, he drifted along in this tranquil state, waiting for whatever might come next.

The scent of rosemary suffused his now-limited perception with the faint undertone of horse. Rane. He would have smiled had he a body. Did she still carry his heart? It would be good to be whole before God collected him.

A pinpoint of warmth began where his forehead would have been if he'd still been alive. It spread over him, first a sweet ache followed by prickling pain. His eyes flew open as his awareness planted itself back into his body. His lungs inhaled a deep, cleansing breath, and the world came into focus.

By the world, he meant Rane. Her lovely, heart-shaped face hovered over his, and her eyes brimmed with crystalline tears. Her dark curtain of hair closed them off from their surroundings.

"Where am I?"

Through still-numb lips, the words were as clear as he could make them. They sounded as if they came from a tired, drunken version of himself.

"In Avora," she said, a faint smile on her lips. "Everything is okay. Your name has been cleared, and Jocelyn will pay for her crimes. She's confessed to everything: the murder of the guard, the magical coercion of Alize, and your attempted murder."

"You've been a busy princess."

"You have no idea."

Nevar cupped her cheek—holy God, he had hands again! He was then gifted with a big, wet swipe of the tongue from a highly enthusiastic Bash.

"Bash!" Rane said, her cheeks coloring beautifully.

"Miss me, dog?"

Bash woofed, gave him another lick, and trotted off to the fireplace. She curled up, still keeping guard over them both.

"She did. I did, too."

"What happened?"

"Jocelyn poisoned you. I located an antidote, of sorts."

"Of sorts?"

"Fairy magic."

Fairy magic? It was a little too much. He could get the complete story later, when his body and mind were more cooperative.

"Kiss me again? On the lips?" he asked instead.

She obliged, and the salt of her tears mixed with the sweet taste of her mouth.

Rane pulled away and locked her gaze to his. "I never got the chance to tell you something. If you'd died, I would've regretted it for the rest of my life."

His heart thumped in his chest. "Oh?"

"I love you."

"I love you, too."

Nevar rested his forehead on hers, and peace settled on them. He loved and was loved in return. What else could he possibly want? Maybe the odd trip to Lorea would be enough. Maybe he'd grow wings and fly home.

Someone cleared their throat loudly and with annoyance. Rane pulled back.

"What is going on?" King Rowan's voice carried through the room, a little too loud for his newly awakened senses. Nevar grimaced.

"He's awake," Rane said, a smidgeon of mirth in her voice. "Hyssop gave me the antidote. I was administering it."

"Ah."

Heavy footsteps approached. Nevar sat up and blinked, clearing the residual haze from his vision. He was on the massive table in the Council Chamber. King Rowan, Queen Beatrice, Rane, and both her siblings stood next to it. Nevar swung his legs over the edge of the table, and a wave of dizziness crashed into him. He caught himself before his legs buckled, almost slipping back into the green nothingness of the poison.

"No, no, please don't," Queen Beatrice said with alarm.

"Thank you, Your Majesty," he said. He decided not to add that if he tried again, he'd merely end up back where he'd started.

"We owe you an apology for assuming your guilt with little evidence to support it," King Rowan said.

"I didn't give you much help on that front, but my stepmother left me little choice. She threatened my family. I've seen how you and your family act. What would you do to protect them? I did what I could while giving myself a chance to live."

"You are welcome back to our court. I will send notice immediately to King Armel."

"What will happen to Jocelyn?" Did he truly care? No, but he did want to ensure she never interfered with him or his family ever again.

"If she is tried under Lorean law and found guilty, the decision will rest with me whether to imprison or exile her."

Lorea was more merciful than Teruelle. If Jocelyn were tried at home, her life would be on the line. Nevar wasn't sure prison or exile would be enough to keep her from abusing power again, but it wasn't his call. It would have to do.

King Rowan sighed. "And now, our negotiations must begin again."

The queen placed a hand on his arm. "We made a fair agreement once. It won't take nearly as long this time. It's a pity Otero needs Lord Nevar now that Hyssop has exposed the baroness's crimes."

"What do you mean, my lady?" Nevar's mind raced to keep up, but it was like reading a thick text immediately upon awakening. He couldn't quite connect the dots.

"Your stepmother was dosing your father with the same poison as you," the queen said quietly, but with a hint of a smile on her face. "A much lower dose. It should clear his system in the next few weeks. He will be fine but weak for a while. Someone needs to handle the business of Otero while he recovers."

Nevar failed at suppressing the wide smile forming on his face. He didn't want to leave but hearing his father would be fine after all this time was news almost too good to be true. It seemed everything was coming up roses. Except he'd be far away from Rane, and they still couldn't be together. He was no longer a wanted fugitive, but that didn't change the difference between their stations or his responsibilities at home. What could Nevar possibly offer worth giving up their daughter's hand in marriage?

The germ of the idea from the night they'd said goodbye unfolded and bloomed into a full-fledged plan. He caught Rane's eye.

"Do you trust me?" he mouthed.

She gave a sharp nod, barely perceptible.

"Do you believe the agreement the baroness negotiated is fair to both Teruelle and Lorea?" Nevar asked the king. Time, after all, was as valuable a commodity as most others.

The king's eyes widened in surprise. "Yes, but—"

"I am certain if you petition King Armel to reinstate me as ambassador, he will do so. After looking over the agreement, if I agree with your assessment, I am more than willing to sign it, saving us all the time and energy it would take to renegotiate. I only have one condition."

The barest hint of a smile formed on Rane's face. She saw where this was going.

"Name it," King Rowan said.

Queen Beatrice shot a sharp glance at her husband.

Here went everything. "The crown princess's hand in marriage."

"No, absolutely not," the king protested, a red haze of anger creeping up his face and fire lighting his eyes. "Her destiny is here, as the heir to the Lorean throne. She can't be your baroness."

It was true, she couldn't be Baroness of Otero, but once his father recovered, Leon could govern Otero and train Orom to become Baron. Nevar could be Rane's prince.

"I appreciate that, Your Majesty. I am willing to come to the Lorean court once my father's recuperation is complete."

Queen Beatrice's glare slid from her husband and darted between Nevar and Rane. Her eyes narrowed in suspicion, then widened as she put the pieces of the puzzle together.

"Mineral rights are a low price to pay for the future queen's hand, Lord Nevar. Why should I agree to this merely to save a few weeks?" King Rowan glowered at Nevar, tapping his foot impatiently.

Rane cleared her throat. The king and queen turned their heads toward her.

"I am willing to make this sacrifice for our kingdom." Her voice was calm and clear, but her eyes sparkled in amusement.

"Wait," Ebon said, confusion on his face. "I thought—ow!"

Betony kicked him soundly in the shin.

"Hush, Ebon. Let the adults talk," the fey girl said, a smirk on her angelic face as she winked at her sister.

"I taught you better than to accept the first offer, Rane." the king said. "We promised you some say. I would rather see you happy than accept an offer when other avenues to solve the problem are available."

"Rowan," Queen Beatrice said, "I believe they are both more than amenable to the idea."

"No, I don't believe Rane would—"

"Look at them."

The king's gaze raked his daughter from top to bottom and did the same to Nevar. Realization slowly settled in his eyes. He pressed his lips together, as though hiding a smile.

"They've only known each other a fortnight," King Rowan protested weakly.

"It works that way sometimes," the queen said.

"Will he make you happy, Rane?"

She darted a glance at Nevar, and a beautiful, full smile spread across her lips as she stood on her tiptoes. "He already does, Father."

"Fine," the king said with an exasperated sigh. "I will add it to the agreement. Will that suit all parties involved?"

"Yes," Rane said, her voice a little too innocent.

"Yes, Your Majesty, thank you," Nevar said calmly and authoritatively, everything he wasn't feeling at the moment. All he wanted to do was sweep Rane into his arms and kiss her in celebration.

The king addressed Nevar. "Your quarters are available. We will send a missive to your king immediately. We should sign the agreement on schedule. You can then head home and help your father in his recovery. We'll set a date for the wedding when you have a better idea how long that might take. Welcome to the family."

With a last, hard look, King Rowan took his wife's arm. Queen Beatrice gestured to Ebon and Betony, who followed them out reluctantly.

"What was that all about?" Ebon asked as they left.

"Don't worry, dear brother. I'll explain it in small words so you'll understand," Betony said with loving amusement. She pulled the door shut behind them, leaving Nevar and Rane alone.

As soon as the door shut, Rane planted herself in front of him, tears welling in her eyes.

"I almost lost you." She cupped his face. "I don't know—"

He pulled her into his arms, wrapping them around her waist. "Hush. I'm here now. Everything worked out."

"You are as brilliant as you are beautiful."

"Not that brilliant. I mean, I almost died before I thought of it."

"It never would have occurred to me to make the agreement contingent on something I wanted."

"We'll make a good team." A deep satisfaction lodged in his heart. "After spending most of my life learning from a conniving, evil stepmother, I'm able to think like one. I'll be the politician, and you can be the queen. What happens now?"

"Now? No one's expecting us anywhere for a few days. Do you have any ideas?"

"Oh, one or two."

"Say it again, Nevar."

"I love you, Ranunculus."

She swatted at him, but he caught her hand and entwined his fingers with hers. He kissed the back of her hand, and Rane smiled at him, her green eyes lighting up his entire world.

"Don't call me that."

"It suits you." He bit back his own smile.

"Do I look like a fucking flower?" she asked with a chuckle.

"No, you look like a princess. My princess. I will love you until my dying breath, Rane." He meant it with every fiber of his being.

Her smile softened, and she stepped closer in his embrace. "I love you too, Nevar."

He lowered his head and kissed her, heady with the feel of her in his arms. It was where she belonged, where he belonged.

Epilogue

Like everything else in her life, Rane's happily ever after began with an accident. She tore through the halls, encased in white silk overlaid in lace, and a long, white veil trailing behind her. She was late for her own damn wedding.

Taking a corner too quickly, Rane grabbed onto a statue to keep upright. Once her slippered feet gained traction, she continued her race against the clock. The bells rang out as she skidded to a halt, overcompensating and bumping one of the statues standing to either side of the throne room doors. Her arms windmilled as she attempted to keep her feet, but it was a losing battle. The statue hit the floor with a boom that echoed through the hall and down the past two years.

"Idoya's tits," she said, expecting to land next to the now-shattered piece of marble.

Instead of a hard stone floor, strong, warm arms encircled her. She admired the molten bronze eyes of her prince. Well, he would be as soon as this wedding was over.

"There's my princess," Nevar said, a wide smile on his lips as he examined the broken statue. "What did your great-grandfather ever do to deserve this fate?"

"It was great-great-grandpa, and I'm sure he did something worthy of ending up gravel in the castle halls if he was the least bit interesting."

He stood her on her feet, and she smoothed the layers of silk and lace. Nevar set the veil right and brushed a loose strand of her hair out of her face, leaving his hand on her cheek.

"You're late." A devilish gleam shone in his eyes.

Heat flooded her face, but she kept her voice even. "*Someone*, and I'm not naming names, kept me up indecently late last night. He even knew I was getting married today."

Nevar chuckled and gave her a peck on the cheek.

"That's supposed to come after the ceremony, my lord." Heat washed through her of an entirely different sort, from a simple peck on the cheek. Holy goddess, how was she going to survive a lifetime of this?

"I hadn't seen you in months, and you expected anything else, Your Highness?"

He hooked her arm through his. He was in a velvet sapphire blue doublet, embroidered with silver flowers, beautifully rendered ranunculus. Her flower. A crisp, white tunic over black leather breeches, and the fairy-wrought sword at his side completed his outfit. He cut almost as magnificent figure clothed as he had naked last night.

The throne room door cracked open, and Betony poked out her head.

"There you are. The guests are getting restless." She stepped into the hall and thrust a bouquet in her sister's general direction.

Rane gripped the bundle of yellow ranunculus, bright and cheery on this cloudy day. Bet glanced at the ruined statue.

"Another one, Rane? I'm beginning to think you have no respect for our ancestors." Her tone was disappointed, but the smile on her face belied her words. "Are you ready?"

"I have never been more ready for anything in my life."

"Good," Nevar said. "If you'd answered anything else, I'd walk."

Betony knocked, and two guards swung the throne room doors open, but to Rane and Nevar, it was as though they were alone in the great room.

"Really? You'd walk away from all this just because I answered a question wrong?" Rane gestured wildly at the sumptuous hall and her own curvy body.

"Oh, no doubt. Correct answers are important. How could I possibly tie my fate to someone who got a question like that wrong?"

"Well, if you want to go, now's the time."

"No, I'll hang around. See what happens next."

Rane opened her mouth for a final retort, but Betony brought reality crashing down.

"Shut up. You two are giving Baron Leon heartburn, the poor man. He's suffered enough," she hissed.

"Oh, right," Rane said instead, forever grateful his witch of a wife was locked away in the deepest, darkest cell in Lorea.

The faces in the crowd grew clear. Relatives, guests, important courtiers. Hyssop sat next to Queen Beatrice, smiles on both their faces. King Rowan waited on the dais to perform the ceremony. And next to Nevar's father, who was finally well enough to travel, Orom bounced on his toes, trying to get a glimpse of the couple as they made their way down the aisle, looking like a smaller version of her groom.

They reached the dais and stepped up as they'd rehearsed yesterday. Facing Nevar with both her hands in his, Rane was exactly where she belonged. Her godmother was right. Love was the only thing that truly mattered. When Nevar kissed her at the end of the ceremony, she knew without a doubt he believed the same.

And they lived happily ever after.

The End

Acknowledgments

One of these days, I will be able to dedicate a book to all the wonderful stepparents out there. This is not that book. Sorry, evil stepparent is one of the important tropes in Snow White. However, I was blessed with two of the best stepmothers out there. Michele and Nancy, thank you from the bottom of my heart for being wonderful bonus moms.

When I was very young, maybe seven years old or so, I received An Illustrated Junior Library Edition of *Grimms' Fairy Tales*. I read it over and over, fascinated by the illustrations and how the stories differed from the Disney versions, both simpler and more complex, and a hell of a lot meaner (you don't want to know what happened to Cinderella's stepsisters). I can't remember who gave it to me, but it is still a treasured possession and the skeleton upon which I loosely draped my retelling.

If you're interested in learning more about royal families in the Middle Ages and the lengths they would go to keep power, may I suggest listening to the British History Podcast. Jamie has spent more than a decade on British history, most of it between the Romans and the Norman invasion, and there are plenty of stories that would put George RR Martin to shame.

I found thoughtful and kind beta readers for this book on the Critique Match website. Thanks to Katherine, JA, Melissa O, and Melissa C. Your comments and suggestions helped improve this book. Shoutout to Elisabeth G for looking at my blurb. Thanks also to Gail Delaney, my editor, who suggested the title. I thank whatever deity or saint in charge of social media for sending you across my TikTok FYP. Give Tommy a scritch from me.

And of course, my family: parents, steps, siblings, grandparents, in-laws, niblings, spouse, and kids. I love you all, and none of this would be possible without you.

If you've ever wondered how to support an author, may I suggest leaving a review of their book? Leave it anywhere you can—the retailer where you bought it, StoryGraph, Goodreads, social media, blogs. A fifteen-second video, some stars, or a couple of sentences can help us out a lot

About the Author

Emily Michel read her first fairy tale before kindergarten and has been fascinated with speculative fiction of all kinds ever since. She's traveled the world as a military family member, calling many places in the US and Europe home. She settled in Arizona a few years ago with her husband and kids.

When not writing, Emily reads, walks, crochets, and pets her feline overlords. Emily has volunteered her time to community organizations for the past twenty years and looks forward to taking a break in 2022 to concentrate on her writing and editing, which is a nice way of saying she's tired and needs some "me time."

Socially awkward and extremely introverted, she nevertheless participates in social media. Check out @EmiMiWriter on Twitter, Facebook, Instagram, Pinterest, and even, dear God, TikTok. If you want to be the first to know release dates, cover reveals, and sales, sign up for her newsletter at EmilyMichelAuthor.com.

Books by Emily Michel

Magic & Monsters Series
Witch Hazel & Wolfsbane
Devil's Claw & Moonstone
Brimstone & Silver

Memory Duology
A Memory of Wings
Book 2 coming soon

The Lorean Tales
Blood Magic and Brandy

CPSIA information can be obtained
at www.ICGtesting.com
Printed in the USA
LVHW021834280322
714614LV00004B/72